Praise for Jenna Leigh's *The Wolf's Heart*

5 Lips "...an engrossing and exceptional book! The dialog is fresh and witty and the action intense... This is one book you MUST read!"

~ *Tara Renee, Two Lips Reviews*

4.5 Blue Ribbons "Jenna Leigh is on the top of my list for excellent paranormal reads... especially ones involving werewolves."

~ *Angel, Romance Junkies*

Five Roses "Ms. Leigh has done a great job with THE WOLF'S HEART. ...well written, paced beautifully ...a page turner!"

~ *Robin S., My Book Cravings*

Five Stars "The Wolf's Heart by Jenna Leigh is not just another werewolf tale, it is so much more, it is a hilariously witty story... a total pleasure to read.. spicy and passionate, filled with characters you love and hate, and best of all thoroughly enjoyable."

~ *Sheryl, Ecataromance*

Winner of the Reviewer's Choice Award: "The Wolf's Heart flows beautifully... This is a book that you won't stop until the end and when you finished it leaves you with a happy feeling that you like to come away with a good romance novel."

~ *Rosalynn, Historical Book Club*

Five Angels "The Wolf's Heart of the Lune Wolf series is a definite keeper and I am looking forward to more from this outstanding author and her new series."

~ *Dana P., Fallen Angel Reviews*

"The Wolf's Heart is a paranormal will hold you tight as you try to figure out all the who's, what's, when's and where's ahead of the plotline."

~ *Jo, Joyfully Reviewed*

Four Hearts "If you enjoy a fast paced, suspenseful romance that walks on the wild side, The Wolf's Heart is a winner!"

~ *Patrice, The Romance Studio*

The Wolf's Heart

Jenna Leigh

A Samhain Publishing, Ltd. publication.

Samhain Publishing, Ltd.
577 Mulberry Street, Suite 1520
Macon, GA 31201
www.samhainpublishing.com

The Wolf's Heart

Print ISBN: 1-59998-770-8
Digital ISBN: 1-59998-515-2

Editing by Angie James
Cover by Anne Cain

First Samhain Publishing, Ltd. electronic publication: June 2007
First Samhain Publishing, Ltd. print publication: April 2008

Dedication

For Bill, who knows when to be the big bad wolf and when to give me puppy dog eyes. For not one but two Angela's, the first whose prize for this story gave me confidence to keep on going and the second who said *yes*. And last but not least, for those Mad Cows who in the midnight hour always cry more, more, more.

Prologue

Phoenix, Arizona

"On a dark summer night, would you offer your throat to the wolf with the red roses?" ~Meat Loaf

She ran through the woods, icy terror shooting up her spine with each footfall behind her. The footsteps sounded strange, not like hers at all. Sweat stung her eyes and she impatiently wiped it away. *"Elaine."* The name slithered deep into the recesses of her brain.

She stumbled, almost falling to the forest floor. Redwoods and pines lined the path she traveled. Roots made the way treacherous. Her breath steamed out into the cool air in short bursts. She began to tire. She couldn't stop because he would catch her. The images of what he wanted to do to her flashed through her mind and galvanized her steps. She poured on the speed.

"Elaine." There it was again, her name. It was a command for her to submit, to obey. Never.

"Go away!" She turned to scream at him. The sight that met her eyes stopped her in mid-stride, for it wasn't a man that pursued her, no, not at all. This was something else, a monster from a child's nightmare. She'd had plenty of those—realistic, vivid and terrifying. Here was the cause of them all. But who, or more importantly, *what* was he?

He stood in shadows, at least seven feet tall and about half that wide across the shoulders. His legs were large, muscled, but deformed somehow. He wasn't moving and her curious nature got the better of her. His amber eyes glowed brightly in the darkness.

"*I'll never leave you, Elaine.*" The beast took a step forward, still shrouded in darkness. Fear welled up inside her when he moved, prowling toward her. The moonlight crept between the trees, illuminating him enough for her to see the teeth, the claws and the desire.

She turned to run but a root from a nearby tree proved her downfall. And what a fall it was, over the side of a cliff she could have sworn wasn't there a moment ago. She yelled, her arms windmilling into the air in a futile attempt to stop herself from falling onto the sharp rocks below.

The last thing she saw was the monster watching her with a smile on his horrifyingly familiar face.

Elaine sat up with a scream lodged in her throat. She gasped for breath and pressed her hand to her heart when she found herself safe in bed. It was all a dream, The Dream, rather, one she'd had for the past ten years. Always it ended with that creature watching her. The look on his face was always the same too, hungry. Hungry for her.

She rubbed her eyes and stood with a stretch and groan as she looked out her window. The sun was just beginning to lighten the horizon. She may as well get up and make coffee. She had a big day ahead; one that made her heart beat even faster than the dream. But not from fear, instead, it was...excitement.

Chapter One

Lainie stared at the massive black doors that led to Bei International's CEO's office and bit her lower lip in trepidation. She hadn't seen the man inside in over ten years. How had the time changed him? Would he be the same?

There was only one way to find out.

She straightened the hem of her skirt and made sure her hair was still up in its clip. After knocking on the door, she took a deep breath to calm her nerves and waited for the call to enter.

"Miss Westerbrook?" A deep voice made her whirl and put her hand to her throat. She looked up for what seemed like forever.

"Yes," she found her voice, proud that it didn't quaver.

The owner of the voice had short spiky blond hair and dark gray eyes. A dark business suit clothed a body that told of hours spent at the gym. When he smiled, his cheeks produced two deep dimples.

"I'm Elaine Westerbrook," she continued, holding out her hand.

After a few seconds, he took it between his finger and thumb. She raised her brow at him in question and he laughed. "Forgive me, I'm told I don't know my own strength. I'd hate to hurt you." He smiled politely but she swore she detected a touch of menace. "My name is Kane."

Maybe it was just paranoia but she didn't think so. The instincts that made her a good reporter told her she was right. However, even she'd admit that she had a wild imagination. "I'm sure you wouldn't do something like that, huh, Kane?" She injected her tone with just the right combination of sweet flirtatiousness.

"Not on purpose." He took another long look at her before opening the door for her. A good thing, as she doubted she could have moved it herself.

He stepped inside and cleared his throat. "Mr. Bei, Ms. Westerbrook is here to see you." With another heart-stopping smile, he left her alone with his boss.

Lainie waited for the man in question to turn. He didn't at first, just continued to look out the window. How rude, and how typical of a man of his standing.

"Marcus."

At the sound of his name, his shoulders stiffened and he slowly turned to stare at her. His lips curled into the same beautiful smile that stole its way into her dreams at night.

Marcus stood a little over six feet. His slanted eyes told of his Asian ancestry; however, she saw his mother's Native American heritage there as well. He'd been blessed with the best of all his genes. Tall, dark and deadly didn't even begin to describe him. The man was some USDA prime, genuine beefcake, the man to whom she'd compared all other men she'd ever dated and found them lacking. Life was so bloody unfair.

"Lainie, long time no see." His voice had changed over the years to a deep baritone.

"Ten years." She tried to relax, but found she couldn't. Her stomach fluttered as she took him in.

He'd been a teenager the last time she saw him. Now his shoulders were broader, but the rest was still lean and hard. The light of humor was missing from his eyes, replaced by a look of superiority and disdain. His hair was still inky black and straight. It was longer than she remembered. This was a surprise; she would have thought that he would have it short, to suit his tycoon persona. Apparently not, as it reached the shoulders of his charcoal-colored suit, nothing off the rack for him.

Marcus Bei, once the friend of her childhood, was now the head of his father's software company. Bei International was a worldwide operation and this man was at the helm.

"You still look exactly the same." He finally moved forward, gesturing for her to sit in the chair across from his desk. He politely waited until she'd done so before sitting down himself.

"Surely not!" She laughed to cover her nervousness. "I was so gawky back then."

He gave her a probing glance which she didn't attempt to interpret before he leaned forward, lacing his fingers together on top of his desk.

She stared at those long fingers, strong and capable, and shivered but covered it by shifting in her chair.

"What can I do for you, Elaine?" He pinned her with his dark gaze.

"I have a favor to ask," she began, only to be interrupted by a short bark of laughter. "What? It's only a small one. I—"

"Just spit it out." His words made her look up, and she noted that his eyes matched his tone perfectly; flat, hard and empty. It seemed he had changed, and not for the better.

"Never mind. This was a mistake. I'll get my story by myself with no help from you." She wished she'd never come here at all. He only made her remember happier times in her life, before she lost the small amount of security she'd gained in her teen years.

She stalked across the black marble floor, her heels clicking out a staccato rhythm that matched the pounding of her heart. She was furious and didn't care if he knew it. She reached her hand out and grasped the handle, jerking it with all her might. It barely budged. Was the damned thing made of lead?

A hand appeared over the top of her head and pushed the door shut. "What in the hell are you doing?" She turned to glare up at him, thankful she'd worn heels. At least she wasn't staring at his breastbone. At 5'4", she used to think she was average, but the world seemed to have grown taller when she wasn't looking.

Marcus loomed over her, probably on purpose. "I thought you wanted a favor, Lainie." He drawled her nickname and if he wasn't leering, she'd turn in her press pass right now.

"You said no."

"I don't even know what your favor is, so how could I refuse?" He had a smirk on his face she wanted to knock right off. Belatedly, she remembered how he used to tease her when they were younger. He hadn't changed all that much.

Strangely enough, that was comforting. She straightened to her full height and attempted to look down her nose at him. "I want you to take me to the Caulder Ball."

He blinked in surprise and triumph surged through her veins. Ha, he never saw that coming. "Why?"

"Something strange is going on in his company." She kept her answer purposefully vague. "I need to get close to see how high up it goes." She knew he had an invitation. All the bigwigs did.

"What sort of strange goings-on?" He leaned forward and she tried to lean back but the door halted her progress. He moved a little nearer. Did he sniff her? He did! She'd showered just this morning.

She opened her mouth to tell him off when he fitted his lower body snugly against hers.

"You smell nice, Lainie. Almost good enough to eat." He sniffed her neck again.

"Are you on drugs?" She shoved at him but he was like a stone wall, not even budging an inch. "Marcus! Get the hell off me!"

"If I give you this favor..." he moved back, but only slightly, "...what do I get in return?"

"My undying gratitude?" she ventured. When he only arched his brow she snapped, "What do you want, my firstborn?"

"That could be arranged." His grin turned wolfish. "I could make a donation to the cause, if you'd like."

Marcus waited for Lainie to digest his words. He knew the minute she became aware of their meaning because her green eyes lit with fury. Here came the sparks. He anticipated her next move with relish because he hadn't felt this riled up in a long time. Marcus ruled his emotions with an ironclad fist. He had to, being who and what he was. There was no other option for a man in his position.

When she'd contacted his office and asked to see him, the first response had been a definite no, and then he'd changed his mind, three different times. He was all too aware of his lack of control around this particular woman. Even ten years didn't erase the memory of the clamoring of his heart, the pounding in his ears and the howling in his brain. He'd learned his lesson the hard way. Always keep your emotions in check.

Since then, he had. He practiced meditation; he made sure not to get into situations that would test his limits. And he sure as hell stayed away from Lainie Westerbrook, the teen temptress all grown up into a sexy beauty who still had the ability to make him hard as a rock just by walking into the room.

He snapped back to attention when she poked him in the chest, emphasizing each word with a stab of her finger. "Do you seriously think I'd consider sleeping with you for a story?" His lips quirked, but he hid the smile quickly, well aware of her hot temper. "Are you listening to me?"

"Nope." His laconic response had her glaring daggers at him.

"Why in the hell not?"

"I can see down your shirt."

"Marcus Bei!" She clenched her hands into fists. "You're being deliberately crude."

"No, I'm being honest." He smiled in an attempt to placate the little she-demon before she got started. Naw, he wanted her to explode. That way he got to pick up the pieces in the aftermath.

"Why aren't we friends anymore?" Her question sounded wistful to his ears. "I missed you."

His brain whirled at the quick change of subject. He'd forgotten the twists and turns of her conversations. Marcus turned and began to pace. "Don't you remember what happened?"

He saw the flush creeping up her neck with no small amount of satisfaction. She walked to the couch situated over by the windows and sat down. "I don't know what you're talking about."

"Don't lie to me or yourself." He ran his fingers through his hair and stalked around the room. His blood heated in remembrance. "I almost did something that would have scarred you for life. Me, one of the people you trusted most in the world."

"But you didn't." Her voice was a whisper of sound.

"I didn't want to stop. If you'd stayed, I would have tried it again."

She sat stiffly on the couch, her head bowed and shoulders trembling. Cursing himself for a fool, he sat beside her. She didn't move away and his heart warmed slightly because of that one small detail. "I almost took something from you, whether you were willing or not."

She raised her head and smiled, wetting her lips with her tongue, and he groaned. "Marcus, you silly, stupid man." Damn her, she still had the same effect on him as always.

"How's that?" He frowned at her.

"You stopped."

It took him a second to figure out exactly what she meant by that. When the light dawned, his mouth fell open. Her smile lit up her whole face in that instant. "Lainie, you don't know what you're saying."

"I'm not an idiot, Marcus. I wasn't experienced at the time. But I damn well wasn't as innocent as you thought." She tossed her head back and laughed. "Why do you think I ran away? I was scared. I knew if you put your hands on me again, I would never want you to stop."

He sat there, shocked into silence. His whole outlook on life had been born in that moment, with honor warring with shame and desire. The fact that he had resisted taking her had always seen him through some of his darkest times. And he'd had some dark ones.

He looked at her again, seeing her in a new light. The sweet child, the teen who had tempted him beyond reason and now the adult all melded together into one cohesive whole. Lainie was his for the taking. After all this time, he could have what he wanted with no guilt, and no regrets.

Son of a bitch. He cursed silently as his thoughts screeched to a halt. No way in hell could he touch her; even if she did want him, she only saw what was on the surface. Marcus wasn't what he appeared to be.

She saw a nice, honorable, safe man who had been a friend, someone she'd known since childhood. He was that person, but beneath that thin coating of civility was a ravening beast waiting for his chance to create chaos, destruction and above all else gain possession of this tempting treat.

The kick in the ass was, in addition to being a rich, sought-after tycoon, he was the leader of Arizona's own wolf pack. How do you tell a prospective lover that you turn furry on the full moon? And if you tell her, how do you ever let her go?

Finally, he decided to let her make her own decision, albeit an uninformed one. Sliding one arm over the back of the couch, he placed the other on the cushion beside her hip, effectively hemming her in with his arms. "What are you offering me? Be specific and please, be very sure."

"I'm offering us a chance to get to know each other again, Marcus." Her eyes narrowed in either anger or desire, he could smell both warring within her. "I need to get information. I think someone is kidnapping people and doing experiments on them, and you sit here yammering about what you think you're gonna get out of the deal."

He leaned even closer, his mouth a whisper of breath from her own, filing away what she'd said to check out later. For now, he had more important goals in mind. "We can negotiate that right now. I'm willing to accept an oral contract." He winked and pointed at the floor between his knees. He kept his voice light, but the image of her naked and kneeling on the floor in front of him made his dick swell even more. The minute she'd walked in, everything stood at attention, now his libido was at red alert. Explosion was imminent.

"No," she spat. "You're welcome to kneel, though." Her lips curved into a smirk. "All the better for you to kiss my ass."

"There's the sweet little Lainie-puss I remember so well." He sat back and dragged her onto his lap. When she struggled to get up, he purred, "Ooh, baby, that feels good. Do it again." She straightened and glared at him. Marcus laughed and pulled her into a warm hug. "I missed you, too."

She had her hair up in one of those vaguely scary hinged clips so he pinched it open and tossed it over his shoulder. When she was a little girl, her hair had been blonde, but now it was darker, richer, with streaks of red, brown and honey gold shot through the wavy strands. He ran his fingers through it, reveling in the silky texture before lifting a handful to his nose and inhaling flowers, herbs and some other indefinable scent that was all Lainie.

"Will you stop sniffing me?" She jerked her hair out of his grasp. "I swear. You're like one of the dope dogs down at customs or something."

"You smell good." He gave her an easy grin.

"Thank you, I think." She looked at him as if he were deranged, and maybe he was. If so, it was her fault. She squirmed beneath his scrutiny, making him harden even more beneath her thighs.

Her hair fell down around her shoulders, framing a soft, oval face with high cheekbones, a straight nose with a slightly tilted end. Her pink lips were soft and full. Just the sight of them had him aching to slide either his tongue or his cock between them—hell, he was easy.

The stubborn chin she now jutted out at him spoiled the overall symmetry of her face. "Are you quite through with your inspection?" Her haughty question brought him out of his daze.

"No, the strip search is next." He leered.

"Never mind, I'll get into the ball on my own." She scrambled to get out of his lap. "I don't need your help."

He grabbed her wrists in one hand and pulled her back down. She let herself fall much harder than necessary and smiled sweetly at his winded grunt and wince. "Damn, are you trying to break it?"

"Yep," she admitted.

"Here's the deal, Cinderella. You want to go to the ball and I want to get to know you again. We both have something the other person wants so I don't see why we can't make a deal." He thought that was reasonable.

Lainie didn't seem to agree if her expression was anything to go by. After a second or two though, she stopped struggling and he could practically hear the wheels turning in her brain. "Fine, but no sex." He choked and she rolled her eyes. "I meant no sex unless we both agree it is beneficial to the continuation of our relationship."

"You make it sound so..." he paused for the right word, "...healthy." He curled his lip and she let out a delightfully sweet laugh that made his chest ache.

"Sex is healthy. The benefits of a good sex life have been scientifically proven to help promote good skin, shiny hair and lower your cholesterol," Lainie spouted off like an announcer from an infomercial.

"I mean—oh, never mind." He twirled a lock of her hair around his fingers. "So, do we have a deal or what?"

"Yeah, yeah, if that's the way you want it, I guess I'll have to go along with it." She sighed gustily and rolled her eyes, but he could tell she was fighting a smile.

He let her hair go and tipped up her chin. "Shall we seal the bargain?"

"I can't shake hands because you have both of mine," she pointed out.

"I'm sure we can think of something else." His fingers fanned out across her cheek, turning her face toward his own. He slid his hand into her hair and cupped the back of her head, pulling her close to him. "Kiss me, Lainie." His voice was hoarse with the need he'd held in check since she walked in the door.

She brushed her lips teasingly across his, barely making contact, until he thought he was about to explode before her tongue slid against his lips, and darted inside. A breathy sigh escaped her as she dragged her hands out of his now-slack hold, curling her fingers in his hair, tugging gently.

Whimpering softly, she rubbed herself against him like a cat and he lost all semblance of control, taking over despite his attempts to hold back. Growling softly, he slanted his mouth across hers, deepening the kiss.

With fumbled movements, he undid the buttons on her shirt, desperate to touch her bare skin. She bucked against his hands when they cupped her breasts, her nipples hardening against his palms through the lace of her bra.

He knew he could have her right now if he wanted and perversely that thought had him pulling back. He grinned when she tugged on his hair in an effort to deepen the kiss again.

"Lainie," he whispered and her lashes fluttered open revealing dazed green eyes gone dark with passion. Marcus chuckled. "I think that seals our bargain just about right."

She licked her lips. "Well, no, actually." He frowned down at her. "But this one might." She straddled his lap, her skirt hiking up over her thighs. He appreciated the view until she moved in for the kill. This time, she didn't allow him to move. Her tongue played sweetly inside his mouth, coaxing and then retreating in a teasing little dance that left him hard and hungry for her body beneath him. Finally, she pulled away, and gave him a saucy grin.

Once he got his breath back, he began to think that this wasn't such a good idea. Maybe he could trick her into doing something else, goad her into chickening out on the deal.

"What are you planning, Marcus?" Her voice was low and husky, her lips curved in a smile that made his hackles rise.

"If I told you, I'd have to fuck you." He grinned, trying to extricate himself from the honeyed web she'd already started to weave around him.

"You're so full of shit." She laughed and shook her head.

"That's why my eyes are brown, darlin'." He tugged on a curl that fell in her eyes.

She snorted and stood, smoothing down her skirt before picking up the jacket she'd laid on the back of the couch. "I'd better go. So, see you Friday?" When he still sat there, looking up at her, she prodded his leg with hers. "Marcus?"

"No."

"You said our bargain was sealed with a kiss." She put her hand on her hip and glared at him.

"I did and it is. But you won't be seeing me on Friday." He shrugged.

"That's the day of the ball!" She stamped her foot.

"Yeah, but this is only Monday, Lainie. You and I have to get to know each other much better before then." He gave her the most disarming smile he had and it was a doozy.

Of course, she fell for it, staying within his reach, when she should have known better. Until he got the information on this criminal, she was going nowhere.

"What do you mean?"

"You'll be at my beck and call twenty-four/seven." With that pronouncement, he stood and pulled her into his arms. And if he had his way, she'd never leave him again.

Lainie tried to process what he said but his hands were cupping her butt, lifting her against him. The bulge of his arousal was distraction enough without him grinding his hips against her, thank you very much. "Stop it."

"Why?" He pulled her a little closer.

God, he smelled nice. "Because." She glared up at him.

"Honey, that isn't an answer." He grinned and nibbled on her mouth, pulling back when she tried to bite him in earnest. "You like it, I can tell."

"Oh, bullshit!" She pinched his side, and he winced. "You can't tell anything. Unlike boys," she sneered, "women are not so obvious with their desires."

"I'm not a boy, I'm a man, and I can tell when a woman wants me." He stared directly into her eyes and she could swear he was looking deep into her soul, finding out her inner secrets. "Your heart's pounding, your skin is flushed and you're breathing fast. Oh, and you're licking your lips. Keep doing that, I like it."

"Maybe I'm just pissed, did you think of that?" In reality she couldn't help but be flattered by the hungry looks he kept giving her. Now she knew how a piece of chocolate cake felt when it met her in a dark kitchen after a long day of dieting.

"I don't think pissed is the term I'd choose." He shook his head at her. "I think hot and bothered is more in line with what you're feeling."

She closed her mouth, refusing to answer. When she tried to pull away again, he let her go. "Who are you after at the Caulder Corporation, Lainie?"

"The big man himself, Jacob Caulder." She knew Jacob was involved and she aimed to find out how.

Marcus sputtered for a few minutes before he threw up his hands and stalked away, only to turn and charge her like an angry bull. "Have you lost your mind?"

"I most certainly have not!" She stood her ground.

"I won't allow it!"

"You don't have any say in the matter. You ain't my damn daddy!" She winced at the *ain't*. She hadn't said that word in a long time.

He growled, like a dog or a wolf, and she froze, instinctively knowing she shouldn't move. Even as she did it, she wondered at her reaction, it had been automatic.

He pulled his hair and stomped away to stare out the window again. "Elaine." Her name came out low and rough. "I don't want you to do this. It's too dangerous."

"I have to, it's my job."

"You could just live with me; you wouldn't have to work, if you didn't want to." He placed his palms on the window and leaned his forehead against it. "I'd take care of you," he pleaded.

"No." She ignored the way his offer to take care of her made her go all gooey inside. "I'm good at my job. I love it. It's who I am."

"Lainie." His shoulders drooped and he sighed. "Fine, I'll help you. But you'll have to listen to me. Jacob is dangerous."

"Dangerous how?"

"I can't explain it."

"Can't, or won't?" She moved to stand beside him, enjoying the view of the city. Phoenix was a beautiful place. She wondered if that was why he relocated the company here.

"Can't." He speared her with a glance and she barely choked back a gasp. His eyes had changed to an eerie gold color.

The room started closing in around her and some errant thought tickled at the back of her brain, almost breaking through. He blinked and his eyes changed back to their regular dark brown. She shook her head, dismissing it as a trick of the light.

Chapter Two

"Come on, I'll take you home," he spoke, bringing her out of the small trance she'd fallen into.

"You know where I live?" She stiffened, watching him warily.

"Yeah." He didn't admit that he'd kept track of her, and he sure as hell wasn't stupid enough to tell her that his company had funded her college scholarship. Lainie was sweet, for the most part, but she did believe in vengeance and she was sneaky as hell about getting it.

"I haven't lived here that long." If she was waiting for him to give her more information, she'd be waiting a while. He didn't dare give her any more than he had to, but sometimes it seemed like she sensed clues just by smell.

If Lainie were a dog, she wouldn't be a Pomeranian, or one of the other toy breeds like her looks suggested. Instead, the woman had to be half bloodhound because she'd sniffed out more stories than most reporters twice her age.

Marcus just gave her the same affably blank expression that served politicians and CEOs in good stead in the boardroom and beyond. "Did you move here because of me?"

"No, I did not." Her face went bright red. "I didn't even know the paper wanted me to move until the last minute."

Lainie worried her bottom lip with her teeth. Damn, he wanted to do that for her.

He put his arm out for her to take. When she did after a moment's hesitation, he led her to the door, holding it open for her. This seemed to discomfit her, so he kept doing it. It was nothing she could complain about, but it put her off balance and he needed all the help he could get with her.

Finally, when they reached the parking garage, she demanded an answer, her curiosity overwhelming her pride. "How do you know where I live?"

"I am a man of many talents." Marcus spread his arms wide. He leaned closer and leered. "Guess which one I do best?"

She opened and closed her mouth, and he rocked back on his heels, enjoying the special occasion. A speechless Lainie, he hadn't been sure this creature really existed. He got a little too overconfident though, because she stepped closer to him and spoke in a low, seductive whisper that had his whole body at attention.

"Marcus, I'm sure you're a wonderful lover…" she ticked the words off on her fingers, "…kind, strong, caring, forceful." She licked her lips and sighed softly. "Full of shit." With that, she turned and headed toward the limo that stood waiting.

Since she hadn't changed her tone, it took him a few seconds to hear her last remark. "Hey!" He hurried after her, grumbling the whole way.

Lainie smirked as she settled into the back of the limo. She'd got the last word in that time. No easy feat, with his gorgeous smile distracting her. Marcus wasn't smiling when he got into the car, but he slid in until his body was flush against hers.

"Excuse me?" She lifted a brow and indicated the rest of the seat that was free because he was practically sitting in her lap. "Do you mind?"

"No, I don't mind it at all. You're soft, cute and you smell nice." He put his arm on the back of the seat, thus moving himself even closer. She tried scooting over but he followed until she was pressed against the door on one side and his hot, hard body on the other.

"I can't breathe!" she warned in a low voice. "I still get carsick."

He moved away quickly enough after that. "You hurked a hell of a lot for such a little girl."

"I didn't do it that much."

"Yeah, you did," he teased.

She kept her eyes on the horizon, as she always did when she felt nauseous. But she wondered if it was actual sickness she felt in the pit of her belly. The swirling sensation had started the minute she walked into his office. No, to be honest, it started the moment she decided to see him again. She was an idiot, a fool and a dumbass. She stopped her bout of self-castigation, which only made her feel more like tossing the three-taco lunch she should have thought twice about.

"Whatever." She flicked her hand around airily. "So, what's our arrangement, besides your inherent need to control everything? I mean, we could date every night and still not know anything about each other."

"Why won't you look at me?"

"Because, I may hurk as you put it, and how crude does that word sound? Watching the horizon helps." She took a shaky breath and at the count of three, let it out.

"Hurk's a good word." He sounded like he was pouting and she smiled. "How about, hurl, ralph, worship at the porcelain altar, drive the big white bus, the Technicolor yawn—"

"Enough!" She turned to glare at him. "Are you trying to make me do it?" He looked puzzled at her ire. Boys, no matter how much they grew up, remained goofy as hell at times. Despite that, or maybe because of it, her resistance to him melted a little more.

"No. I don't want to have to pay the bill to clean it off my seats. The smell lingers forever." He wrinkled his nose in distaste.

"Marcus, you haven't changed at all." Silence met her remark, lasting the rest of the ride to her house.

As they pulled up, he took in the exterior of her house. It was made of adobe, like a lot of the homes in the area, not too big, not too small. Cozy and comfortable looking. The small cactus garden out front showed she was ecologically conscious, not that he'd ever doubted it. A gravel walk, neatly raked and free of weeds, led up to the small front porch that contained a swing at one end and more deciduous plants clustered around the door and the posts. All in all, it was warmly welcoming. The feeling lasted until they reached the front porch where something caused his hackles to rise, literally.

He shoved the growl down, unwilling to show her his other side before he was sure he could trust her with the truth. "What is that?" He knew he snarled, but couldn't help himself. He was very aware that his driver, Mick, leaned against the hood of the limo while he waited. Marcus knew this would go straight back to his people, embellished with all the bells and whistles.

Lainie, alarmed by his thunderous expression, whirled to see what he pointed at, and laughed when she spied the object of his disdain. “Oh Marcus, it’s just Fluffy!”

Fluffy was a huge orange cat, and apparently he knew what Marcus was, because he gave the man a smug smile when Lainie picked him up and cuddled him. “Hi there, baby. How have you been?” she cooed while the cat purred and rubbed his head on her jaw.

Marcus showed the cat his teeth. This only served to make the cat purr louder and mew at Lainie.

“Aw, he missed me. Isn’t he sweet? Do you want to pet him?”

“No!” He stepped back. “That is, I’m allergic to them. Does he have to come inside with us?”

“Who said you get to come in?” She smirked.

“I did. I never took you for a...” he barely repressed a shudder, “...cat person.”

“Think about it, they’re independent, they don’t whine constantly, you can leave them alone all day and not come home to messes on the rug. They’re the perfect pet for someone on the go.” Lainie put the cat in the swing and brushed stray hairs off her suit. “Dogs are too needy, like babies.” She frowned and looked toward the driver who’d snorted with suppressed laughter.

“Dogs are loyal,” Marcus informed her rather, yes, he’d admit it, doggedly.

“So are cats, to a certain extent.”

“Ha! They aren’t loyal, they’re users.” Marcus curled his lip at the cat.

Lainie stepped into the crossfire, interrupting the staring contest. "Before you whip out the pistols at dawn, let me clue you in, he isn't mine."

"Oh?" Marcus tried not to look too happy about that. He must have failed because she laughed, a sweet, melodic sound that both soothed and aroused him.

"He's the neighbor's cat. She lets me borrow him at the end of the day for a little cuddling time. He's always happy to oblige me too. Aren't you, Fluffy?" She leaned down and gave the cat a kiss.

Marcus gagged. If she only knew what those animals got up to when they groomed themselves, she wouldn't be so quick to— He broke off guiltily when he recalled that he could actually do that too, in his other form. Not that he did, of course, never.

"Come on in." She went to put the key in the lock and stopped when it opened under her hand.

Marcus shoved her behind him so fast she didn't even have time to blink. The porch creaked and he knew Mick was there. He didn't get those muscles from driving the limo; he was one of Marcus's bodyguards. Not that Marcus needed them, but he had to keep up appearances. A show of strength kept the wolves at bay, in his case, literally.

"Mick?"

"Yeah, boss?" Mick's tone was respectful, but not subservient. In the public eye, they had to be careful. Nobody needed to know his employees would walk through fire for him. Boss had been decided on, instead of my liege, my king or my lord. That would attract too much notice, not a good thing for the fur wearers. PETA would never understand.

"Go around back." The driver immediately loped around the house, his speed just shy of too fast. Marcus could smell Lainie's anger and indignation without even looking at her. "You stand right here until I tell you it's safe," he ordered before pushing the door open with his foot.

"I will not."

"Do it." His tone made her straighten and open her mouth. He turned his head and glared, cowing her into sullen submission.

She folded her arms and stepped over to the swing. "Fine, I'm sure Fluffy will protect me."

"Yeah, if someone runs out, throw the little fucker in his face." With that, he entered the house and instantly smelled the invader. A soft scraping noise alerted him to someone else's presence and he ran in the direction it had come from, hoping for a fight. It would relieve the pressure. Anger wasn't a good emotion for his kind; it caused all sorts of physiological changes.

When he let his negative emotions, like anger and jealousy, gain control, he became more wolf-like in both looks and nature. If he got his hands on the person responsible for breaking into Lainie's home, biting him would be only the beginning.

He careened around the corner, entering the tiny kitchen at full speed. He and the chauffeur collided and crashed to the floor in a heap. "Goddamnit." Marcus winced when the full weight of the larger man pinned him to the floor.

"Sorry, boss." Mick was still young and made mistakes. Luckily, Marcus forgave easily. If his father had still been in power, that wouldn't have been the case at all. The old man liked to punish, and being a smart man, he had various torments he liked to employ. The memory of howls and screams still echoed in Marcus's head at night.

He refused to be that sort of Lupin. He didn't think it made him better to have the pack beaten into submission. He preferred to lead by example. It had worked for the past five years. He had no reason to believe it wouldn't continue to do so. "It's fine, Mick. He's long gone anyway." If he'd been paying attention before, he would have realized that; some big bad wolf he turned out to be.

"Do I need to leave you two alone?" Lainie stood in the doorway with the cat in her arms. "I think he's gone. If he wasn't before, you scared him away with all that noise you made."

Mick stood and pulled Marcus up so fast his feet left the floor. Like he said, young, but the boy ate his damn veggies. He was strong as an ox. He looked like a choirboy, with his light blond hair and blue eyes, but looks were deceiving because this "boy" could and would tear you apart if ordered to.

"Yeah." Marcus brushed off his suit, ignoring her comment. "I know."

"I'm calling the police." Her voice quavered ever so slightly, belying the calm expression on her face.

"I wouldn't." He put his hand out, but the hissing cat stopped him in mid-reach.

"Why?" Her question made him rack his brains for a logical reason.

"Because, I think I know who did it." He was actually one hundred percent sure who it was, or at least who ordered it.

"Who?"

Instead of answering her directly, he glared at the cat. "Put him out, will you? He gives me the willies staring at me like that."

"God, you're such a goober." But she put the cat outside, then folded her arms, obviously waiting for his answer.

"How long have you been investigating Caulder?" He silenced Mick with a look. The other man closed his mouth with an audible snap and waited.

"About a month or so, I guess." She tapped her nails on her chin. "Are you saying he did this?"

"I know he did it, or he had it done. This is probably only the beginning."

"But, nothing was touched. It doesn't look like anyone was even here. What if I just left the door unlocked?" She was second-guessing herself; he knew it as well as she did.

"Lainie, please stop kidding yourself." He put his hand up. "Why don't we take a look around and make sure everything is like it should be?"

"Fine." She took a deep breath.

"Mick?"

"Yes, sir?"

"Watch the doors." The other man got into position. "Lead the way, darlin'. I want the grand tour." His easy smile hid the churning emotions inside him. Possessiveness and rage were at the forefront but all of these were coated in a haze of fear for her safety. He didn't like it, and neither did the wolf residing inside him. To feel it for a woman he'd thought of as his own for so long made it even worse.

She walked ahead of him into her bedroom and her soft cry of distress had him racing to find out what was wrong. He stopped in the doorway and stared at the destruction. The mattress and bedding were off the frame, both ripped almost to shreds. But what made the rage grow bright red was the fact that all her underthings had been pulled out of the drawers and strewn about the room, some in pieces.

One pair of particularly sexy black thongs hung from the blade of the ceiling fan. He sighed with regret. He'd have liked to see her in those. It wasn't to be because they were ripped and dangling by one strap. The fan, turned on when Lainie threw the switch, began to whir. The underwear flew from their perch and landed on Marcus's shoulder.

"Well, shit," she began, embarrassment pinkening her cheeks. "Give me those. Did you smell... That's so gross. They are clean, you know."

Just as he'd thought, it was another werewolf. One of Jacob's people, he'd bet. "You're coming home with me," he told her, tossing the underwear in the middle of the ruined mattress.

"What?" She looked shocked at the thought.

"I mean it. No arguments." He would tie her up and throw her in the car. "If you want your things, I'll have them brought to the house, but you won't be staying here, not tonight."

Chapter Three

Marcus kept his cell phone plastered to his ear, ignoring the thunderous glares Lainie kept sending in his direction. "Yeah, Kane, in her house." The man's low whistle answered him. He knew his voice must convey his anger, so he tried to tamp it back down.

It wasn't happening; the invasion of her space, the touching of her things, was a personal affront to him. She'd been a part of his life for six years before their separation. He'd cared for her, laughed with her, spoke with her on the phone when they weren't close enough to visit otherwise.

When she'd been a child, he'd been her protector. As she'd grown, he'd become her confidant, the one she told all her troubles to, but never had he felt like her brother. They'd never meshed that way. Lainie stayed with them for two weeks after they'd taken her from his father's facility. Then, inexplicably, his uncle said she'd have to leave.

Marcus hated him for taking her and it must have shown on his face that day, because Uncle David led him outside and put his heavy hand on his shoulder. "Son, you don't understand now, and God help me, I hope you never do, but I have to get her away from here. She'll visit, I promise."

"Why does she have to go?" He loved Lainie. In such a brief period of time, she'd wormed her way into his heart. Oh, it had been an innocent love. She looked at him with hero worship in her eyes. He'd been the one to save her so she was his.

"For her safety." Whatever that meant, Marcus didn't get to find out, because at that moment Lainie came out the door with her meager belongings. Though his father had bought her all sorts of clothes, she only took a few things. Marcus's heart lightened when he noticed her wearing the flannel shirt he'd wrapped around her. She wore it like a jacket, refused to part with it.

He recalled how her bottom lip quivered before she dropped her bag and hurled herself at him. She'd wrapped her arms around his waist and cried against his chest. Her hair tickled his nose when he kissed the top of her head.

"You're a good man, Marcus," his uncle said—not a good boy, but a man. That day he'd felt less a man and more a child than any other time in his life. He'd felt like crying but he had to look strong, for her.

"Uncle says we'll see each other a lot," he promised, and smiled for her benefit.

"Okay." Lainie smiled through her tears. "Thank you," she whispered.

"You're welcome." He knew she didn't really remember anything about the night he and his uncle came to rescue her, but she knew enough to say that.

David bent down and picked up Lainie's bag. "Come on, Lainie. We have a long way to go." He put out his hand and she took it. "She'll be fine, safe." There was that word again, and the emphasis on it that made Marcus feel as if he were missing something important. But he'd been distracted when David's eyes suddenly went cold. Marcus whirled and met the impassive gaze of his father.

"Goodbye, Elaine." Samuel's voice, as always, was deep and smooth.

"Goodbye, Mr. Bei," she chirped and waved as David pulled her toward his pickup.

Marcus watched them leave then glared at his father. "Why?"

"Don't question me." The smoothness left the man's voice to be replaced by contempt. "Go see to your mother."

The reminder made his shoulders slump. She was pregnant, and not doing well. He hurried through the house, intending to do just that when his father's voice stopped him. "Women are not worth the trouble, remember that. Use them, discard them, and then move on."

Marcus quelled his disgust and stalked back to the secret room his mother now slept in during the last weeks of her pregnancy. She was in wolf form, stuck this way until the birth of her latest litter. He'd been the only survivor of her other litter.

Diana Bei wasn't a strong woman, despite being a werewolf; she'd not been well since his birth. If he'd have known it was the last time that he'd see her alive, maybe he'd have taken a little more time with her that day.

He stopped looking into the past, with all the pain and hate that waited there. Instead, his gaze focused on the present Lainie, superimposing her over the little girl she'd been. "Ready?" He put his hand out and she took it automatically. He didn't immediately lead her toward the car, just stood there watching her.

Finally, her patience snapped. "What is it?"

"I was remembering what a pretty little girl you used to be."

"Uh huh." She gave him a look of patent disbelief.

"Come on, let's go home." It was a slip of the tongue, but he meant it in every sense of the word.

Once they got into the car, she gazed pensively out the window, and he didn't think it was motion sickness this time.

"What's wrong?" His voice was soft, but her shoulders still jerked. "You're a million miles away."

"Oh, just wondering. Why would Caulder have someone do that to my house? How does he even know I'm investigating him? I've been careful." Lainie pulled on her lower lip in thought. "I moved here because of him, you know."

"Have you ever even met him?"

"No, but I've seen his picture in newspapers and magazines, of course. Yours too." She grinned at him impishly. "All those pretty ladies you keep company with, Marcus." She ignored his scowl, continuing her story.

"I got a phone call from an anonymous source that Jacob Caulder was involved in trafficking. At first, I thought they meant drugs or stolen goods, but when I got to looking, I noticed something strange.

"Whenever Jacob went abroad, which he does a lot, under the pretext of buying up land for his development company, people would go missing. Not a lot, only a dozen or so, but they were always women and young girls." She grimaced in distaste. "I wouldn't have caught it even then if not for a friend of mine."

"A friend of yours is missing?" Marcus prompted when she stopped talking.

"Jade Marks and I went to college together. She was in journalism too, but she works for anthropological journals. She's a genius, and like most, wouldn't notice anything happening until it was too late." Lainie looked sad for a moment. "When we were roommates, I was forever helping her find her things."

She took a deep breath and laced her fingers together in her lap. “But now, she’s gone. And the last person she spoke with was me.”

“What did she say?” Marcus watched her become more agitated.

She scrambled to get her thoughts together. Whenever she tried to think about this, she got dizzy and sick. Like the dreams, it haunted her. She hated it.

“She thought someone was following her. I laughed at her and called her paranoid.” Lainie put her fist to her mouth. “She told me, ‘just because you’re paranoid don’t mean you aren’t also right’. Then, the phone cut off and that was it.” Except it wasn’t, something else had happened, something that made Lainie break out into a sweat.

“Lainie?” Marcus’s voice sounded like it was coming from another room. Waves of nausea flowed through her, making her panic in her attempt to open the window. His hand slid beneath her own, depressing the button so the window came down, letting in blessedly cool night air. *When had it gotten dark?* she wondered idly. He stroked her back. His lips slid over her temple and she sighed. “I’ll help you.” His voice, so assured, so familiar, sounded like heaven to her.

“I don’t think anyone can help me, Marcus,” she whispered.

“Why?”

“I think I’m going insane. Because you see, when she called—” Lainie pressed her lips together and took another breath, determined to force the words out. “I heard it.” The memory that was more like a dream came welling up from a deep place within the recesses of her mind. Like a cancer, it began to spread, leaving chaos in its wake.

Marcus nudged her gently. “It?”

"On her cell, when she dropped it. I heard the struggle, then growling, Marcus, like an animal. I heard them howling. I've heard that sound before, I just can't for the life of me remember when. Those weren't animals."

"Maybe they were." Marcus tightened his hold on her hand. "She was in a Third-World country; there are animals that growl, right?"

"Yeah, but um, they don't speak." Lainie laughed, a bitter sound edging on hysterical. "They don't speak and they don't stand up on two legs. God, she had a picture phone, Marcus. Somehow, she sent that picture to me before they got to her. But what I saw was impossible." She shivered, and added a silent, except in my nightmares.

"What picture?"

"It was something unreal." Her whole body trembled with the effort of the telling. It was hard, her memory was resisting, but she fought against it and this time, maybe because Marcus was here with her, she won. "A werewolf like in the movies."

"Do you have the picture?"

"No, see, that's the strangest thing. I remember being hysterical and calling someone. Then, I don't remember anything after that. When I woke up the picture was gone."

"Who did you call?"

A strange reluctance stole over her, as if it were something she was supposed to keep secret. That was silly of course, this was Marcus, so with a shrug, she told him who she'd called in a panic that night. "Your uncle."

"Lainie, honey. Don't lie to me." Marcus pulled her around to face him, pinning her with his intense stare.

"What?"

“Don’t! That shit isn’t funny! If you have a ‘friend’ that’s fine. Hell, I love a challenge. I know I’m more man than any other you’ve had. So don’t lie to me about my uncle.”

“I’m not lying.” She shoved at him.

“Yes, you are, you have to be.” He released her and ran a shaky hand over his face. “My uncle’s been dead for about eight years.”

Lainie shook her head back and forth slowly. “Marcus, I don’t know how to tell you this, but I saw your uncle just last week. He’s always been in my life. He’s been a foster parent to me, both he and Joanna.”

“Joanna?” Incredulity was replaced by white-hot anger so apparent it burned her skin where they touched. “Where is that bitch?”

“I beg your damn pardon? She’s not a bitch, but you’re an asshole!”

“Father said Joanna killed...” He pressed his lips together and narrowed his eyes in suspicion. “What the hell is going on?”

“I wish I knew. But, I do know you’re scaring me. Maybe I should just stay at a hotel,” Lainie began, only to have him turn on her and snarl.

He leaned over until they were nose to nose. “You, sweetheart, are going nowhere but with me.”

“Look, darling, I can go where I want.” She gritted the words out past clenched teeth.

His lip curled up and she thought his teeth seemed sharper but he closed his mouth tight after that, refusing to either speak or look at her. She contemplated jumping out of the moving vehicle; the tension inside the car was slowly choking her.

He must have read her intentions because he hauled her up against his side and smiled. "Welcome to the Bei home, Lainie."

She jerked her head forward. The partition between them and the driver came down to give her a glimpse of the estate. It was breathtaking, but the sight was spoiled by the ominous sound of the gates clanging shut coming through the open window. Suddenly, she felt like a prisoner.

Chapter Four

Lights blazed, illuminating the large home. It was made of weathered gray stone, shaped in an elongated "E" without the middle leg. Instead, a large portico stood over the gravel-paved circular drive.

"Goodnight, Mick." Marcus smiled at his driver. "I won't be needing you anymore."

"Uh, yes, sir." Mick raised his brow, puzzled, and then his face lit with understanding. "Oh, night." He tipped his hat at her and grinned.

"Goodnight, Mick." Lainie glared up at Marcus. If he was insinuating what she thought he was, he was gonna come up short as the saying went.

The light came on, making Lainie squint in the sudden brightness, barely able to make out the outline of a man standing in the doorway in a suit. Sheesh, he had a butler?

"Sir?"

"Hello, Allen." Marcus took Lainie's arm and led her up the wide stone steps, laughing. "Nothing went horribly wrong while I was gone I hope?"

"No, sir." Allen looked like he thought she was something that had gone wrong. Thick black brows lowered over a pair of icy blue eyes as he stared at her silently. Somehow she doubted those wrinkles around them were laugh lines.

But she attempted to make friends. "My name's Lainie, nice to meet you." She held out her hand and smiled.

He hesitated before shaking her hand very gently. Did they all act this way? "You as well, miss."

"Come into the living room. We'll talk there." Marcus led her toward a set of doors and somehow, Allen beat them there, opening the doors for them. "Thanks, we'll call if we need anything."

They both sounded so polite. There was something strange in the way Allen and the others acted, but she couldn't quite put her finger on it. As she sat, it came to her; they acted like servants. No, the word she wanted was subservient, heavy on the sub. Ew, surely Marcus wasn't one of those kinky spanker men. If so, she would have to end it before it began.

Although, maybe not. Lainie shook her head to clear her thoughts.

"What are you thinking?" His voice vibrated against the skin beneath her ear.

"Nothing!" she replied quickly, ignoring the heated flush that crept up her cheeks. Thank God, he couldn't read her mind; she'd die right here on the spot.

When he accepted her answer she sighed with relief and looked around. The room seemed cavernous with a sunken fireplace set in the middle of the floor. A chimney rose up to the peaked ceiling, all but disappearing into the darkness. Large leather sofas and deep-seated chairs were clustered around the central fixture, making the room warm and inviting.

He pressed the button on a remote and panels on the far wall opened revealing a TV.

"This is nice." Her eyes widened. "You've come up in the world, just a little." His family had been well-off a decade ago, but she knew for a fact he'd made his company into something much more than it had ever been under the control of Samuel Bei.

"Software pays. Nerds rule." Marcus grinned and flipped the stations until he found a music channel.

"You are so not a nerd, sweetie." She laughed at him.

"Yes, I am. Beneath the wickedly handsome and debonair exterior, beats the heart of a true computer-loving nerd."

"I hear ya, nerd muffin." Was she flirting with him? Yes, she was. She did it rather well, if she did say so herself.

"Don't believe me, but don't say I didn't warn you." He sat back and put his arm behind her on the sofa. "How have the years treated you ?"

"I've been great. How about you?" The heat from his body radiated into her bones. He would be a lovely accessory on a cold winter night.

"Just fine, honey, but I don't want to talk about me. I haven't seen you since you were sixteen. Catch me up." Without warning, he turned his head toward her and gave her that piercing stare again. "Starting with why you never called me again, how it is you've seen David and I haven't and basically everything." His hand cupped her shoulder and squeezed gently.

She bit her lower lip. "Because David said it might be best not to. It was him I called the day when you and I almost..." She paused and blushed, unable to complete the sentence, but her stupid mistake still lived on in her memory.

Marcus finished for her. "When we acted like a couple of stupid kids and it got out of control?"

"Close enough. Anyway, David took me back to Joanna."

"Joanna?" Marcus broke in on her story. "Not Joanna Michaels?"

"Yes, why?"

"Lainie, she is—" He closed his mouth.

"She is what?"

"Nothing, honey, keep talking." He waited, but it was in vain. She sat with her arms folded, glaring at him. "What?"

"I refuse to tell you anything else until you tell me what the hell is up with you."

"I'm not really sure what you mean." But he did, she could tell just by looking at him.

"I'm kind of tired; can I go to my room now?" She stood, leaving him no choice; either he could get up and take her there, or let her wander around his house unescorted. She'd bet on the former because it was a sure thing.

Marcus stood with a sigh of defeat. "Fine, babe, let's go to bed. I'm tired too." She raised her brow at him but said nothing, just let him lead her toward the stairs in the main hall.

The silence lasted until he stopped outside the door to her room. "Here we are. I hope you find everything to your liking." He retreated into formality, well aware she'd throw it right back in his face.

"Thank you."

He was right, she sounded so calm and cool it made him grit his teeth. As Lupin, he needed the information but he didn't want to force the issue. From her expression, he could tell he wasn't getting anything else from her tonight. But he'd like to know if a man he'd thought dead for the past eight years wasn't. He'd been alive all this time visiting with Lainie. The question was, who he was more jealous of—Lainie or David.

"Why so quiet?" She stood close enough that it seemed natural to just lean down and kiss her. He was surprised she didn't pull away. Instead, she melted against him, putting her arms around his waist. He nudged her mouth open and tasted her. Her soft sigh was like sweet music in his ears.

He lifted her slightly, grinding his hips against her, desperate to get as close as possible. His fingers pulled at the hem of her skirt. She wore stockings, and the contrast between them and the silky skin of her thighs made his body tighten. He wanted her beneath him, screaming and begging.

Marcus pulled his mouth away from hers with a gasp. "Lainie, go in your room." His voice shook. He looked down into her eyes, clouded with passion, and his control started to slip. "Go, right now. Lock the door." He forced himself to step back.

She whirled to do as he asked and it took all he had not to grab her and pull her back. She risked a glance over her shoulder and whatever she saw in his face must have frightened her. "Goodnight, Marcus, sweet dreams." She slammed the door and the click of the lock echoed in the silence of the hallway.

He'd picked this room for her for three very important reasons. One, it was on the second floor. Two, the door was thick and lined with steel, and three, the room was right next to his, with a connecting door, no less. Right now, he pressed his head against the wood that hid the steel core and sighed. "Sweet dreams to you too."

When he inhaled, he could still smell her. He could also feel the change coming; he'd held his emotions in check too long. Quickly, he moved through the house, running by the time he reached the door to the gardens. He took off his jacket and then his tie followed, falling on the ground.

Soon, he stood naked in the moonlight, allowing it to bathe his skin. With a thought, he started to change. His hands curved into claws, fur black as the night appeared and he fell down on all fours, groaning slightly with the effort. The wolf shook himself and lifted his head to the sky with a long, low howl. It was good to be free again.

With one last look back to where he knew her room to be, he turned and ran into the warm desert night, howling his cares to the bright orb hanging low in the sky. The moon was almost full.

Marcus was the Lupin for a reason. He had the unique ability to control his change throughout the month. Only during the full moon did he actually need to and then only for a short time. Otherwise, he could shift into his wolf form at will.

One other had been able to do this—David Crow. Not only did his uncle have the ability to change into a wolf, but also a bear and an eagle. His uncle had been special. Or was "had" the right word now? According to Lainie he was alive and well and sending her Christmas cards.

Marcus growled and dug into the loose dirt with his claws, running up the small rise behind his house. He glanced back at it, glistening like a jewel in the dim light. She was inside his home now, what could be the greatest treasure of his life, or his greatest torment depending on his point of view. He'd changed his mind about that at least ten times today alone.

She messed with his equilibrium, and he wasn't sure he liked that. But it was all balanced out by the fact that she made him feel alive again. He'd been holding his emotions in check for so long that he did it automatically. Now, however, he had the feeling she would break his control. He only hoped they both survived the experience.

Chapter Five

"Damn." Lainie whistled softly, taking in the contents of the room. Dark rose rugs were scattered over the floors. A fireplace, smaller than the one downstairs, but made of the same stone, sat in the far right corner by the large sliding-glass window. A down comforter covered the bed in a shade slightly lighter than the rugs, with mountains of pillows ranging from blush pink to almost red, interspersed with a few green and ivory.

The green stripe on the chaise lounge and rugged stone on the floor and the fireplace broke up the color scheme, barely saving it from being too feminine.

Her bags sat on the small bench at the foot of the bed waiting to be unpacked. She was moving to do just that when a soft howl echoed in the distance. She hurried to peer out of the large glass doors that led onto the balcony outside her room.

Nothing but the cacti loomed in the darkness beneath the almost-full moon. With a shiver, she turned and went back to putting away her things. She didn't have that much with her but Marcus had promised the rest of her things would arrive tomorrow.

She decided all her furnishings would fit into this room with no trouble at all. Not that she'd tell him that, it might give him ideas to move her here. The big idiot was as bossy as ever.

With a bored sigh, she decided to explore her immediate surroundings and went to the door she thought led to the bathroom. Instead, when she unlocked it, she found another room, as beautifully appointed as her own. Done in earthy browns and dark greens and blues, very masculine, and she knew just what man it belonged to. How convenient that it had a connecting door.

She gritted her teeth and tapped her foot on the floor. Someone wanted their midnight girl-snack close at hand. Had she seemed that easy? With a laugh, she decided she didn't really care. Despite all his shortcomings, he still made her feel more alive than she had in years.

He also had the ability to make her angrier than she'd been in years too. His controlling attitude was one of the things she hadn't missed at all. If he thought he could subdue her like his servants, he was setting himself up for disappointment.

Another howl echoed through the night. Lainie wrapped her arms around herself and wondered where Marcus was. She wouldn't mind a little company right now. Wolves disturbed and fascinated her. They always captured her attention when they came on TV. Beautiful, strong and wild, they called to some level deep within her psyche, one she didn't want to examine too closely. As she made her way through her teens and adulthood, she realized there were some subjects she shouldn't dwell on too long. When she tried, she got sick to her stomach and suffered from what amounted to panic attacks. The sight of a wolf with its prey had the ability to make her feel numb with shock and heated with something else.

She hated feeling out of control, hated knowing she didn't understand herself fully. In an age of self-analysis and getting in touch with your mind, she didn't have access to a lot of her childhood memories.

David told her she blocked them because they were traumatic. Joanna said to try and force them would be even more so. Sometimes Lainie wondered why they'd always been against her remembering things. It was as if they were hiding important revelations from her. Marcus would hide things from her as well, "for her own good" of course. He'd feel he was protecting her from whatever would make her upset. She wasn't a child any longer, nor was she fragile.

With that thought, she stalked to the remaining door and flung it open to reveal a richly appointed bathroom, also in shades of pink. "Ew, it's like someone puked up Pepto in here." On further inspection, it reminded her of a seashell. However, she would never admit that she liked anything pink, so she put that on her list of grievances. She wanted to have something against Marcus, something to keep her from just falling into his bed without the slightest resistance.

"Pink is my favorite color." She sang to herself while running the large and yes, pink tub full of the hottest water she could stand. She wondered if she'd use it all up and force him to take a cold shower. Her mouth turned up in an evil grin at the thought. "I hope so, maybe that will cool him off." She took off her clothes, tossing them at the hamper. She'd worry about washing things later. Tonight, she was too tired to do more than bathe and get into bed.

She lay back and stretched her legs out in the tub. This was much nicer than hers. She wouldn't get used to it though, because she wasn't staying. No matter how luxurious the accommodations, it was still a prison.

She scrubbed her hair with much more vigor than needed, then dunked her head beneath the surface to rinse. When she popped back up and opened her eyes, she got a bit of a shock. A huge black wolf stood in the doorway.

"Oh shit, oh shit," she breathed.

In answer, the wolf licked his lips and walked even farther into the room.

"Ooh, no! Go away. Shoo!" She flicked her wet hands at him.

He flinched when the water hit him in the face and stopped, staring at her with a pair of glowing golden eyes. The contrast between his fur and eyes made his stare even more intense. He was the biggest wolf she'd ever seen. Not that she had seen all that many, come to think of it, not in real life, anyway. If they stood side by side, his shoulder would be level with her hip.

She wouldn't be standing beside him, however, not by a freaking long shot. "I said to git!" she yelled.

Instead, he moved closer.

She squealed and slid back in the tub, promptly going under with a strangled yelp. After much splashing and screaming, she resurfaced and came face-to-face with him. "Urk?" she managed.

He sniffed her arm where it rested on the edge of the tub, and then licked it, gently.

She waited with her eyes squinted, expecting him to bite down on her bare flesh. When nothing happened, she chanced another glance at him.

He was grinning at her; there was no other word for it. His tongue lolled out and he panted.

"Oh. My. God!" she squealed. "Are you a freakin' pet?"

He leaned forward, pushing his nose beneath her hand.

"I guess that's a yes." She giggled when he licked her wet fingers. "Are you the howler?" She reached out and scratched his ears.

With a sigh, he sat and put his muzzle on the side of the tub.

"This is so cool. Leave it to Marcus to have a wolf as a pet." She stood and reached for the towel she'd left on the floor beside the tub.

"Back up, pretty puppy." She pushed at him until he stepped out of her way.

He watched her as she dried off with one of the huge pink towels. "I'm glad you're here. I was getting lonely." She put her gown on and started out of the room.

"You want to sleep with me? If Marcus don't like it, tough." She turned off the lights and got into bed with him trailing her every step. The animal leapt onto the foot of the bed. She grinned at him until he crawled up to put his head on the pillow beside hers. "Hey, down at the bottom." She pointed but he ignored her. "Oh, fine." It wasn't as if she could move him anyway. He looked like he weighed a ton. "Goodnight, puppy."

He barked and looked insulted.

"Well, sorry, I don't know your name. Tomorrow I'll ask Marcus. I won't tell him that you slept in here with me. It will be our little secret." She turned over so that she faced him.

She wondered how he got in until she saw that the door to the balcony hadn't shut all the way. With another look at the huge canine lying between her and the door, she decided it didn't matter. Anything that came in would have to go through him, and while he'd been nice to her, she had a feeling he'd go for the throat if he felt threatened.

Her eyes drifted closed and she smiled when he pressed his nose against her cheek, almost like a kiss. "Aw, how sweet." Then she frowned. "Ew, dogs lick their butts, gross. No, no," Lainie muttered, wrapping her arm around his neck. She pushed at him until he rested his head on her chest. "There, now, be still or get down." And with that, she drifted off to sleep.

Marcus lay in his wolf form wondering if he would expire from the torment of it all. Instead of changing back to his human self, he'd leapt up on the balcony and pressed his nose to the glass. He'd been surprised that the door slid open but decided he may as well go in and check on her. The sounds of water splashing led him to the bathroom and once he saw her in there naked, there was no way he was going to let such an opportunity pass. He'd walked in and looked his fill. Lainie as an adult was a hell of a lot better than he remembered. When she'd screamed, he again thought of leaving.

When she'd slipped in the tub, he'd gone over to make sure she came back up. At least, this was what he told himself. In reality, he wanted to look at her up close.

She'd popped up and stared at him with those wide green eyes. There was fear there, but beneath it all, he sensed fascination. Who wouldn't be? He was a wolf, anyone would love the opportunity to touch one if it was safe enough to do so. When he'd nudged her hand for a scratch, she'd complied.

When she'd said that he was Marcus's pet, he knew it would be fine, at least for now. Then there had been the drying off... He'd almost shifted then and taken her, especially when she bent over to dry her legs. Jesus, the woman gave him a case of the blue balls.

She sighed in her sleep and buried her nails in the scruff of his neck before moving on to the ears. He whined softly. Hell, the woman was diabolical.

Chapter Six

Marcus woke in mid-snore. He was still a wolf, but he'd been about to shift back to his human form. He opened his eyes and snuck a look at Lainie. She lay flat on her back, asleep, with her mouth half-open. His heart flipped. She looked angelic and innocent, all the things he wasn't.

Did he have the right to spoil her with his touch? He slipped out of the bed and padded over to the connecting door. The answer was an unequivocal no. Would he do the honorable thing and keep himself from her? Probably not. He'd never been someone who denied himself what he wanted in life.

Marcus moved into his room and headed for the bath, intending to wash off the results of a night spent running in wolf form through the desert. He stood in the bathroom and looked at the mosaic tiles beneath his paws. He couldn't actually see the colors, not as well as in his human form. He concentrated and the bone-grinding shift began.

Slowly, the greens and yellows of the tiles came into focus, then the blues and finally the reds hit his vision. He flexed his fingers, and then his toes. He stood and stretched, his joints popping back into place effortlessly. With a small sigh, he shook himself and stepped into the shower.

When he emerged, he put on his boxer briefs, intending to go back into the room with Lainie; he'd share her bed as a human too. She'd be less inclined to freak out if he at least wore his underwear, though he preferred to sleep nude. Then he put on a pair of silk pajama bottoms with the idea that the more he had to take off, the more time he'd have to think.

He stared at the door, undecided. If he took this final step, there would be no going back. Once he had her, he never intended to let her go.

Ten years was a long time to carry a hard-on for one woman, but he had. He stalked toward the balcony door instead of the connecting one. Ten fucking years. He sighed as he stood outside looking at the stars.

Marcus leaned on the rail, wishing he could go back and change what had happened the summer Lainie waltzed into his life. Now he thought of it as the summer of his awakening. What a fucking joke.

The Lainie he remembered before that had been tiny and cute, a little girl who aroused his protective instinct. His lips quirked in a half smile recalling that as a teen she'd aroused something else entirely.

He'd been her knight in shining armor, not that she really recalled the incident involved. He remembered it vividly and rage burned in his chest. Uncle David or more than likely, Joanna, had wiped that horrible night in his father's lab from her mind...or had they? Maybe it was lying in wait, ready to jump out at the worst possible time.

Lainie had been his friend, his ray of sunshine, innocent and sweet. She'd had a serious case of hero worship for him. One that made his chest swell with pride. When they were kids she'd come to visit every single summer. He looked forward to those visits for the whole year. Hell, he'd been innocent too until she came to visit that last summer.

Marcus, his cousin Jordan and his two friends, Ben and Stephen, were in his room the day she arrived.

"Hey, man, I hear a car." Jordan peered out the window then did a double take. "Who in the fuck is that?"

"Who?" Marcus didn't move from his slouched position by the bed.

"Hell, I don't know, but I want me a piece of that." Jordan grinned and wiggled his brows.

"You don't know what to do with that," Stephen breathed, peering though the crack in the curtain. "But I do."

"Shit, both of you are idiots." Ben lay with his hands behind his head, looking up at the ceiling. "Neither of you have ever gotten lucky."

Good-natured ribbing and jibes flew back and forth until the voice he heard at least once a week on the phone called out, "Marcus?"

He rolled his eyes and made a face at the other boys. "Man, it's just Lainie." Her hurried footsteps sounded on the tiles, so he turned to catch her as she hurled herself into his arms. His blood turned to ice, before fire and a feeling of possessiveness foreign to him quickly replaced it.

"Marcus!" Her eyes glowed with happiness. "I'm here!" Her arms tightened around his waist. She buried her face against his chest and giggled. "Did I surprise you? I came early this year." At that, she danced away, whirling around, arms out from her sides.

He stared. She wore a pair of simple cutoffs and a white tank top. But what she did to that outfit was surely illegal. Her breasts had ripened to full mounds that strained the thin fabric, and the denim hugged the firm curves of her ass. In a word, Lainie was hot.

"Uh," he managed before she flew back at him, smiling in that trusting way she had. She gave him another hug and his dick went berserk.

"How you been? What ya doin'? Oh, hi." She noticed the others in the room. None of them slouched or lounged now, they all sat up straight and stared at her.

"Hi there, sweetheart." Ben was the first to break the tension-laden silence. He pushed his hair out of his face and smiled at her, his blue eyes sparkling.

"My name is Lainie, what's yours?"

"Oh, sorry." Belatedly Marcus remembered his manners. "This is Ben, Stephen and that's Jordan, my cousin on my dad's side." He glared at them all but that only made it worse. "This is Lainie."

"Yeah, we're practically family, Lainie, come sit over here by me." Jordan patted the window seat.

"Oh, okay, but I need to go and put my stuff up first. See y'all in a little while," she promised, going up on her toes to kiss Marcus's cheek. "I missed you." With that, she breezed out of the room, unaware that she'd started his blood pounding in his veins, particularly below the belt.

"Damn! Dude, where the hell you been hiding that fine piece of ass?" This remark from Stephen brought guffaws from the other two, but it only made Marcus burn with rage. Something clamored inside him at the sight of her. Lust, hunger and desire all rolled up in a package of possessiveness that howled the word *mine*.

He'd had sex, hell he was almost eighteen. His dad had chosen one of the pack bitches for him. But Lainie had just burned the other woman's image from his brain.

"Dude." Ben laughed. "Set us up." He jerked his head in the direction Lainie had just taken and it was all Marcus could do not to leap on him and tear out his throat. They wouldn't touch her; he'd kill them if they did. The irony of it was, neither would Marcus.

The next week was hell for Marcus. The only thing that made it bearable was that Lainie remained oblivious to his attraction to her. All of it went right over her head. He was suspicious of her innocence now, but back then he'd only felt guilt. Surely the little brat hadn't been *that* unaware.

The day *it* happened was hot and sunny. And he'd been desperate to get away from her, the smell of the lotion she put on her skin, her own sweet scent beneath, so he'd gone to help the groundskeepers repair the fence behind the house.

The workmen had long since gone and a storm cloud was brewing by the time Marcus quit digging postholes. He was tired, sweaty and in a pissed-off mood, all because Lainie was in the pool in a bikini.

Well, that wasn't the real reason. There was also the fact that his friends were more than likely still there looking at her in that silly excuse for a swimsuit. When he'd left, they were all hanging around just to gawk at her. She'd been chattering about some music video she liked.

It was a testament to how hot she looked that the three admitted to liking the Backstreet Boys. It was at that point that he'd left before he killed them or threw up, or both. Teenage boys did not like boy bands or they didn't admit it out loud.

He'd left the pool, with their laughter ringing in his ears. He imagined her kissing one of his friends or even letting him sneak into her room. He wouldn't set foot in her room now. He couldn't risk it. Too damn bad, she didn't feel any compunction about slipping into his room and bouncing up and down on his bed to wake him.

He shoved the posthole diggers deeper into the hard-packed earth. “Fuck it.” He sat in the shade of a small, weathered old pine that held on for dear life on top of the hill.

The wind blew from the east, the same direction of the house. He raised his nose and inhaled, happy for the cooling sensation on his sweaty skin. However, on the breeze, there was a smell. Lainie.

Marcus sat with his shoulders hunched, curling his body in on itself. His stomach cramped, radiating from his abdomen to his thighs. He made a sound between a whine and a howl. But she kept coming closer, unaware she was stepping into a hornet's nest.

“Hey, Marcus, I thought you might be thirsty.” She stood right behind him before he knew it. “There's a storm brewing too, you better come inside.”

The storm brewing above paled in comparison to the one inside his body. He looked over his shoulder and took in the long tanned legs exposed by the yellow dress she wore. The wind pressed the fabric against her body, delineating the soft curves of her thighs and breasts.

“Marcus?” She looked around and spied the towel he'd brought out with him.

He sat in silence while she smoothed it out to sit on so as not to get her dress dirty.

“Are you all right? Here's your tea.” She handed him a large lidded cup.

He tried to thank her for her thoughtfulness, but couldn't get the words past his throat. Instead, he chugged the tea down, hoping to quench his thirst for other things. “I'm fine,” he finally managed.

"Do you think maybe we could go to town later?" She twisted her fingers in her skirt, drawing his attention to her legs again.

"No."

"Oh." Her head bowed and he felt like an asshole. "That's okay, I'm sure you're tired. So, you want to come on home? We could go for a swim, that would cool you off." Not if she wore that damn bikini, it wouldn't. He smiled at her and something must have shown in his face then, something that scared her.

Lainie's eyes widened and she froze in place.

He leaned forward and tugged on the hem of her dress. "Somethin' wrong?"

"N-no," she whispered back, but he heard her heart speed up, and watched when she wet her lips with her tongue.

"I like the dress." He inched the hem up a little. His whole body screamed for him to take her and the only thing that kept him from doing so were the memories of the way she used to be.

"Thanks. I got it last week when Ms. Sarah took me to town." She smoothed the skirt down and flipped her hair back.

Marcus just stared at her, smiling when she flushed and looked away. His hand slid closer and she jumped when it met the skin of her thigh. She turned her head and opened her mouth, probably to ask him what the hell he was doing.

She never got the chance. He pushed her down on the ground and lay on top of her. He wedged his body between her legs and grabbed her wrists with one hand. "Why did you come out here?"

"Get off." Her hips bucked in an attempt to push him off her. She only succeeded in pressing herself against the bulge in his jeans. She froze, watching him closely.

"Why?" he ground out.

"To bring you something to drink."

"I want something else, and I think you do too." He leaned closer.

"What?" Her voice was faint.

"This." He kissed her, softly, tasting the sweetness of her lip gloss before he delved inside and tasted her own heady flavor. His free hand moved to the top of her dress, pulling it down to expose her breasts to his gaze. "You are beautiful."

Soft creamy mounds trembled with each breath she took, the dark pink nipples hardening before his eyes. He leaned down and took one into his mouth, moaning at the taste. He watched her eyes as he sucked hard, flicking the tip with his tongue before biting it. She gave a high keening cry. He plumped her other breast in his hand, squeezing it.

"Marcus."

"Shh." He rocked his pelvis against her. "You want it, I can smell it. You're wet for me. All for me."

"I am not." She sounded shocked to the core.

"Yes. For me." His hand left her breast to trail down to the end of the skirt. He pulled it up, slowly exposing a pair of pink lacy panties. He slid his fingers down the front of them, encountering the soft, springy curls covering her sex. Just as he thought, she was wet and warm, ready. He flicked his thumb up the center of her slit, rubbing against the nub of flesh hidden in the silky folds.

She sucked in her breath, drawing his attention back to her breasts. He groaned and latched onto her nipple, biting and sucking, at the same time cupping her pussy in his hand. Gently, he pushed a finger inside and she went wild in his arms. The scent of her filled the air around them; she inadvertently aroused him even further.

She screamed, but he only pushed harder, another finger joining the first, stretching her, sliding in and out. Her desire spiked, he smelled it. She tightened around his fingers. He circled her clit and her pussy tensed again. Her mouth fell open and her eyes closed as she arched her hips upwards. "Oh God, Marcus."

"Mine." He moved his hand to his pants. He pulled his cock free and pressed it against her. She opened her eyes wide when he slid her panties to one side. Slowly, he began to enter her.

She kicked at him. He pulled her a little closer, holding her despite her struggles. He eased farther into her tight, slick opening, and she clenched around him again.

Finally, one foot found purchase, and the grinding pain in his thigh snapped him out of his lust-filled haze. Marcus raised his head from her breast and the mark he'd left there to meet her panic-stricken gaze. Her innocence was there for any fool to see. Ice sluiced through his veins, banking his desire instantly. Regret took its place. "Oh, God, Lainie, I'm so sorry." He gathered her in his arms.

She tried to get away at first but she must have realized whatever happened was over, because she stopped fighting and just held on, her whole frame wracked with sobs.

He righted her clothes and rocked back and forth, cradling her in his arms, his hand rubbing her back soothingly. "I'm sorry, so fuckin' sorry," he whispered, hoping to make it right, but knowing everything had changed forever.

Seconds later, he knew just how they had changed. He looked at his hand and saw to his horror that fur was sprouting on it. He was going through his first shift, now, at the worst possible time. "Lainie." His voice thickened. "I want you to go to the house, right now. Go to the house, honey. But don't run." He sounded desperate even to his own ears.

She looked up at him, her eyes filled with tears. But she nodded and moved to stand. He did so as well, wanting nothing more than to throw her back down on the ground and finish what he started.

"I'm sorry," she whispered and turned. Despite his warning, she did run.

He started toward her, only to fall down on the ground in pain. He gritted his teeth, groaning in agony. Suddenly the clouds let loose what they'd been promising and rain drenched his fevered form.

He stared in fascinated horror as his arms shortened and twisted. He crossed his eyes watching as a muzzle appeared. Slowly, he put his hands to his ears and felt the points. Fur sprouted from his skin, black and thick. His fingers clenched before forming into paws. With a low ripping noise, his jeans gave way as his spine bowed and shortened. The last thing he screamed was her name in a voice that became a howl at the end.

The wolf sensed prey running in the distance. He lowered his head and sniffed the ground. Despite the rain, he could scent his quarry. He leapt forward, his four-legged stride eating up the distance between them. But, something strange happened when he got closer. He didn't want to hurt her at all. The wolf sniffed the air again, hung back, and watched instead of attacking as his first instinct told him to do.

She slipped and fell on one knee and sobbed with terror.

He hid behind a bush when she turned to scan the way she'd just come. He would find her again. There was no hurry; the wolf was much more patient than the man—in this at least.

Marcus came back to the present with a raging hard-on and a pissed-off disposition. The source of all his angst resided in the next room. She was his and had been for a long time. Of course, he'd made himself stay away from her since that day. His uncle had sure spent a lot of time with her though.

He narrowed his eyes and wondered at their relationship. Deep in his heart, he knew David Crow would never take advantage of the child Lainie had been. Unlike some people, Marcus included. "What a dumbass I've been."

To hear her tell it though, she hadn't been all that afraid of him that day. More afraid of how they'd been together, how they'd reacted to one another. "You're all grown up now, Lainie, let's see just how much." He stalked across the balcony and pushed her door open.

Chapter Seven

The moon illuminated the room and the woman lying on the bed well enough for him to see her chest rise and fall with even breaths. She snored slightly. He smiled at how sweet she looked. "Lainie." It was only after he whispered her name that he realized it was late. She might not appreciate being awakened at this hour, especially for what he had in mind.

He turned to go before she found him looming over her like some psycho. In his haste, he hit his toe on the bed frame. So of course, she woke up right as he yelped and started hopping around the room on one foot. Oh yeah, dead sexy.

"Marcus, what time is it?" She tried to see the clock, but her hair kept falling in her eyes, despite her repeated attempts to rake it back. Finally, the red numbers on the clock came into focus. "It's two in the mornin'." She swallowed to clear her throat. "What do you want?" She narrowed her eyes at him. "I know you didn't wake me up for some damn booty call."

Rearing her head back, she opened her mouth to give him hell, but he slid into bed with a grin he'd surely borrowed from the devil himself. "No, I just wanted to hold you."

"Honey, I was born at night, but it wasn't last night." Despite her snort of derision at his blatant lie, she peered at him from beneath her lashes.

He lay on his side, facing her with one arm propped beneath his head as if waiting for her to succumb to temptation and jump his bones. She had to admit, the thought was very tempting. That dark hair of his, damp and messy, made her want to run her fingers through it. He took a deep breath and her mouth watered as his abdomen muscles rippled one by one. His lips wore a hint of a smile that seemed to invite her to kiss him. Again. Just the memory of their kisses alone had her blood heating.

When he still lay there, waiting, she knew that she'd have to be the one to make the first move. Well, she wouldn't make it easy on him by a long shot. With a devilish grin of her own, she walked her fingers up his chest, happy to note that he shivered in response to even that light touch. Circling the flat brown disc of his nipple, she waited until it hardened before she asked a question. "Where's the dog?"

"Dog? What dog?" He seemed dazed for a second, before he shook his head. "Oh, him, well, he's outside, where he belongs."

"I liked him," she admitted. "What's his name?"

"Who?" Marcus appeared to be having trouble following the conversation and he kept staring at her chest.

"The dog!" She glanced down. "What are you looking at?" When she saw that the twins were trying to escape, she quickly pulled her gown back up, ignoring his sigh.

"His name? Uh—Scooby."

"You're jokin', right?"

"I like the damn name." He sounded insulted. "Do you really expect me to talk about the dog when all my blood has migrated..." he jerked her against him so that she couldn't help but be aware of what he was talking about, "...south?"

"Everybody keeps saying the South's gonna rise again. I guess you just proved them right." Lainie grinned up at him, half expecting another smart comment. But he surprised her by covering her mouth with his, so gently at first that it almost tickled. When she opened for him and he slid inside, she shivered and shifted her body closer to his.

He slid his fingers down her neck to her shoulders, and finally her breasts. Cupping them in his palms, he rubbed the soft material of her gown across the hardened peaks. She shifted her legs restlessly to relieve the pressure building between them.

When he stopped and tugged her gown over her head, she swiped her hair back and found him staring at her with a slightly goofy grin on his face. "I've been waiting for this for a long time, Lainie." Reaching out, he circled the peak of one breast with his fingertips and sighed.

She returned the grin and tugged on his hand. "Yeah, me too."

He put one hand on either side of her head, caging her in with his arms, and leaned down to kiss a path from her mouth down to her throat, stopping to nuzzle the hollow. She swallowed hard when his teeth skated lightly over her skin. Before she could protest or ask for more, he slicked his tongue down the curve of her breast, nibbling as he went, moving in circles, teasing her until she arched her back, trying to make him do what she wanted. Finally, after she mewed in protest because he missed the mark yet again, he flicked his tongue against the furled peak, sucking it in his mouth.

Burying his face between her breasts, he inhaled deeply. "You smell so good, Lainie," he whispered, grinding his hips against hers, his cock sliding over her pussy.

She opened her legs wider so that each time he moved, he brushed against her clit. He must have realized it because he thrust against her and rotated his hips. Every stroke took her higher until she was gasping for breath, on the very edge of completion. “Please.”

“Please what?” Scooting down in the bed, he kissed her belly, nipping the skin above her navel, skimming his hands up and down the insides of her thighs. Hooking his thumbs on each side of her panties, he slid them off and threw them in the far corner of the room. She shifted her hips, offering herself to him, and his lips curled back from his teeth.

Her body stiffened. He stared up into her wide eyes and forced himself to slow down. He could tell she was nervous, and really couldn't blame her. She surely had questions, but he didn't have brain cells left to answer them right now. He moved back up to lie beside her, determined to hold himself in check when all he wanted was to plunge inside her and take. “I won't hurt you. But the first time may not be slow or easy. Lainie, I've wanted you for a long time.”

Lainie reached up and tangled her hands in his hair, using it to pull him back to her. “Maybe I don't want slow and easy. Did you ever think about that?”

He tugged on her lower lip with his teeth and she responded, opening her mouth to suck his tongue hungrily. He slowed the kiss down, softly caressing her mouth with his own. She sighed and wrapped her arms around his neck, clutching his shoulders with her hands. When he moved away, she uttered a wordless protest that died in her throat as he began to trail his way to her jaw then her neck. He intended to take his time, no matter what his libido screamed right now. His teeth lightly scraped the skin between her neck and shoulder, and then he bit down. She said his name again and this time it sounded like a plea for more.

His mouth watered at the taste of her, he wanted to feast on her body in more ways than one. She cried out and stiffened when his hand glided down between her legs, stroking the silky folds. Marcus thrust inside her heat with trembling fingers. The sweetness of her response was slowly driving him insane. She grabbed his wrist but instead of stopping him, she rocked back and forth, her muscles clenching around his fingers. He found the spot he was looking for and pressed inward, tightening his hold when she shuddered. He chuckled and did it again.

He took her wrists in his hand and began to kiss his way back down her body. She whispered his name in a grumpy tone when he again skipped the very part begging for his touch.

When he finally ran his tongue across her clit, circling it, then spearing it with his tongue, her body came off the bed and she screamed his name. He spread her open and plunged his tongue inside her. She squirmed, trying to pull her hands out of his, but he just tightened his hold. He devoured her, lapping at her, sliding past then flicking her clit when she wasn't expecting it.

She was on the very precipice when he stopped once more. With a low screech, she moved her hips. Nothing happened so she glared at him with narrowed eyes. "Tell me what you want, Lainie," he said, then ran his tongue along the outer edge of her sex. He licked the rim of her pussy, barely sliding inside her hot, wet entrance.

In answer, she kicked him hard enough to make him grunt. "What in the hell do you think?" Then her hands were free because he had shoved his own under her buttocks and lifted her to his mouth, sucking her clit between his teeth, biting down on the little nub. Digging her heels into the mattress, she lunged upwards, exploding against his mouth, the waves of ecstasy cresting over her without stopping.

Taking the little peak into his mouth, he rolled his tongue back and forth until she cried out again. He held her close when she shuddered, then pressed a soft kiss on her thigh. “Baby, you taste so damn good.”

When Lainie came back to her senses, she was trying to push him away and pull him against her all at once. She didn't really know what she had said or did, but Marcus was laughing. When he started back up her body, she made her move, flipping him over on his back, straddling his hips to hold him down. She had no illusions about being strong enough to keep him in this position; she intended to use more subtle methods, like bribery. First, she had to get her breath back.

Collapsing on his chest, she snuck her fingers under his waistband, brushing them across the head of his erection. He sucked in his breath with a hiss but she ignored him, tugging his pants off. After she’d looked her fill, she grinned up at him. “It’s my turn. Now put your hands behind your head, please.”

He did what she said, but gave her a look that let her know he would only play for so long.

Lainie ran her hands over his chest in little circles, concentrating on his ribcage when she discovered he was ticklish. Then she went on to bigger and better things. Kissing a path from his chest to his navel, she paused at the top of his boxer briefs before flicking her tongue down inside the waistband to touch the tip of him. “You taste good too, Marcus.”

“Lainie,” he groaned.

She eyed him wickedly, saying in a low voice, “Payback is a bitch.” When he took his hands from behind his head, fisting them in the bedcovers, she stopped and pointed. “Back behind your head, please.”

He grunted, but complied.

Inch by inch she slid his underwear down his hips and then off his ankles, smoothing her hands back up his body, He lay with his eyes closed and his jaw clenched so hard the tendons of his neck stood out. Should she take pity on him? Nah, not yet. She pushed his legs apart, raking her nails up his muscled thighs. “God, you’re pretty.”

“Men aren’t pretty.” His voice was hoarse.

“This is a work of art.” She gripped his cock and squeezed the heated flesh, smoothing her thumb over the head.

“It’s going to be Old Faithful if you don’t stop,” he warned. “Lainie, you’re killin’ me.”

“Aw, poor baby. I’ll kiss it and make it better.” And she did just that. He was hot and hard in her mouth, and smooth as silk. After skimming her teeth across the pulse throbbing at the underside of the wide flared head, she had to hurry to catch the small drop of pearly fluid that slid out of the opening at the top.

He kept his hands behind his head. She had to hand it to him; he was controlling himself very well. Much better than her, in fact, because she was about to explode again just from touching him. “You’re doing really good, sweetie.” But she wasn't finished yet, not by a long shot. She squeezed the base of his shaft and swirled the tip of her tongue around the tip of his erection.

“Yeah, I am, ain’t I—” he began just as she sucked him all the way inside. Cupping his sac with her fingers, she bit down harder on the flared tip, her teeth raking over the sensitive skin. “Oh God, that's it!” He took his hands out from behind his head and flipped her on her back.

Marcus stared at her lying with her dark hair fanned out on the pillow. She looked soft and sweet. Even as he thought it, she gave him a wicked smile and wiggled beneath him. He laughed and said the first thing that came to his mind. "You're beautiful."

She shook her head. He kissed her and when he pulled away, her eyes were almost black with desire. He knew his own were glowing and he wondered what she was thinking right now.

He entered her slowly, stretching her to her fullest. Her eyes widened and she gasped. He stopped and began to withdraw but she was having none of that. She grabbed his ass and pulled him back toward her. "Marcus, I want you inside me now. Don't make me hurt you."

He thrust inside her to the hilt. She whimpered, pressing her face against his neck. He began stroking in and out, holding her against him with one hand while the other slipped between them. His fingers found her clit, circling it in time with his thrusts.

When she moaned in the back of her throat and squeezed her thighs together, gripping him, he lost control and began to thrust harder. He could hear her gasps but could no longer tell if it was from pleasure or pain.

He sat up, bringing her with him, and her head fell back. He leaned down to take her nipple in his mouth. He grabbed her hips, rocking her back and forth, gently at first then harder. Her legs were spread wide and with each movement, her clit brushed against his belly.

Her nails dug into his shoulders and with a soft cry, she clenched around him in rapid bursts, her pussy milking his cock, pulling his orgasm from him. With a low growl, he pulled her close, burying his face against her neck, keeping his mouth shut to hide his fangs. His muscles tightened with the force of keeping his animal side down. *Not now. Please, not now,* he repeated silently, rocking back and forth still buried deep inside her until he got himself back under control.

After a few minutes, he looked into her eyes and said the only word he could manage. "Damn."

"Yeah." She slumped bonelessly against him with a laugh and he joined in, unable to help himself.

Lainie felt him slide out of her and wondered what the hell she'd been thinking. At the first sign of interest, she'd caved to her own lusts and— Oh, screw it. She'd enjoyed it and he had too, very much so. Besides, she was tired of fighting the feelings she'd always had for him.

The day she'd run away from him, she left a part of herself back there on that hill. For her, it hadn't been a loss of innocence, not a physical one, at least. But a sense of self had developed of how others perceived her, saw her.

Strangely enough, her self-confidence stemmed from the fact that this man, at least, found her physically attractive. She smiled bitterly at the thought. His loss of self-control was something she'd secretly found exciting.

Fantasies had sprung up in her fertile teenaged imagination. He would come after her, take her away. They'd live happily ever after, and some strange, misty scenes involving the two of them in bed that left her body taut with anticipation and frustration.

But he hadn't, and one day she woke up to the fact that he never would. She lived with Joanna, went to school in a rural area and had been advised to stay away from Marcus and the others up until now. Why had she been allowed to come back? She'd thought he didn't want her around, that had been the reason she'd given herself for the exile.

Or was it? Did David have more to do with it than she'd suspected? And what was it Marcus said about him being dead? David was one of the most vibrant people she knew. He certainly wasn't dead, that was for damn sure. He was her rock, a combination of father, confidant, psychiatrist and above all, friend.

Panic welled up in her at the very thought of him dying. He couldn't die, he was still a very young man, and he barely looked thirty. Now that she thought on it, that puzzled her. There was a niggling sense of disquiet running through her head. She wasn't supposed to think of this sort of thing. It would only make her upset. Why didn't she think of something else instead?

"Lainie." Marcus interrupted her musings. "Something wrong?" He pushed a lock of hair behind her ear and kissed her forehead.

"No."

"So, this, us." He tweaked her nose, laughing when she tried to bite him. "This is okay with you?"

"What is this, us, anyway?"

"I don't have a clue."

His admission made her feel a little better about her own inability to figure out just what they were doing. "Me either."

"I think maybe there is a clue, here, though." Skimming his hand up the inside of her thigh, he circled the opening of her sex, barely sliding his fingers inside her.

"I don't think so." Her voice quavered. "But you're welcome to keep looking, if it makes you feel better."

"Treasure hunting? I like that idea." He flipped her onto her back and her laughter rang out in the darkness.

Chapter Eight

Jacob Caulder scanned a document sent up from his lab with a satisfied sigh. Things were going according to plan. The phone rang, and he grimaced at the interruption. "Caulder."

"Sir, the woman you wanted me to watch... She's contacted Mr. Bei." The caller stopped talking long enough to strike a match and exhale shakily.

"Did you do what I asked?" Jacob Caulder settled back in his chair. A knock at the door interrupted him. "Enter." The door opened and his newest pet walked in.

"I went to her house. I didn't find anything."

"Did you make it so she knows you were there?" Jacob beckoned the woman closer. She looked terrified. He grinned at her and her eyes widened. Smart girl, she had reason to be scared.

"Yeah, that part was fun."

"I'm sure it was." He put his hand over the receiver. "Bring your fuckin' ass here now! Don't make me come get you."

The little blonde hurried over to him with tears in her eyes. She trembled when he pulled her onto his lap. His hand slid up the smooth expanse of her back, left bare by the dress she wore.

"Where was I?" Jacob ripped the strap off the dress. He cupped her breast in his hand, squeezing it until she gasped. "She'll know someone's been there but Marcus Bei will know it was you, Lars."

There was silence on the other end of the phone. Apparently, his newest employee hadn't thought of that. The idiot would learn the hard way.

"I have to go." Lars's voice broke and he started coughing.

"Yeah, you better." Jacob hung up the phone and filled both hands with the woman's breasts. "Now, I can give you my undivided attention. Isn't that nice?"

She refused to meet his gaze; instead, she stared at a point right over his shoulder.

Jacob grasped her chin and forced her to look at him. "Do not push me. Have you already forgotten what happened the last time?"

"No, sir."

"I think you have." He stood, picking her up.

She started crying, silent tears falling onto the flawless skin of her breasts, and he licked his way down to the peak, sucking hard. She shivered and tried to pull away.

"Let's have a refresher, shall we?"

He put the nosy reporter and the young Lupin in the back of his mind. Instead, he focused all his attention on the pretty little piece of ass he'd culled from the last expedition. The cream of the crop, she was small, with waist-length blonde hair and big blue eyes.

When he'd first got a look at her, hiding in the back of the cage, her eyes had drawn his attention, full of innocence and fear. Now, they just held fear. He'd taken the innocence, reveling in the screams that echoed in his ears. "Little Bibi". He didn't know her real name; he'd given her a new one. She answered to it, after a fashion.

She'd last until he tired of her, or killed her. Whichever came first, it was all the same to him. In the end, she was disposable. Her genetic makeup wasn't compatible with the Lune Gene, so she was just for fun. His teeth grazed her neck as he carried her through the door of the private suite located off his office.

She whimpered, but didn't move otherwise. Good, she was learning. "Take the dress off." He let her feet slide to the floor. She hurried to obey, giving him a view of her sweet ass when she turned and laid the dress over the foot of the bed.

"Bend over." His hands were at his belt, undoing it. He freed his cock and pumped it once with his fist.

She hesitated and that was her first mistake.

He slammed her face down on the bed and smothered her screams in the covers. Soon the only sounds in the room were his grunts as he pounded into her. Little Bibi had outlived her usefulness today, it seemed.

Much later, he sat in his office while one of his unobtrusive staff carried Bibi's remains down to the incinerator. Stroking his chin, he picked up the files on the Breeders. Elaine Westerbrook was a potential candidate, though it was unknown whether she qualified for the Lune Elixir. Maybe he'd play with her next and find out.

Chapter Nine

The next morning, Lainie woke to the sound of Marcus telling his secretary to hold all his calls and reschedule any meetings he might have. She peered out from under the covers, watching him as he stood at the doors that led onto the balcony.

Her eyes opened a little wider to take in the lovely view. He was beautiful; his legs were long and lanky, muscular but not bulky. Today he wore a pair of old jeans that molded themselves to his ass and a T-shirt just tight enough to show the rippling of the muscles in his back when he moved. "I don't care, tell them anything you want. I'm not coming in today."

"Marcus. Go to work, I don't need a babysitter." She sat on the side of the bed, wrapping the sheet around her.

He whirled around and grinned at her. "Let me call you back, Dee." He hung up the phone and moved toward the bed. Her gaze drifted up and down his frame as he approached. He prowled; there was no other word for the graceful and self-assured way he moved.

"Good morning." He sat on the side of the bed and looked down at her with a strange smile on his face.

"What?" She put her hand to her hair to do something to tame it, but he stopped her.

"You look cute. Leave it."

"Go to work. I mean it." She frowned at him when he laughed. "What the hell is so funny?"

He shook his head and shrugged. "Are you hungry?"

"Maybe, are you cooking?" He was horrible at it, or he used to be.

"No."

"Then, yes, I am starved." Her grin was unrepentant even in the face of his scowl.

"I'm not that bad."

"Yeah, you are." She threw the covers back and stood with a stretch. She'd gotten up sometime in the night and put her gown back on. She hadn't been able to find her underwear though. She spied them in the corner now and flushed in remembrance of how he'd flung them there.

"Meet me downstairs." He shut the door behind him and she hurried to get dressed.

Once she finished, she opened the door to her room and looked out into the hall. "Where the hell is the kitchen?" she wondered aloud.

"Ma'am."

"Shit!" She whirled and faced Allen. "Oh, sorry, you scared me."

"I apologize." He had a pained expression on his face.

"It's okay."

"If you will follow me to the breakfast room." Marcus had a breakfast room? She was a little out of her depth here. She and Joanna lived in a six-room cabin. They had the one room for eating and cooking. It was called the damn kitchen.

Allen wasn't the best of conversationalists. All of her attempts to draw him out were, if not rebuffed, then discouraged, albeit politely. He was nice, but he didn't like her and she knew it.

"Here we are, ma'am." He indicated the door to the right.

"Thanks." She gave him her brightest smile, which he returned with another constipated look. Damn, the man needed some fiber.

She forgot all about him when she opened the door to the breakfast room. It faced the east, and the tall windows blazed with the morning light. The room was warm in color and in temperature, and it felt wonderful.

They were at a higher elevation here, and she'd been a little chilly. No more, though; the sun warmed the floor beneath her sock-covered feet. She laughed and wiggled her toes.

"I take it you like the room?" Marcus sat at the table with a coffee cup in one hand and the paper in the other.

The coziness of the scene struck her, making her chest ache with the wish that they could be a real couple. With a small sigh, she put it out of her mind and moved to take the seat he indicated. "I do."

"What's wrong?" He put down his paper and tugged her onto his lap instead.

"Nothing, I was just thinking." She scooted around to get comfortable and the inevitable reaction occurred. The bulge of his arousal pressing against her backside made her roll her eyes. "You have to go to work; we don't have time for that."

"There is always time for 'that' as you put it." He pulled the clip out of her hair. "I like it down." Ignoring her protests, he began feathering kisses from her temple to her ear, so she tipped her head back to give him better access. He inched his hand under her shirt and her nipples hardened beneath the lacy barrier of her bra. He pinched one between his thumb and forefinger, making fire streak from her breast straight to her pussy.

"Are you sure you want me to go to work?" His laughing question had her glaring at him. "Fine." With a sigh of defeat he released her. "Anticipation makes the dick grow harder."

"That's not how that saying goes and you know it."

"You have your proverbs, I have mine."

"Freak." She tried to wiggle free.

"Baby, you ain't seen nothin' yet." He let her stand and smacked her butt.

"Hey!" She whirled with her hands on her hips. He only raised one brow at her. She stuck her nose in the air and sat in her chair, serving herself, trying to ignore his stare.

Soon enough, they finished their breakfast and he stood. "I have a phone conference this morning and I have to meet someone for lunch, but then I'll be back."

"Enjoy your day. I need to call my boss; he'll be worried about me." He nodded absently and kissed her before heading toward the front of the house.

She sat in the morning sun, wondering what was bothering her. When she finally figured it out, she felt stupid. He hadn't said he loved her. While she hadn't made any declarations either, it would have been nice to know to have some clue.

She let out a heartfelt sigh and put her chin on her hands and stared out the window. How did she feel about Marcus? She wasn't actually sure. Aside from some mind-blowing sex the night before, they didn't really know one another anymore.

When they were younger, they'd been close, but sometime in the last ten years, her ability to read him had deserted her. Or had she been fooling herself the whole time? If she couldn't figure him out one way, there was always her favorite pastime that would help her do so.

Lainie, the super sleuth, investigative reporter and all-around snoop. She was nosy, it wasn't just a characteristic trait with her, and she'd made a career out of it after all.

So with Marcus away, the curious cat would play, and hopefully, he wouldn't catch her at it. If he did, she'd plead the fifth, on her knees, maybe naked. She grinned at the thought. He'd be begging by the time she was done.

Chapter Ten

Marcus thought about heading back to the house and chucking his attempts at working today. He couldn't concentrate; he kept remembering Lainie in his arms last night, or this morning rather. She'd responded to every caress, every touch, better than his wildest dreams.

He'd kept his distance, afraid of what he'd do if they encountered each other. That and the fact he knew she'd do much better without him complicating her life with his own particular lifestyle.

The leader of a pack had to do things a certain way. He had to have the appearance, at least, of controlling everyone around him, his subordinates. Lainie, being his lover, was his subordinate in every sense of the word. She wouldn't see it that way and he wasn't ready to make her either. He didn't know if he ever would be.

He would have to move slowly. But he had a feeling time was running out and he was racing toward something. It was her, in a way, but in another it was answers to questions he had about his own origins.

He knew it all started with WWII and the imprisonment of Asian Americans during that time. An encampment high in the Colorado Rockies had been the location of a top-secret experiment, with his father at the forefront. Samuel was a scientist, a brilliant one. Too bad he didn't have a damn conscience to keep from making what was an abomination to some and a potential weapon to others.

Samuel had taken David's magic and used genetic splicing to create a race of werewolves who were slow to age, with other enhanced abilities like speed, keen smell and hearing. While Marcus still didn't understand it all, he did know that only some of the later generations had been able to transform into the Wolfkin, the two-legged and more dangerous creature. The Wolfkin both puzzled and angered his father because the man couldn't change into it himself.

He wondered where his father was, and if he had landed on his feet since he'd been ousted from the pack eight years ago. It had been a combination of voting and fighting that made him leave. When Marcus was old enough, the elders came to him with a proposal about leading the pack after helping him oust Samuel. Of course, he'd agreed, happy to be rid of his father. Marcus knew that his position as Lupin irked Samuel. As if he gave a damn—he hated his father, always had.

David Crow, his maternal uncle, on the other hand, had been like a father to him when he was younger. Marcus had respected him, believed in him and looked up to him. And now to find out David had more than likely faked his own death to disappear out of his life rankled Marcus. Why did he leave?

It came to him suddenly. David left to protect Lainie. There had been some sort of upheaval, Marcus hadn't been high enough in the ranks at the time to know all of it, but he thought it involved breeding mates. David always opposed Marcus's father's wishes. Which meant it was probably morally wrong at the least and ethically reprehensible besides.

"Father, what in the hell were you up to?" Breeders, Lainie and something else. There was a connection there. He knew

Samuel had been grooming Lainie for his own mate, which was sickening to Marcus because she'd been a little kid. He knew that his kind aged differently than humans, so while his father was over eighty, he could live much longer—unless Marcus got lucky and killed him. In his father's sick, twisted mind, teaching Lainie pack ways while she was young was logical. However, that went awry when David came and took her away.

Joanna was an enigma as well. Maybe she wasn't the evil bitch his father always said she was. Samuel hated her, with a passion he usually kept in check. The animosity between the two had been obvious. She wasn't just a human. Her natural psi abilities had been enhanced as a byproduct of the gene-splicing experiment gone wrong. His father fucked up and gave her something he didn't have control over, that was it. Joanna was a dark horse, an unknown. Marcus smiled at that. Well, go on, Joanna.

Lainie had lived with the woman, thought of her as her mother. He sighed and rubbed his eyes. As soon as he got through with this annoying, yet necessary bit of business, he was going home to talk to Lainie about her life with Joanna and his uncle. No more beating around the bush, they were going to get to the bottom of this.

Chapter Eleven

Lainie called her boss and was slightly unsettled when he answered with a panicked note in his voice. "Elaine? Where are you? Are you all right?" Mr. Fargo was never upset; he was stern and quiet, almost cold.

"I'm fine. That's why I called. I do have a lead on this story though; I have a way to get closer to Jacob Caulder." She went on to explain that her house had been broken into and she didn't think it was safe to stay there. She acted as if the move was her idea. It made her seem more mature than it did to be dragged willy-nilly to Marcus's house like a recalcitrant child.

"Where. Are. You?" Each word cracked, making her flinch.

"Oh, sorry." Her face heated up and she was glad he couldn't see it. "I'm staying with an old friend of mine. You might know of him. His name is Marcus Bei."

He sighed gustily. "Thank God."

"Um, what?"

"Look, you just stay there. I'm sure Mr. Bei knows what's best for you. Listen to what he says." His voice took on a jovial note. "I wasn't aware you knew him."

"Yeah, we go back a long way. I've known Marcus for over fifteen years."

"Great." The sound of phones ringing in the background made her slightly homesick for her tiny cubicle. "Look, sweetheart." Her brows went up at the endearment. "You take all the time you need. Mr. Bei is a major shareholder with the company that owns our paper."

"Is he now?" She frowned, wondering if that was why she got her job so damned easily. "You can bet I'll report in every day. The function is Friday. I'll have something in your e-mail by Sunday at the latest," she promised, determined to get proof of Caulder's nefarious activities.

"You do that. Be careful, Caulder is a powerful man." Mr. Fargo sounded strangely afraid.

"The higher they are, the farther they fall."

"Yes, my little bloodhound." The warm chuckle was more like the boss she was used to so she relaxed slightly. "Give Mr. Bei my regards."

"I will." She hung up the phone and pursed her lips. How powerful was Marcus to make her normally arrogant boss toady to him that way? She intended to find out, but not today. She slapped her hands on her knees and stood, heading toward where she thought his home office was. Last night, she'd glimpsed a computer on a large desk as they walked through. She'd been distracted by him, but now that he wasn't here, all her instincts came back online. He was hiding something from her and she intended to find out what it was.

Lainie checked to make sure the coast was clear before she slipped inside the office. She stopped and looked around the room, whistling silently. The desk was antique and huge, made of mahogany and waxed to a high sheen. She had a little prefab one from the local discount store that she used for her own home office.

She clicked the door shut and crept behind the desk. With a nervous laugh, she sat. What was she doing, sneaking up on the damned computer?

She booted it up and cracked her knuckles, wiggling her fingers back and forth. "Come on, hacker skills, do your worst." She'd been friends with a guy in college; he'd taught her a few things about computers in between bouts of sweaty, athletic sex that she'd thoroughly enjoyed.

In a flash of insight, she realized something. The computer whiz had been a lot like Marcus. Time and distance let her see that. So had just about every guy she'd dated for any length of time. She frowned, trying to decide if she should worry over her sanity or feel happy that she'd finally gotten it right. That was how she felt last night. When he put his hands on her, when he slid inside her, she felt right.

She shook herself out of her reverie, unwilling to allow the memory to distract her. Instead, she got busy sneaking in the back door of Marcus's well-protected, state-of-the-art computer. Her mouth watered when she looked at the screen. Damn, this thing was fine. "I wonder how many... Oh please, get a grip, it's just a computer."

After a few minutes, her lust turned to something else. Her heartbeat quickened when she found the file marked *S. Bei, Experiment Files*. She opened it and found a list of files. Another with the title *Breeders* caught her eye. The word resonated in her subconscious. When she thought of Samuel and experiments, she thought of that word. Dread grew in the pit of her belly. She wanted nothing more than to stop reading and forget about the whole thing. She tried to get into the file, but failed repeatedly, so she turned to the one marked Lune Gene instead. It opened without a problem.

"What in the hell did he do?" She looked at the dates, surely that was wrong. Samuel wasn't old enough to have done those things in 1944 was he?

She noticed another file, titled *Progeny.* The files within this database were unprotected, so it was the work of a moment to open them. The first name on the list was Jason Bei. It stated that he was deceased, beside that were the ominous words "experiment failed". She shivered and read on down the list of various names. They had one thing in common, the surname of Bei. Beside each name was either the words "experiment failed" or "subject terminated".

At the bottom was a folder by itself. It was Marcus, of course. Marcus Bei, born 1976 to S. Bei and non-Breeder female. Her brows drew down at that term. "Breeder female, what the hell?" She remembered his mother's name was Diana.

She continued to read. "Marcus Bei is a successful result of the Lune Gene. His intelligence is markedly higher than others in his age group. While he shows signs of stubbornness, he will likely become more malleable as he grows. He has claimed his mate at an early age, even if neither is aware of this yet. It is not known whether the mating was successful. Attempts to locate the Breeder female have not been fruitful. Addendums will be added when further information is available."

"Who in the hell is his mate?" Lainie wondered as she printed everything off as quickly as she could. As the pages shot out, she looked around. The room was nice, lined with books of all sorts. The last page was printing out when a soft footfall outside the room alerted her to someone's presence. She quickly turned the computer off. Her palms began to sweat when she saw the doorknob turning. She dove beneath the desk and peered out from under the bottom edge where it didn't quite meet the floor.

Allen stood in the doorway, his cool and aloof expression missing. Instead, he looked angry. He sniffed the air and frowned. What was with the damn sniffing?

Apparently, her deodorant worked, because with one last sniff, he shut the door. His footsteps slowly faded into the distance and Lainie let out her breath. For a minute, she'd been terrified. She was aware he didn't care for her, or more than likely didn't think she was good enough for Marcus, but he'd looked downright hostile.

At the thought of Marcus, her heart ached. What was this Lune Gene? What did it all mean? And now that she thought of it, where in the hell was Samuel?

She scooted out from under the desk and scooped up the papers. Stopping to think, she grabbed one of the larger books off the shelf, and folding the papers in half, she shoved them inside. For now, that would have to do. She hurried to the door with the book in her hand, pressing her ear to the thick wooden surface before she opened it, intent on running out of the room before she got caught.

Unfortunately, for her, there was someone waiting on the other side. Lainie stared up into a pair of angry eyes that seared her with their intensity. She felt like she was in a spotlight, being questioned without even a word being said. "Hi, Marcus."

"Hello, Lainie." His lips twisted in a parody of a smile. "Making yourself at home, I see. Allen thought he heard someone in there printing something."

"Oh, but I was just getting a book." She held up her book then squeaked, breaking off when his fingers gripped her elbow. He pulled her along with him toward the den, his mouth compressed into a tight line. "Marcus, you're hurting me." He jerked even harder when she dug in her heels. She tried to sit, thinking he would let her go.

Instead, he picked her up, putting her over his shoulder. When she wiggled, his hand came down on her bottom with a resounding *crack*. "Be still." His voice was thick with menace, rumbling beneath her outraged shriek of protest.

"Put me down." She pinched him on the side. "I will not be—" She shut up when he practically threw her on the couch. The book fell on the floor and slid under the coffee table.

He paid it no mind, just leaned down and caged her in with his arms on either side of her head. "Be quiet or I'll make you wish you had." There was something strange about his eyes. They were gold.

A scream bubbled up inside her, but she refused to let it out. She was afraid if she started, she might never stop.

"Sir?"

"What?" Marcus snapped at Allen, who stood unobtrusively at the door.

Had he seen the humiliating way Marcus had brought her in here? She took in the smirk on his face and knew for a fact he had. Her face got hotter, if possible, and she gritted her teeth.

"You have company," Allen said.

"Tell them I'm busy."

"Is that any way to treat your one and only uncle?" David Crow stepped into the room, dwarfing Allen with his presence. He crossed his arms over his chest and looked at the pair frozen in place on the couch. "I hate to interrupt this little lovers' quarrel," his lips twisted, "but you need to know some things I've been putting off telling you for a long time now."

"You!" Marcus snarled. "You lied to me." At that, he leapt at David with his hands stretched out toward his neck.

Lainie never really saw them move. David stepped to one side, moving faster than Marcus did.

Allen silently melted out of the way, leaving the two men to fight it out.

“Elaine?” David called out.

“Yes, sir?” she answered, automatically.

“*Okohke.*” David chanted the word, and she immediately slumped over on the couch.

Chapter Twelve

Marcus stopped and stared in shock. "What did you do to her?" he roared and rushed David again. He quickly realized that his uncle had simply been avoiding his blows and kicks. Now, David turned on him with a snarl and grabbed his arm, wrenching his fingers in a viselike grip.

"What does it look like?" David released him when Marcus's foot connected with his thigh and he went down with a thump and a groan. "Boy, you need to respect your elders."

"I am the Lupin; I don't have to do anything." Marcus sneered in triumph.

"Well, it's about time someone beat the Lupin's bony little ass again, huh?" David rushed him, grabbing him around the waist, their momentum carrying them against the far wall with a crash.

Marcus grunted and tried to break out of his uncle's hold. The man was built like a linebacker, much larger than he was. Physically there was no contest between them. However, Marcus was the smarter of the two, at least he hoped. If not, his uncle was about to kick his ass. He brought both fists down on the other man's broad shoulders; there was a grunt, but no other reaction. David kept him pinned to the wall, slamming him repeatedly against the hard surface. Marcus saw stars, then he growled and shifted his hands until claws formed. He used them to nail David in the sides, and this time, the other man moved just enough for him to use his feet for leverage. He kicked out, hitting the man in both knees, and heard them breaking with a satisfying pop.

David went down with a pained groan. "Fuck that hurts. You sneaky little bastard."

Marcus bent over with his hands on his knees, winded. "You tried to kill me." After a minute, he held out his hand and waited for his uncle to take it.

"Nah, just a little harmless maiming." David took the proffered hand. "That was a good move. Who taught you that one?"

With a grin, Marcus pulled him to his feet. "You."

"Oh, yeah, I forgot." His uncle put his hand on the wall to hold himself up. His knees began to straighten, instantly repairing themselves before he took another step. "Damn." He cracked the vertebrae in his neck by tilting his head back and forth. "I'm too old for this shit."

"Why did you leave me?" Marcus's voice was soft, but the other man turned at the plaintive sound in it.

"Because, with me there, you would never have become the leader you could be. You would have relied on me to advise you, and I wanted you to stand alone. Plus there was Lainie to think of." David winced as he hobbled over to the couch across from her and sat down.

Marcus straightened Lainie from her slumped position before he sat and placed her feet in his lap. She hadn't moved the whole time he and David had fought, which he found weird as hell. "How did you do that? And what did you say?"

"I said a word that doesn't come up in everyday conversation. It means crow. It's a posthypnotic suggestion, she will only do it at mine and one other's commands, so don't worry."

"Joanna, I presume?"

"You got it in one, never said you weren't a smartass." David grinned, then sobered. "I had to get her away. There was a treaty of sorts between your father and me, but if I insisted on keeping her out of the pack much longer, it would have been war. So, I faked my death, placed the blame on Jo and we took Lainie off to the wilds of Canada."

"What do you mean, in the pack?"

"Lainie is a Breeder, Marcus. Surely you knew that. Remember, we saved her from that facility."

"Yeah, I remember, but she doesn't. I guess Joanna did that too. Mind telling me how?"

"Jo's psychic abilities were enhanced by your father's so-called genetic therapy. He wasn't at all pleased with the results in her case. Imagine him creating a woman that can lift a Volkswagen with her mind. A little out of character for him, huh?" David's opinions about Marcus's father were well known, and as Marcus shared them, he didn't bother to disagree.

"So, you took off with her. How come they didn't find you? I mean, we are trackers, it's what we were made for, really."

"Joanna always had her feelers out for the pack, and she'd leave before they were even in the area, most of the time anyway."

Marcus thought on that for a minute. To give himself time to adjust, he rang the maid for some tea, not the hot variety, but ice-cold sweet tea. The drink always made him think of the summers he'd spent back home, a time of innocence. He had a feeling that he was about to lose even more of his innocence tonight.

His uncle had something he wanted to get off his chest, though Marcus wasn't sure he wanted to hear it. However, as the leader of the pack, he had to be sure that he was informed about these things. He also thought it was connected to this investigation Lainie was involved in up to her eyeballs.

The two men waited until the tray was brought. It was a testament to the way Marcus lived that Carrie, the maid, didn't bat an eye at Lainie stretched out on the couch. "Thanks." He smiled at the girl and she looked shyly at David before sashaying out of the room.

"You remember when you snuck in the back of the truck I drove into the facility that night?"

"Yeah." Marcus remembered it with some pride. He'd gotten one over on his uncle and it made him feel like a man. David was hard to trick. It was a game they played. That night, it almost got him killed.

"Remember how you found Lainie?"

Marcus closed his eyes and swallowed the bile that rose to his throat. "Yeah." His hands tightened reflexively on her feet, touching her as if to reassure himself that she was fine. Nothing had happened. He'd saved her.

"She's a Breeder. Joanna was the prototype, you know. A little bit of me, a whole lot of her and way too much of your ignorant father's blind faith in science," David explained.

"I know some of that from the files. My Daddy's a Mad Scientist 101." Marcus waved his hand. "I want to know why and how they got her in the first place."

"He always claimed Mother agreed to the experiment. Some of those women did get paid to birth those kids. Most of the Breeders are women, but not all. There are male Breeders too, but, with the females of our species, it isn't as hard to breed with a human male." He shrugged.

"Yet another case of the female of the species being better than the male, so? I can tell there's something else you aren't telling me." Marcus leaned forward.

"Lainie was to be your father's mate from the first. He contacted her birth mother and made all the arrangements. He was already plotting Diana's demise when he had Lainie's mother inseminated with the Breeder sperm."

"Ick." Marcus grimaced. "Wait. He wanted to kill my mother when I was three, why?"

"Because of me." David's eyes turned bright red. "She wasn't my sister; she was my granddaughter."

Marcus was too tired to even be angry at the lie, because in the end, it didn't matter, David was still family and he still loved him. However, he did want to know one thing. "I still don't get why he wanted to kill Mother because of that."

"You had brothers and sisters."

"Yeah and they're all dead. I read that part in the files I managed to hack from his computer. Even if he called it experiment failed or terminated it means the same thing."

"That's not all. Some weren't born human." His uncle, no he had to stop thinking of him as that, his grandfather put his glass down and took a deep breath.

"What're you saying? None of us are human, we're more than that."

"I mean, they were born as wolves. Only, they're different from the average wolf, caught between two worlds, unable to shift to human, but able to think like one. Your father thought of them as abominations and he blamed Diana for it. You were the only one born as a human."

"How many are there?" Marcus rubbed his face with his hands. He would have never guessed this, not in a million years.

"Over a dozen, I'm not sure how many are left. He tried to kill most of them, but some escaped and are more than likely scattered across the United States and parts of Mexico." David sat back and drank his tea while Marcus assimilated the new horror his father had set loose on the world.

"Shit."

"That about covers it. The point is, when he found he couldn't make any more like you with Diana, he decided someone else would give him the children he wanted. And that's where Lainie came in. He gave her that jacked-up serum at the age of ten so she'd be his, and only his, or so he thought."

"How did you find out about it in the first place?" Marcus had always wondered how he'd known to turn up on that night, just in the nick of time.

David gave him a wry grin. "Who's the one person that would know your daddy's secrets?"

Marcus sat back and thought about it, until it dawned on him. "Mother?"

"Yeah, the sick son of a bitch told her all about it, thinking she couldn't tell me while stuck in wolf form." He scratched his head. "Well, he never counted on Jo being able to pick up her thoughts on that subject. Diana was frantic to stop him. She wasn't jealous of him by then, she just wanted to protect innocent people from being hurt." David sighed. "Too bad your mama was smarter than me."

"Let's hope I take after her." Marcus couldn't resist the jab. "This serum, what the hell does it do?" He didn't really understand that part.

"He invented it especially for Elaine. It imprints a certain male's genetic code in her subconscious. She can find him by not a sense of smell but the physiognomy of that particular male."

A cold chill raced up Marcus's spine. "She was programmed to respond to my father?"

"Yeah. After that he planned to start visiting her. Not sex," he hastened to add when Marcus gagged. "Gifts, visits, making her used to his presence in her life." David laughed.

"What's so funny? That's just sick."

"The thing is, if nothing else, you look a lot like Samuel Bei." He ignored Marcus's scowl. "Enough to fool a ten-year-old brain into thinking that you were the one she was looking for. You stayed around her just long enough for her to imprint onto you, and then, well, the rest is history."

"She's imprinted on me? Like baby ducks on their mamas?"

"Basically, yeah. She likes you, and only you. Everyone has a type, Marcus. Lainie's just happens to be tall, with dark hair and eyes and a nice smile, if I say so myself." David preened.

Marcus knew very well what he was talking about, because his mother had told him countless times when he was a little boy that he had his uncle's smile. He couldn't resist teasing him. "Ew."

"What do you mean, ew? There's nothing wrong with my smile, or yours for that matter." David sounded indignant.

Marcus sobered. "It's just that when we were kids, it was sort of sweet the way she always acted like I was her hero." He knew it sounded stupid, but it had mattered that Lainie looked up to him, especially when his father seemed to hate his guts.

"It stuck in your daddy's craw that she chose you." The older man chuckled at the memory. "He was upset when she went missing from the lab, and got madder when we showed up at the house with her. Not that he could do a damn thing about it without the elders of the pack knowing what he'd done. He deserved me rubbing his nose in it though. The son of a bitch shouldn't fuck with nature; it always fucks you back in the end."

"I got fucked by nature, Uncle David!" Marcus gnashed his teeth. All this time he'd thought maybe, just maybe, he and Lainie had something special. Now, come to find out, it was all genetics. They'd both been blinded by science or some crap.

"What are you bitching about? The woman likes you." David indicated Lainie's prone form. "Do you know how rare that is?"

"You just told me that she has to like me."

"No, I said she is predispositioned to want to have sex with you." David frowned at him. "I didn't say she wanted to be in the same room or even the same state with you. In fact, with a lot of them, that frightens them so much, they run."

"Like she did when she was a teenager?"

"You screwed up." His uncle pointed a finger at him. "I came to get her that day and she was shaking like a leaf. It took all I had not to come beat your ass, boy."

"Yeah, I wish you had. It would have saved me from beating myself up for the past decade about it." Marcus watched his uncle closely when he asked his next question. "You never uh—" He stopped speaking when the other man lifted his head and glared at him.

"No. And I never would. We're not animals. Besides, she was just a baby to me, she still is." He paused. "She was Joanna's baby chick to hover over and coddle. I just provided the muscle to protect her."

"You love her."

"Of course I do. She's funny, smart and she's not scared of a damn thing. She takes no prisoners when it comes to her job. She'll ferret out any and all information she wants, any way she can." The last was said with some pride.

"Yeah, she got into my files today, I think," Marcus admitted.

"What did she see? Anything incriminating? If so, I can have the memories blocked. We've had to do it a few times." The big man pushed a long strand of raven hair out of his face. "Once or twice, your father's men have snuck up on us, and I've had to take care of them. It hasn't happened in a while."

"Yeah, was this before or after I took over?" Marcus spoke with a hard, flat tone in his voice.

"Before you took over, a lot. After he left the pack, once or twice." David spread his hands. "Look, I know you're pissed because I left, but you had all this support, she had nobody. What was I supposed to do? I always kept my ear to the ground about what happened after you moved down here. I was proud of you."

Marcus shrugged. "It all came to a head when I turned twenty-three or so." He folded his hands in his lap, trying to pretend his nails weren't getting longer. "I found out he was testing some of the younger Weres, including Jordan, to see if he could figure out why they changed into the Wolfkin form." He swallowed hard and closed his eyes, trying to regain control. It helped, a little. "Me, Jordan, Ben and Stephen killed most of his supporters one by one until he was forced out. I wanted him to challenge me, but he didn't. Instead, he ran with his tail between his legs."

"Watch him."

"I have been. You don't know how happy it made me when Lainie walked into my office. I'd missed her so much." He reached down and stroked her hair back from her face. "I figured I could at least keep an eye on her if nothing else, especially when she opened her mouth and spouted that Caulder bullshit. Why is she after him?"

David let out a weary sigh. "She called me in the middle of the night so hysterical I could barely make out what she was saying. When I heard the word werewolf, Joanna and I went to her house and tried to erase the memories of the picture of the Wolfkin that Jade sent her on the phone. We couldn't because she knew Jade was missing, and the picture was tied so closely to that. So Joanna did what she calls a shallow bury. Those memories could resurface if she's pushed," David warned.

"Why did she move here?"

With a wry grin, David leaned forward, putting his hands on his knees. "To expose Caulder and hopefully find Jade. But I suggested it because I figured it was time for you two idiots to meet up again. I got tired of the endless parade of the Marcus-wannabe revue."

"What?"

"You weren't listening, were you? I said she likes a certain type. If I showed you pictures of her ex-boyfriends, you'd see the resemblance between them and you. Of course, being that they don't have my wonderful cheekbones in their gene pool, they weren't really up to snuff. But hey, if all men were as hot as me, the ladies wouldn't know what to do with themselves." David's eyes sparkled with mischief.

"Mr. Modesty." Marcus snorted.

"Hmm, you don't seem to be all that modest either." David's expression veered into scary porch daddy, something Marcus hadn't seen since his high-school-dating days. "Before I wake her, there's something I need to say. I know you, Marcus. You're a good man, but if you hurt her, I'll skin your ass. Don't think I won't."

"What the hell?" Marcus was taken aback at the forcefulness of his tone. "I *am* your fuckin' nephew, wait, grandson. What happened to blood is thicker than water?"

"Your blood will be spilled, that's a promise. She may not be mine, but I helped raise her. She got under my skin, despite my attempts to keep it from happening. I didn't want to be close to her because I knew she would be yours one day. It was too weird." He curled his lip. "But, she just..." He held his hands up helplessly.

"I know," Marcus told him.

David looked at him for a long minute. Finally, a smile bloomed across his face. "I know you do. Take care of her, Marcus. She's special."

"I know," Marcus repeated.

"*Mahpe.*" David said another word, which Marcus recognized as Cheyenne.

Lainie opened her eyes and looked around. "What happened?"

"You said you felt faint, and I made you lie down." Marcus hated to lie, but he didn't know what else to tell her. If it were any other person besides David with this power over her, he'd be worried. However, Marcus's own sense of honor came from him; he knew what ethics meant because of this man. She was safe with David, at least. Marcus, well, he was another story entirely.

Lainie noticed David sitting on the other couch. "When did you get here? How are you?" She glanced at Marcus, but he didn't seem too upset about seeing his long-lost relative in his living room.

"A few minutes ago." He smiled at her. "I'm about the same. How have you been?"

"I'm good. How is Joanna?" She didn't want to go into any details about Marcus. Speaking of which, he was staring at her like she had two heads. What was up?

"She's fine too. Are you sure everything's okay?" David stared hard at her, as if searching for something.

"I said it was! Why wouldn't it be? What did he tell you?" She glared at Marcus, who just lifted one brow at her.

"We were just catching up," Marcus interjected before David could say anything.

"Oh, whatever, fine. Don't tell me shit, I'm used to it!" Lainie pouted, folding her arms across her chest. She hated being treated like a child, or worse, an addlebrained twit.

"Elaine." David was the only one who used her full name.

"You act like I don't know my ass from a hole in the ground!" she shot back, coming to her feet. "I'm going to take my book and go to my room. When you wish to treat me like an adult, you know where I'll be." Reaching under the table and snagged it, then, contrary to her terse words, leaned over and gave David a peck on the cheek. "I love you."

"I love you too," he answered automatically, and then flushed when Marcus smirked at him.

Lainie marched out of the room with her nose in the air, anger apparent in every line of her body. They waited until they heard her slam the door to her room upstairs, then both men broke out into sputtered laughter.

"You know she's going to sneak down and try to eavesdrop." David smiled fondly in the direction she'd taken.

Marcus shook his head. "Yeah, I know. She's a nosy little thing."

"Sometimes, I wonder if it's because of all that we've taken from her. If Joanna and I left her access to those memories, she may not have such an ache to find the truth." David pulled on his bottom lip.

"She's had a normal life up 'til now. You've done her a favor," Marcus replied, sitting forward to put his elbows on his knees. "What happens when she finds out the truth about us? It's inevitable, you know. I can't be a man all the time. Plus, I shed." David choked on his tea at the last remark, but let him talk, as if sensing his need to do so. "She's just so wonderful. I think, no, I know she's supposed to be here. It feels right."

"I know, son." David gave him a sad smile.

"Do you really? Have you ever felt it, deep inside, that this is meant to be?"

"I thought I did." David looked away for a minute. "There are others that let their animal side rule. They will attempt to steal her from you. Especially if they find out what she is. Samuel was between a rock and a hard place. He knew she'd imprinted on you, and he wants the children you two could produce. He wants to see his experiment through to fruition."

"He will never get near any of our children." Marcus's voice was low and deadly. "He's not welcome anywhere near this house or Lainie."

David gave him an incredulous look. "You don't know?"

"What?"

"Jacob named Samuel his second, his beta. Sam is the number two in the New Mexico pack. You've got to keep up with the gossip. He's the reason Jacob's been stealing those girls. Your father has started up his so-called enhancements again."

"So, Lainie is right? She isn't just dreaming up conspiracies?"

"Lainie has a twisted imagination, but, no, not in this case. She's right in suspecting Caulder. What she doesn't know, is that the man that pursued her across fifteen states and the Canadian border is mixed up in this too."

"I tried to stop him," Marcus admitted. "I spoke out against the things he did. Those that sided with me stayed on in the pack, those that didn't left or died. Some thought it weakened us but I know the truth."

"You're the Lupin now. You're the alpha male of the pack. Have you thought of how this will affect her? She'll have to appear subservient to you, at least in public. She isn't at all that way." David clenched his fists together. "Maybe if she'd grown up in the pack atmosphere, or been trained to be that way like your father wished, she would know that. But you can't just toss her in there without so much as a by-your-leave."

"I know that. She won't be allowed to come in contact with the pack until I deem her ready." Marcus sounded like what he was—the leader, the ruler, the king.

"You hurt her, and I will make you wish you'd never been born."

"You sound like her daddy." Marcus snorted.

"No, just a friend. If I was her daddy, she'd be off-limits for you, think about that." He grinned devilishly when his grandson wrinkled his nose in disgust.

"Fine, Grandpa." Marcus laughed when David looked thunderstruck.

Both men stopped talking at once. They'd heard it, the soft footfall on the stair. She was sneaking down to listen. "So, you like what the Packers are doing this year?"

"I'm a Steelers fan, you know that," Marcus replied.

"You little bastard." David looked horrified.

"Cheesehead."

"Dickhead!"

"Sir?" Allen interrupted their good-natured diatribe.

"Yeah, what now?" Marcus whipped his head around to glare at the unwitting butler.

"Your guest left the house. I thought you'd like to know."

"Is she just out in the gardens?" Marcus was already walking toward the doors at the other end of the living room.

"No, she scaled the fence and is heading south. At her rate of speed, she's a mile away by now."

"Shit!" The younger man ran out the door, throwing his clothing off as he did so. He became a black blur within seconds, running into the night. There was a break in the fence just big enough for him.

"Hell." David walked outside and followed suit. He moved, swift and gray through the night, nearly invisible. He wouldn't get too close because he had a feeling that this encounter could be embarrassing on both their parts.

Although, he could take pictures for a scrapbook, trot them out and show them to their children. That sort of thing went over well. David's tongue lolled out and he put on more speed. Life was good for a lone wolf.

Chapter Thirteen

The moon was almost full, lighting the road well enough for her to see. She jogged at a steady pace, intent on getting as far away from Marcus as possible. She couldn't think straight with him around. He made her go all squishy in the head. Of course, she had the papers in the satchel she'd secured on her back.

She intended to go over them at the first opportunity. They, meaning he and David, were hiding something from her. Something important. If it were only business between them, she wouldn't care. But she knew it involved her so she should be told.

There was a rustling sound on her left and she flinched, biting her lip to hold back a cry. It was surely a bird or small animal that was probably more scared of her than she was of it. Oh, yeah, right.

The moon went behind a cloud and she cursed when she stumbled over a small rock. "Fuck." She went down on one knee and just sat there holding back tears. "Damn.

"Of all the shit," she grumbled. "I watch those movies and I laugh at those inane bitches that fall down. And what happens to me? I fall the hell down. I'm a horror-movie bimbo. Crap." She pushed her hair out of her eyes, readjusting her ponytail holder.

She stood and put her weight on her foot with a grimace. Limping, but determined to press on, she made a little progress. When she reached a bend in the long two-lane road, she stopped again. This time it was because of the icy tingle of dread creeping up her spine. She straightened and turned to look back where she'd just been. Was that a shadow there in the brush? Dear God, it was. And it was moving. Her dream haunted her, coming to the front of her mind with a vengeance, the familiarity of the setting, a dark and lonely place, her running from an animal. Or, what if it wasn't an animal? What if it was a psycho killer intent on chopping her into bits after making her eat at the table with his dead, stuffed mother?

Okay, calm down. Nobody does that sort of thing anymore. Now, they make you put lotion on your skin and— On second thought, that didn't help at all. "I want my—" Lainie paused. She wanted her Marcus, where in the hell was he?

"Some fuckin' he-man he is. If he were any sort of big and bad dude, he'd be out here picking me up and putting me into the limo against my will. My ass would be safely pissed off in luxury right now instead of scared shitless and injured out communing with nature." Lainie bit her lip and walked a little faster. "No. Here I am, being stalked by some freak with a penchant for fat girls. How dare he? I am in perfect shape. Well, I mean, yeah, I could lose a few pounds. Rat bastard, size discrimination is against the law." She wiped sweat from her forehead and kept limping along. Her language deteriorated and she decided to blame Marcus for that too. If she was going to die, she may as well have a clear conscience. Another rustle, this time closer. She whined and began to hobble even faster. "Marcus, as an alpha male, you totally fuckin' suck—bossy and useless."

The totally fuckin' sucky alpha male was at this moment glaring at David who lay on his back laughing his furry gray ass off. Marcus growled and thought seriously of biting him. He didn't, though, because David bit back, and in the soft spots too. Instead, he waited for the moment to spring. He would take the silly little twit down and scare the shit out of her. His muzzle stretched into a lupine version of a smile. His eyes reflected the gleam of the moon, which was almost full now. Soon he'd feel its pull but tonight was just for fun.

He woofed at David to be still, a command the other wolf ignored. When she came near enough, Marcus crouched down low. As she passed, he leapt out of the brush. In mid-leap, he remembered how much she'd liked his wolf form. Damn. He muffled a yelp of pain as he forced his body to shift too quickly back into its human form. He made it just in time to land on his quarry. However, the results of his ambush were not what he'd hoped.

"You nasty bastard, get off me, you psycho! Ew, naked too. Gross!" Lainie screamed like a banshee.

Marcus's ears rang with her yells until she slammed her fists against his ears and he went blessedly deaf. He knew the peace wouldn't last long. In the meantime, he grappled for her hands before she could do any more damage. "Stop it!" he hissed, wincing as his ears popped. His hearing returned just in time to hear her screech again.

At the sound of his voice, she stopped struggling for a second before she renewed her attack, adding in verbal thrusts for good measure. Women really were the champions of multitasking.

After disparaging his parentage, his weight and his bony pelvis, she glared up at him. "Marcus? Why in the world are you out here naked?"

"*Ohke?*" He attempted to say the word to make her go into that trance state like David did.

"Okay? Okay what?"

Another snort came from the vicinity of the bushes.

"Weirdo! Get off me. Just because I had sex with you doesn't mean you can come running out of the woods and hop on me naked!"

"If you hit me there with your knee once more, so help me I'm gonna..." He trailed off when a pair of high beams hit them both. "Well, fuck."

There was the sound of a car door opening and closing. "Sir?"

"Yes, Mick." Marcus sighed, leaning his forehead on hers. She bit him on the nose. "Ow!"

"Get off me, you heavy shit."

"You weren't complaining about it last night," he couldn't help pointing out. Other things were pointing as well but he refused to allow her the satisfaction of seeing the effect she had on him. "Will you turn off the damned lights?" The minute Mick complied, he stood and walked to the trunk to get his pants.

Lainie blinked for a few minutes, trying to adjust her eyes. She thought she saw another shadow moving behind the car, but wasn't sure. She craned her neck, just as Marcus, clad only in a pair of jeans, came stomping back over to glare at her.

"What did you think you were doing out here in the middle of the night? You could have been killed or worse, attacked by some deranged sex fiend."

"I was," she snapped as she took the hand he extended.

"You were?" He jerked her up off the ground, running his hands over her arms and legs. "Are you all right? Did he hurt you?"

"It was you, you big freak. I'm fine with that sort of thing in the right circumstances, but not now. And another thing..."

Despite her wiggles, he carried her to the car, settling her inside with ease.

"...nasty, naked and sweaty and don't think I didn't feel you poking me with that—that thing!" she continued.

"Lainie," he said, his voice low and calm.

"What?"

"Shut up."

She opened her mouth to tell him what he could do with himself. She took one look at his expression and closed it again.

He was enraged; there was no other word for it. His face was red and his lips were pressed tightly together. "Why did you run off?"

"I, well..." She bowed her head. "I just felt like I should." How could she tell him she'd seen her name on the computer printout, with his father's beside it? What did that mean? Why did it make her stomach hurt just thinking about it?

Chapter Fourteen

Lainie didn't speak while they made their way back home. She glared at him from her corner of the vehicle with her arms folded beneath her breasts. Her knuckles were white. To any other man, she'd just look pissed. However, Marcus could sense the fear beneath the anger. It made him want to hold her, protect her from whatever it was that made her feel this way. "Lainie?" When he said her name, she jumped. "What's wrong?"

"Nothing," she answered quickly. Her throat muscles moved jerkily as she swallowed. She bit her lip, worrying it with her teeth.

The lights from the house lit the car, illuminating her soft skin and burnishing her hair with its golden light. "You're so beautiful," he whispered. He hadn't really meant to say it out loud. But just now, seeing her so still, it came to him how lovely she really was.

Usually she was so animated, her hands and lips in perpetual motion. Her brain worked overtime, that much he did know. But right now, she looked like a still life. And if he painted her portrait, he'd simply call her Beauty. With a wry grin, he shook his head to clear his thoughts. If she was Beauty, that surely made him the Beast. He was so not going there. Disney could kiss his ass. He didn't want to be "cured" or released from some spell.

He loved being a werewolf, but sometimes, late at night, he felt lonesome. Lainie would stay with him for a while, but she'd find out what he was sooner or later. And he had the feeling that when she did find out the truth, she would run as fast as she could. Hell, any intelligent woman would, unless he trapped her here. He discarded that notion as soon as it came into his mind. He wouldn't keep her against her wishes. He wanted her to stay with him of her own free will. That meant she had to love him.

They reached the front of the house and he got out of the car first, scanning the front yard for signs of company before he turned to help her out. "Come on."

She looked at his hand for a few seconds before taking it. Heat flowed through him at the mere touch of her skin on his. "Where did you come from? And why were you naked?" She didn't look him in the eye, just stood there clutching her backpack.

"Well, it's a long story." He pressed his hand to the small of her back.

Her muscles tensed, then quaked.

He smiled as it came to him that half his battle was won.

Lainie was sexually attracted to him, so logic stated love would soon follow. "I'm a good listener." She gave him her best reporter smile. "Talk to me."

"Not tonight." Her shoulders slumped at his reply. "I'm tired. Chasing idiotic women around in the dark takes it out of me."

"You didn't chase me. You jumped on me after scaring the shit out of me." She took a step then gasped when she put her weight on her foot. "Damn."

"Here, allow me." Marcus swept her up in his arms and motioned for Mick to open the door before he walked inside the house and started for the stairs.

"How romantic."

"Hmm, yes, I am a romantic." He ignored her snort of derision. "Don't you believe me?"

"No. You're a man. You've already had sex with me, why should you be romancing me now?"

"Because I want to have sex with you again?" He grinned down at her.

She seemed to think it over. "There is that."

He stopped on the landing and kissed her. She sighed and put her arms around his neck. Marcus walked into his room and slammed the door with his foot. He moved toward the bed but her next words stopped him dead in his tracks.

"Where is your uncle?"

"Shit." With a groan of frustration, he laid her in the middle of the bed. "I'll go see. You stay here and rest your foot."

"I can't have sex while he's in the house!" She struggled to get up.

"He's not in the house."

"How do you know that? Did you kick him out? Marcus!"

"No. Shh." Marcus walked out before she could protest again. A few minutes later, he walked back into the room. "He told Allen that he'd be gone for a while. Something about pizza and beer."

Lainie smiled. "He's a good man, you know."

"I know." But Marcus didn't want to talk about David. He didn't want to talk at all.

Lainie had other ideas, but he figured he could distract her. He was wrong. “I want to know why you were naked.”

“It’s an old Indian custom.” Even he winced at that lame excuse.

Lainie didn’t buy it either. “Bullshit.”

“Look, what I was doing is irrelevant! You were out on a deserted highway. You are the guilty party here, not me.” Marcus decided to take the offensive.

Lainie stared at him mutinously. Her full lips were pursed in a pout that made him either want to spank her or kiss her. Both of those were nice options. “Elaine, tell me what you thought you were doing running off that way.”

“I don’t have to tell you jack shit.” Her chin was at that determined angle he remembered from their childhood days.

“Yes, honey, you do.” He put his chin at an even higher angle.

She still sat in the middle of the bed. He leaned down and grabbed her knees, jerking her to the edge. She started to squirm but he knelt down and grabbed her wrists. Her mouth was halfway to his hand, her teeth bared.

“If you bite me, I will bite you back.” He watched to see if she bought his threat.

Her gaze met his over the top of his knuckles. She paused for a minute, as if trying to gauge the seriousness of his words.

He licked his lips, waiting. When she didn’t bite, he continued. “Spill it.”

“Fine! I heard you talking, when you said something about Samuel; I thought he was coming here, so I left.” She stared at a spot over his shoulder, refusing to meet his gaze.

“He can’t hurt you now, I’m here.” Marcus put his other hand on her neck, stroking the soft skin beneath her ear.

"You were there the last time." She finally met his eyes.

"What are you talking about?" Marcus prodded, but she closed her mouth, refusing to say another word. "Lainie, I want to help, but you gotta talk to me." He pulled her onto his lap. "Tell me."

"He um..." Her body trembled. "He came into my room. He wasn't supposed to be home, but he came in one night."

"What did my father do?" His teeth itched and his skin tingled. Rage boiled through his veins. He'd just been a wolf, which was the only thing that stopped him from transforming now, right in front of her.

"I was about fourteen. I woke up and at first I thought it was you standing over me. We'd watched a scary movie, and I thought you were being mean and trying to scare me." She smiled. "You would do that."

"I would not."

"Marcus, you put on a damn hockey mask and chased me through the yard." She never forgot anything.

"I was fifteen when I did that!" He inhaled deeply, trying to calm down. "That's not the point. What happened?"

"I thought it was you, so I pretended to be asleep to see what you would do. And really, I was just waiting for my chance to scare the crap out of you," she admitted.

He chuckled, visualizing her waiting to jump up at him. Her next words killed any amusement he felt.

"He sat on the edge of the bed and put his hand over my mouth. That's when I knew it wasn't you." The shaking got worse. "He told me that I was his. He said—" She stopped talking for a second and took another deep breath. "He said that I'd never escape, and if I knew what was good for me, I'd just lie back and take it." Tears gathered in her eyes, but she blinked them back.

"What did you do? Why didn't you tell me?"

"He started to take off his clothes. When he let me go, I ran."

"Where?"

"To you." Her laugh had a bitter sound to it. "You woke up and I told you I'd had a nightmare. So, you let me sleep on the other side of you, closest to the wall."

Undiluted rage washed over him as he recalled that night. She'd still been little Lainie—to him but not his father, apparently. "That's just sick."

"I know! That's why I didn't ever want to come back when he was going to be there."

"I'm so sorry." He cradled her head against his shoulder, rocking her back and forth. "Why didn't you tell me then?"

"What could you do? You were just a kid too."

"I was..." He paused. "Yeah, you're right."

"You were there so I got through the night. When I woke up the next morning, he was nowhere around. I tried to convince myself it was a dream, but I knew." She grimaced. "Then, you went all freakin' postal that summer and I never came back again."

"Yeah, about that—"

"It wasn't the same thing." Her skin flushed, starting at her neck and going straight up to her hairline.

"How so?"

"Marcus!" She sat up and glared at him. "I loved you. That's how it was different."

"Lainie, I loved you too, but it didn't make it right. You were just a little baby. I should have controlled myself."

"You did, in the end." She caressed his jaw with her fingers.

"But what if I hadn't?" He bit his words off. "I didn't want to."

"I didn't really want you to either. The feelings that hit me were scary as hell. It felt like heat in my blood, and when you touched me, I went up in flames." She licked her lips. "I have a confession to make."

"What's that?" He lay back, pulling her with him. She wiggled around, tucking her head beneath his chin.

Lainie chewed on her nail, wondering how she should go about telling this man she'd set out to seduce him all those years ago. He'd been the ultimate teenage fantasy, charming, handsome, sweet and gentle. At least, she'd thought so, until that day when he attempted to take her further than she'd wanted.

"Lainie." He slid his hands underneath her shirt stroking them up and down her spine. When he began to knead the muscles there, she melted against him with a sigh.

"When I came to your house that summer, I'd decided that you were going to be my boyfriend."

"Did you now?" He sounded amused.

"Yes, I did. Shut up." She pinched him on the side. "The minute I saw you again, I wanted to—okay, I really didn't know what I wanted, but that's beside the point. I wanted something and I set out to get it. But you proved to be more of a challenge than the boys back home."

"What boys back home?" He didn't sound too happy about that. She put her face against his chest to hide her grin.

"The point is, they were always after me to go out with them, but I didn't want to. I wanted something else, and when I saw you, I knew what it was." She sat up and looked into his eyes to see his reaction to her next statement.

"Before I came out to where you were that day, I prepared myself." She smiled when he raised his brow at her. "Shaved my legs, put on my favorite dress, the one that showed off my tan and made my boobs look bigger."

Marcus's hands strayed up the front of her shirt, cupping her breasts in his hands. "They're big enough now." He squeezed them, lifting them in his hands. His thumbs stroked her nipples to hardened points.

Her eyes crossed. "Stop that, you're distracting me." She pushed his hands back down. She sat astride his hips, very aware of the bulge of his arousal pressing against her through their jeans. "I fixed you a glass of tea, so I'd have an excuse to come see you."

She paused as she remembered the feeling of anticipation. All she'd been expecting was maybe a kiss, one of those nice, soft ones like in all the movies. What she'd gotten was much more primal and ultimately terrifying. Her own reaction had been just as strong, so much so that she'd fled from him when all she'd really wanted was to pull him inside her and hold him there forever.

"There you were, without your shirt." She tickled his bare ribs with a grin. "Hot and sweaty and hot."

"You said that twice."

"Two different meanings though, keep up." She kept her voice light and teasing. "At first, I didn't even think you noticed me, but then once I sat down, I could tell you did."

"You bit off more than you could chew, Lainie." Marcus frowned.

"I know that now. But then, I didn't. So, imagine my surprise when you just pounced on me. I felt like I was being..." She paused to find the right word. "Devoured."

"Eating you up did cross my mind."

She glared down at him. "You scared the crap out of me. I didn't know what to do. I couldn't breathe, couldn't think, so I ran. Pretty stupid, huh?" She lowered her head, ashamed for teasing him. But, she thought she knew what to do to make it up to him.

He watched her for a long moment, taking in all the changes time had wrought and all the wonderful ways she was still the same. "No. You were sweet, innocent and silly, but then again, you were only sixteen. Looking back, it was a damn wonder we didn't do anything before. Why in the hell did they allow you to come see me each year? I was a hormonal wreck, you know?" Besides being a damn werewolf, he added silently.

"I begged to go. And whined, and made a nuisance of myself until Joanna threw up her hands and chucked me out at your house." She grinned. "I loved you. You were my best friend in the whole world, my only friend really. You let me call you. You answered my letters. You were wonderful."

He shrugged, feeling uncomfortable. He'd done all those things because he believed in the philosophy that when you save someone's life, they become your responsibility. Add to that the fact she practically treated him like a god during his early teens and you had a potent cocktail for his continued goodwill. She'd been a little pest, but she'd been his pest.

He put his hands around her waist and tipped her forward so she lay on his chest again. Her breasts slid against him with each breath she took. He gritted his teeth at the sensation, but didn't want to upset the uneasy peace that existed right now. She wasn't asking questions so he didn't have to scramble for plausible lies. He knew it was only a matter of time, but he was dreading the death of that look in her eyes.

She'd said she loved him. But was she talking about the Lainie from the past, or the one from the present? He wished he knew, but was afraid that if he asked the question, the answer would break his heart.

"Marcus, you said that you were out doing a secret Indian ritual." She trailed her fingers up and down his chest, ruining his concentration. "Why did it involve you being naked again? I don't think you ever said."

"I can't tell you." He closed his eyes with a groan. She circled his nipples with the tips of her fingers, lightly scratching her nails up and down his chest.

"Why not?"

"David won't let me." Marcus was happy to put the blame on someone else's shoulders. He hissed and opened his eyes when she pinched both of his nipples. "Don't start things you don't want to finish, Lainie."

"Who says I won't?" She raised one brow at him and smiled wickedly. "Maybe I'll start it and finish it too." She waited for a beat. "I'll leave the naked jogging thing for now, but only because I have more important things on my mind." She hopped off the bed and out of his reach before he could grab her. With a mysterious smile, she pulled her shirt off.

Immediately, he sat up and started to come toward her. "No!" She put up her hand. "Stay back and watch me."

Marcus flopped back on the bed and put his hands behind his head. He crossed his legs at the ankles and tried to pretend he didn't have a care in the world. In fact, he was about to explode, and all she'd taken off was her shirt. "What are you doing?" He swallowed hard to get the words out past the lump in his throat.

"What does it look like?" She slid her jeans down over her hips, turning her back on him when she did so. Her ass was almost within reach of his hand. It took all he had not to grab her.

The swishing sound of the denim brought him out of his daze with a snap. She threw them out of the way and turned back to face him. She took off her socks and flicked them out of the way with her toes.

He smiled at the sight of them, long and thin, with the ability to pinch the shit out of you when you least expected it. That small, quirky memory helped him calm down slightly. Then he looked at her standing there in a white bra and panties. The creamy swells of her breasts overflowed the cups and the dark circles of her nipples showed through the lacy fabric. He wanted to know how they'd taste, if they'd be salty from her exertions, with the hint of sweetness beneath.

He inhaled, breathing in the scent of the lotion she wore, a light, clean fragrance he couldn't identify. Beneath he detected something that made his nostrils flair. Her arousal.

She smelled hot, spicy and he knew she'd be wet for him. He could pull her down on the bed and take her from behind without even worrying about whether she was ready or not. He knew she was, more than ready. Marcus's gaze crept downward, over her belly, the tiny ring in her navel making him smile.

He looked at the apex of her thighs and licked his lips. "Lainie."

She slid her hands up her belly, cupping her breasts, lifting them.

He gave a low whine of need. "What the hell are you trying to do, drive me crazy?"

Lainie undid her hair from the band holding it in place, allowing the long tresses to fall free. She raked them back from her face, tossing her head. She didn't answer. Instead, with a flick of her wrist, she released the catch on the bra and peeled it from her breasts, one cup at a time.

"Oh shit." He caught the bra she tossed to him. He pressed it to his face, narrowing his eyes to thin slits.

"Marcus, are you looking?" She sounded like a temptress, a siren, teasing him with what he knew he'd get, eventually. It was well worth the wait, he knew that.

"I haven't blinked yet," he assured her, grinning and tossing the bra onto the bed. "Carry on, darlin', I don't know what you've got in that diabolical brain of yours, but I'm game."

"Game? This isn't a game." She smoothed her hands over her stomach, flicking the ring with her little finger. The charm on it made a tiny jingling sound. Then she moved back up again. She molded her hands to her breasts, cupping them, tweaking the hard rosy nipples between her thumb and forefingers.

His already engorged shaft pulsed once; he ached to take her but didn't want to miss whatever she had in store for him next. He wasn't disappointed.

Her head fell back and she sighed. "Mm." She licked her lips and pulled her nipples a little harder.

"Baby." His voice was breathless and slightly higher in pitch. "I'll be happy to do that for you...and that too!"

Lainie's hands had left her breasts and moved slowly down her abdomen. She paused at the top of her panties; he smiled and waited for her to take them off. Apparently, she had other plans. With a wicked smile, she slid one hand down the front of her underwear. Her eyes met his, never wavering when she began to circle the bud of her clit.

His breathing quickened with each stroke of her fingers. In the silence of the room, he could even hear the slicking noises when she thrust her fingers within her pussy. "Lainie, please."

"Watch me," she commanded and placed her foot on the bed beside his hip, spreading her thighs. Her panties were so wet he could see her fingers through the white silk. That was it. He sat up and jerked her down onto the bed with him.

She struggled for a minute, unwilling to give him the upper hand.

He reached out and ripped the underwear away, and watched her pleasuring herself. He almost stopped her, but became hypnotized by the sight of her long fingers sliding in and out of the wet, glistening folds of her sex.

She pinched her clit between her fingernails, lifting her hips in imitation of the way they'd made love just last night. "Marcus." Her voice sounded soft and thready; she was on the brink of release. "Fuck me." With one last thrust of her fingers, she came with a low groan.

He watched in astonishment when she licked her fingers clean. He pulled her hand to his mouth and did it too, scraping his teeth across her skin.

She smiled up at him knowingly.

Marcus pulled his pants off, almost ripping them in his haste. "I don't know what the hell you were trying to prove by doing that, but I'll be glad to let you know, it worked." He sucked her lip and bit it, barely stopping before he drew blood. Almost angrily, he batted her hands away from her sex. "Mine," he told her, his voice low and harsh. She laughed, a husky, sweet sound that told him she had no clue how jealous he'd been when he watched her fuck herself.

"I'll let you borrow it." She smiled lazily at him, her eyes dark and heavy lidded from pleasure.

"You know, as nice as that was to watch, and yeah, it was..." He pulled her wrists up and looped the bra over them. Before she figured out what he was doing, he had them tied to the headboard. "I think I should show you just how it's done."

She tugged at her bonds. Her breasts bounced with each movement, drawing his attention to them.

"Like here, for instance." He leaned down and kissed first one breast then the other, barely brushing his lips across the pebbled surfaces. "You were pretty rough. Maybe they liked it?" He met her eyes and winked. "Let's see." He squeezed her right breast, rolling the nipple between his fingers, as she had. He tugged the peak, twisting to the point of pain. Lainie arched up with a gasp. "I think you were right." He rubbed his palm across her breast and she hissed.

"Let's see about this one." He licked her nipple and blew on it. "It's hard too, and sweet, how about another taste, hmm?" A soft stroke with his tongue, knowing she wanted him to do more. But, she'd teased him, and he intended to return the favor, in spades.

His teeth grazed her nipple and she mewled. "Marcus."

He tugged with his teeth then sucked the nub into his mouth. He squeezed the soft mound, slicking his tongue across the soft creamy flesh of her upper breast, biting hard enough to leave a mark.

"Oh God, yes."

He slid down her body, grinning when she whimpered. He pulled her legs apart and looked at her. Her pussy glistened and even as he watched a small bead of moisture slid from between the curls. He moved forward and caught it on his tongue. She hissed, bucking her hips toward his mouth. "Not yet," he told her.

"What are you doing?"

"Watching your pussy weep for me." He blew a stream of air, aiming it at her clit.

"How do you know it's for you?" She squirmed slightly, but he pushed her legs farther apart, sliding them under his arms, effectively trapping them.

In this position, her outer lips slowly parted, revealing the dark pink flesh inside. He blew again, and she twitched. With a hungry smile, he made his move.

"Marcus." She practically shrieked when he pressed his mouth to her inner thigh. "I want—"

"What you want is no longer an issue," he informed her. She tried to wiggle away again. He clamped his arms down on her legs, pushing them even farther apart until her sex was totally exposed to his gaze.

He pressed his lips to the soft skin where her thigh joined her torso and sucked.

"Marcus?" Her voice held a beseeching quality. She groaned when he just licked her skin. Goose bumps rose up on her flesh and she shivered in his arms.

"I'm making another mark, right here." He made a small X mark with his tongue, and sucked the flesh into his mouth hard. She opened her eyes wide and looked down at him. His gaze never left her face. She watched him, hypnotized by the sight of his tongue gliding over her flesh.

He tilted his head slightly and nibbled the inner edge of her slit. The wet, creamy juices clung to his tongue when he flicked it inside with darting little strokes designed to frustrate her. It worked; she screeched. "What is it, Lainie? Can't stand to be teased?" He waited until she got the point. He wasn't disappointed.

"Fuck you."

"Not yet," he answered before he thrust his tongue inside her. He concentrated and his tongue thickened, roughening slightly. He curled it upwards, flicking it inside her until he found the very spot that made her scream. "Beg me." He stopped and whispered the command. She shook her head, refusing to do so. His tongue slid in and out of her, thrusting and coiling. Her pussy clenched around it, the muscles almost capturing the appendage. He moved his arms, pressing his hands against her inner thighs. His fingers slid around her ass, squeezing.

He used his thumbs to spread her open. The small pink nub slid out from beneath the folds surrounding it. He lunged forward, capturing it between his lips. She hiccupped, sobbing with the force of her climax. He didn't stop, only scraped it with his teeth, bringing another dimension in, one she seemed to like. "You're soaking wet, baby."

"Please."

He sucked her into his mouth, biting gently. She creamed for him again and he stole another lick, at the opening of her passage. "Damn, you taste good."

"Oh, God, Marcus, please."

"I don't know." He paused to lick the nub again, smiling when she shuddered. The entrance to her sex clenched, tightening and opening with her orgasm. "I think you need a little more instruction."

"I won't be tied to this bed forever." She glared at him. "And when I get loose, you'll be sorry."

"Was that a threat?" he asked, his voice low and hard. He lay poised to put his mouth back on her again. Even as she watched, he licked the side of her sex.

"No," she told him quickly. "It wasn't."

"I think it was." He buried his face against her, ignoring her thighs clenching around his face. Instead, he devoured her, reveling in the taste and smell of her. She screamed his name with the next climax.

"Please, just stop. I won't—" She stuttered, unable to form the next word.

He caught her clit between his teeth again, this time, tugging slightly so that it distended. His tongue lapped at the tip, and she shuddered.

He finally noticed the tears. With one more lick, he stopped, laying his head on her belly. He stroked her thighs, circling the mark on her leg with his finger. Even that touch made her jerk and her breath rasp harshly in her throat.

He moved beside her, running his hands over her breasts and belly. Each time he got close to her sex, her muscles clenched. "Are you gonna tease me like that again?"

She glared at him, not speaking.

"Ah, Lainie. Don't be mad." He kissed her and she opened her mouth easily enough. Too easily, it turned out because she bit him. Aroused by what amounted to love play for him, he squeezed her breasts harder than before.

He turned her over on her belly. "What are you doing?" Her question ended on a gasp when he pulled her up on her knees and plunged his cock inside her so hard his balls slapped against her clit.

Her pussy squeezed him, the muscles dancing around his shaft as she stretched to accommodate him. "I asked you a question." He thrust again, grabbing her waist and pulling her back against him.

"Fuck you, Marcus," she answered, unwilling to give in.

"That's what we're doing." He squeezed her ass, caressing the soft globes of flesh. His thumb slid into the cleft, stroking the tight little hole there. She tried to jerk away, but he just pulled her closer, never breaking the rhythm of his strokes.

Everything he did aroused her to a fever pitch. Lainie was unable to contain a moan when he squeezed her ass again. His thumb pressed a little harder against her anus. Her body clenched tight, but her pussy grew even wetter. "Marcus." She hissed his name.

In response, he smacked his hand down on her ass hard enough to sting. "Hey!" She glared at him over her shoulder. He grinned back at her, looking like a marauding pirate. "Don't do that shit again."

But he did, and then rubbed the reddened flesh. She bucked her hips back against him. His movements became more savage. He looked positively feral. He plunged, stealing her breath with the impetus of his strokes.

He slid one hand to her breasts, tweaking first one nipple then the other. His free hand moved to the curls between her legs, finding her clit. She braced her legs further apart, taking him inside as far as she could. "Yes, harder." Her voice was hoarse from her screams.

"Put your hands on the headboard and hold on." He could barely draw in enough oxygen to get the words out.

He filled her, his cock bumped the entrance to her womb and she keened softly, thrusting back against him. "Marcus, don't stop. Please, right there." She stiffened, squeezing her thighs together.

"Damn, Lainie." His body tightened, tingles beginning in the base of his spine, radiating outward to his balls. He slid his arm around her belly, lifting her against him as he ground his hips against her. He swelled inside her and she cried out as it took her over the edge.

Marcus was past all reason, his eyes narrowed and he knew they'd changed to the amber color of his wolf form. He reached up and ripped the bra off the headboard, uncaring that the wood splintered as well. He wanted her as close as possible and this wasn't doing it for him.

He lifted her in his arms, sliding to the edge of the bed. Here, she was at just the right height. He slid back inside her with a grunt and leaned down to skim his teeth over her spine. She arched her back against his mouth. He bit her neck, holding her in place. She screamed and bucked her hips up to meet his thrusts, her ass pressing into his abdomen. He tasted blood and his balls tightened. "Baby, let go."

She couldn't or wouldn't and then it was too late. This time, their mating had been too primitive, arousing every instinct he'd suppressed the first time so he wouldn't scare her. His self-control left him. His head fell back and he howled long and hard. His cock swelled, trapping him as he poured his seed inside her.

She clenched her fingers in the coverlet, closing her eyes tightly. Her pussy quivered around him, milking each and every drop.

With each heartbeat, his cock throbbed. The juices of her sex sluiced down onto his balls and thighs, warm and wet. "Lainie, just lie still," he whispered against her ear. He kissed her, smoothing his hands up and down her arms. He couldn't pull out of her right now, not without hurting her and himself.

"Marcus, you're squishing me," she told him, her voice muffled. She tried to wiggle out from under him, gasping when she found that they were still connected. "Oh that feels..." She trailed off and moved her hips. "Nice."

He moaned, gritting his teeth. “If you don’t stop, we’ll be starting over.”

“What was the reason for all of this?” She snuggled against him with a happy sigh.

“To teach you a lesson.”

“Oh,” she replied in a faint voice, “I’ll be sure to do it again then. But, let’s wait a little while. I don’t know if I’m up to any more of your brand of teaching right now.” She turned her head and smiled at him sleepily, her lashes growing heavy even as he watched. “Are we going to stay this way all night?”

“Yes, damn it.” He moved them both up on the bed, turning her on her side. “Like spoons.”

She giggled then yawned. “More like tab A goes into slot B, but I’m not complaining. If you do decide to start your next lesson, be sure and wake me up first.”

He pressed his forehead against her shoulder and muffled an exasperated laugh. So much for teaching her a lesson. She thought it was all a game. “Lainie, that’s not—”

Her light snore interrupted him. Astonishingly, she fell asleep while his cock was buried inside her. He had a long wait until he could do the same.

Chapter Fifteen

On the fourth day of her stay at Marcus's house, Lainie woke, squinting her eyes in the bright morning sun. She stretched then winced when her muscles protested the movement.

Remembering the reasons she was so sore brought a smile to her face. Since the night she'd tried to escape, she'd been in this bed or on the floor or… Her smile widened when she spied Marcus standing outside in a pair of cutoff sweatpants and nothing else. He was one fine specimen of a man. She propped her head on her hand and lay on her side, watching as he moved through the complex steps of his morning exercises.

Through the half-opened door, the loud whooshing of his exhales reached her. His legs were about hip width apart and slightly bent at the knees. He moved his hands slowly, making the motions as graceful as any dance.

She continued to stare, fascinated by the play of muscles rippling down his back. The sight of his sweaty form made the muscles of her pussy tighten. She moved her thighs restlessly on the bed and grimaced at the sticky residue left over from the night before. He'd been domineering and possessive again. Despite her modern woman's way of thinking, she admitting that she liked it a hell of a lot. Did this make her a closet sub? And if so, was Marcus a leather-wearing dominatrix? No, that was the lady one. What the hell was a man one called? A domino, domineer, dominus? She'd have do a cyber search on that later, or she'd go crazy.

Lainie slid from the bed and hurried into the bathroom, pausing to stare at her reflection in the mirror over the sink. She looked like she'd been well loved—more like well used. Leaning closer to see the fading bite mark on her breast, she noticed something strange about it. The indentions from his incisors were a lot deeper than they should be. She curled her lip to examine her own.

She twisted and turned, noting the marks on her body, telling the tale of how she'd spent her nights. Small bruises on her wrists and hips where he'd held her down. The mark on her thigh was an outright hickey though. She looked like she'd been in a fight. With a snarl to rival any 80s pop star, she sang out, "Love is a battlefield." Then smothered her laughter behind her hands and went to shower.

Marcus paused with his hand raised to knock when the sound of what he thought were sobs made him pause. Had he hurt or scared her? Now she'd run and he couldn't blame her in the least. His shoulders drooped. Wait, he could still salvage this. All he had to do was make it up to her. He twisted the knob and entered the steamy bathroom.

Lainie was in the shower stall. Glass blocks came halfway up, leaving the rest of the area open. A large skylight above illuminated her soapy skin. Marcus leaned on the partition and just enjoyed the view. She didn't look scared or upset. On the contrary, she seemed content as she stood beneath one of the sprayers lathering her hair. The scent of his shampoo teased his nostrils and he smiled, liking that she shared his scent. He'd liked her smelling like his come last night too, but this would do just as well. He'd marked her as his own. Without even knowing it, she would be advertising that fact to any other werewolf she met.

With each movement of her hands in her hair, her breasts bounced. He watched the soft mounds of flesh moving rhythmically and licked his lips in anticipation. Her eyes opened and she sputtered with shock. "Ack! Shit! My eyes!" She tried to climb the wall, but her feet couldn't get purchase on the slick tile. "What are you trying to do, give me a heart attack?" She brought her arms up in an attempt to shield her nudity from his gaze.

"Why are you doing that?"

"I always wash my hair." She blinked to clear her eyes then wrinkled her nose. "Don't you?"

He sighed and rolled his eyes. "I meant that I've seen you naked. So why are you covering up now?"

"For all I knew you were a psycho, sneaking in here while I'm in the shower." She bowed her head under the spray.

"This is my bathroom, I don't have to sneak." In a flash he was in front of her with his arms folded across his chest. His clothes lay in a puddle on the bathroom floor.

"How do you move so damn fast?" She backed up when he came into the stall with her.

"I'm just that good." He pulled her hands away from her breasts and sucked in his breath. "Oh, God, I'm so sorry. Is that why you were crying?" He took in the deep bruising of the skin right above her nipple. It looked even worse today.

She frowned, tilting her head to one side. "When was I crying?"

He gave her a sheepish grin. "A few minutes ago. I was listening at the door."

She blushed. “No, I was laughing about something else.” She pointed at the bruise. “This, well, this I kind of liked at the time.”

“Did you now?”

“Yeah.”

He stroked the skin around the mark then leaned down and kissed it. “Still sorry.”

“Still gonna make you pay.” She giggled and flicked water on him.

“How?”

“Oh, maybe by doing this.” She licked a path down his chest, pausing to spear his navel with her tongue. “Mm, nice and salty.”

Marcus watched her slide to her knees and take his cock in her hands. She handed him her sponge and then squeezed him. With a wicked smile, she arched her brow. “Are we going to exfoliate, or fornicate?”

“Urk?”

“Ooh, I like a man with an extended vocabulary.” Before he could think of a reply, she opened her mouth and took him in. She licked the head, flicking the sensitive spot where the tip began to flare out. He moved to lean against the wall. His knees were buckling and she hadn’t even really gotten started.

“Lainie, baby.”

She bit him hard enough to sting. He hissed and froze in place, his hand moving to her hair. She let him slide out of her mouth and glared. “Don’t call me that.”

“Why?”

“I like when you call me darlin’.”

“Oh, fine, darlin’,” he said, gritting his teeth.

She immediately sucked him inside the warm, wet cavern of her mouth. She opened wide to take him all in. When she hummed low in her throat, it vibrated up the length of his shaft, straight to his balls.

He tangled his fingers in her hair for purchase and pumped his hips, fucking her mouth. She curled her hand around the base of him and held on for the ride. Her cheeks moved in and out with each thrust. Her fingers cupped his sac, sliding wetly over the surface. When she pulled away he let her go, thinking she needed to stop, so he was surprised when she moved farther down and licked the underside of his cock. "Do you like this?" she asked in a low, husky voice.

"Yes." He barely got the word out. All the blood had left his brain and headed straight to his dick. She flicked her tongue like a whip on the veined surface from below. She curled it around him, and nipped at the skin, lightly tugging on it. "Oh yeah, baby."

He opened his eyes when she laughed. She was watching him, her green eyes glowing wickedly. She rubbed her cheek against his thigh and then licked his balls. "Lainie!" He held his breath when she did it again, sucking the swiftly tightening skin.

She bit down and he shuddered. If she kept this up, he'd lose it before he ever got to the next level. "Stop," he gasped.

"You didn't stop the last time," she pointed out.

"But you can do it more than once without a break, darlin'."

"I suppose that does mean girls rule and boys drool." She pondered this while she slowly circled the little spot right behind his balls with her fingers. He went up on his toes when her nails raked over him again.

"Yeah, drooling." He caved to her vast feminine superiority. She rewarded him by sucking his cock into her mouth again. He hit the back of her throat, but she didn't stop and he damn well wasn't going to argue about it too much. With a shout, he spilled his seed into her mouth, unable to take another minute of the torment. She made a little humming noise and licked the head of his cock once more before she got to her feet.

With a smug grin she handed him the sponge he'd let drop to the floor and presented her back. "Go ahead, bath boy, and wash me."

He looked at the sponge then the soap, and smiled. "Sure, darlin'." He emphasized the endearment and lathered the sponge. "Anything you want."

"That's right." She giggled when he ran the sponge down her back, then squeaked when he began to slather the soap between her legs. "I got there already."

"Aw, well, I'm just making sure you didn't miss anything." His finger slid into the folds of her sex to circle her clit. She shuddered and put her hands on the wall to brace herself. His fingers thrust inside her once and she moaned.

Marcus turned her around so he could watch her face. He slid the sponge over her nipples. They hardened into little pink nubs of flesh. "Like berries and whipped cream."

"You can taste them." She fluttered her lashes. "You need your mouth washed out with soap."

"I will, later," he promised, and she pretended to pout. Her eyes glazed over a second later when he returned to his task of washing her.

"Bath slaves kneel, right?" He led her over to the bench in the corner of the stall.

"Yes."

He pulled one of the detachable showerheads from its holder and knelt down between her knees. His body was wedged between her thighs, exposing her sex to his gaze and more importantly to the stream of water he aimed at her clit.

"Marcus!" She tried to shield herself with her hands but he just grabbed her wrists and held them above her head.

"You can't tell me you've never done this to yourself." Her breasts tilted up, her nipples pointing impudently at his face. He bit one, enjoying the mewling sounds she made. "That you haven't run the hot water over your clit, felt the pulse of it on your pussy lips then zipped it back to the middle." He did what he said and she screamed when the first orgasm hit her.

"Oh God." Her mouth was open and with each breath, her right breast slid against his cheek.

"Open your eyes," he commanded. She had to struggle to do so, but when she did she became captured by his intense stare. "You are beautiful when you come for me," he told her, then circled her nubbin again with the water. "Once more."

She wiggled but it was no use, his lower body was wedged between her legs holding them apart and his hand held hers captive high above her head. "Marcus, it's too much." He angled the stream, playing it over the entrance to her sex, pulsing it over the outer lips before darting it inside to hit her core again.

He slid back enough to plunge his shaft deep inside her sex, letting her go to pull her hips forward so he could fuck her as hard as he wanted. With a frustrated hiss, he turned her over on her belly and plunged back inside. For a few minutes, there were only the sounds of their flesh slapping together.

Holding her hip with one hand, he pressed the showerhead right against her clit, and her muscles spasmed around his cock. It took everything he had but this time, he pulled out to spill his seed onto the small of her back.

His heart thundered in his ears as he slowly regained control of himself. Methodically, he cupped some of the cooling water in his hands and carefully washed the evidence of their lovemaking off her body. His hand trembled when he reached up to turn off the faucet, but he forced it to stop. With precise movements, he took her in his arms and held her, breathing in and out until finally, he felt human again. Or as close as he ever got.

With a satisfied sigh, he stood and started toward the bedroom. Lainie opened her eyes and gave him a languid look. "Marcus Bei, you're something else."

"You have no idea, darlin'." He hefted her high in his arms and nibbled on her neck to make her squeal. She really didn't, he thought, sobering for a minute. No idea how "something else" he actually was. He shook off the dark mood that threatened and lay down beside her on the bed.

She stretched her arms over her head and grinned when he stared at her breasts. "Boys are so easy."

"Mm." Marcus reached out and licked her nipple. "Girls aren't too hard."

"We're going to have to slow down." She grimaced at the new soreness in her thighs. "I won't be able to walk much less dance at that darned ball."

"What ball?"

"The Caulder Ball!" She smacked him. "The reason for this whole mess."

He scowled at her choice of words.

"Oh, honey, I didn't mean it—" she began but he shrugged her hand off and stood to get dressed, retreating into the cold, aloof persona he presented to the world. "Marcus."

"I just remembered I have to go into the office," he lied, pulling a suit and tie out of his closet.

She came to him and wrapped her arms around his waist. "I didn't mean us. Not that. I meant—"

"Save it, I know what you meant."

She watched him go, silent and withdrawn. He looked so hard right now, unreachable and remote. She sighed and tried one more time. "I'll miss you."

"Yeah, me too." He gave her a halfhearted smile and left the room, slowly closing the door behind him.

Staring at the closed door, she worried a sore spot on her lip with her tongue, debating whether to follow him to his office or not. Finally, she decided against it. Instead, she dressed and went downstairs where she found a very cold note from Marcus reminding her that she had to get a dress for the ball.

After she'd eaten and wandered around the house for a while, she got bored. "Hey, Al?" The butler hunched his shoulders at the shortening of his name. She'd done it on purpose to vex him. So what? She didn't have much else to occupy her time.

"Yes, ma'am?" He turned and gave her his coldest glare.

"Where's Mick?"

"He just got back from town and is waiting for you to get ready to leave." Allen sniffed and looked her up and down. "If you are going to buy a dress, I suggest you put on more suitable attire."

"Why?" She looked down at her sweatshirt and jeans. "It's easy to get out of."

"You will be going to an exclusive shop, owned by the wife of one of Mr. Bei's associates. Do you wish them to think that you are a ragamuffin?"

"Ragamuffin? Who in the hell do you think you are? And who uses that word anymore?" she scoffed and folded her arms, meeting his glare with one of her own. "And while we're on the subject, what do you have against me?"

"I have no idea what you mean." Allen straightened his cuffs and made another sniffing noise.

"Do you use cocaine?" she asked him, narrowing her eyes in suspicion.

"I most certainly do not!" He looked affronted at the very possibility, even more so than he usually did in her presence.

"Then stop with all the sniffing. If you don't have anything against me, why do you treat me like you do?" She refused to give it up. If, as Marcus said, they were going to try this relationship thing out, she would be here a lot. She refused to be made to feel unwelcome in his house by the damned butler.

"I don't know what you mean," he repeated, blinking rapidly.

"Sure you don't." She curled her lip. Then inspiration dawned. "What do you think I should wear? I have no idea what the proper dress code is for an exclusive boutique. I'm more a department-store type of person, if you must know."

"You don't need to tell me that, ma'am." His snide reply made her grit her teeth. However, you can take the girl out of the south, but you can't take the south out of the girl. In other words, she could bullshit with the best of them.

"Well, you dress so nice and all." She drawled her words out and fluttered her lashes. "I'm sure you'd be able to help me choose. I don't have much though, that man tore all my things up when he broke in." She sighed, and let tears fill her eyes. "I don't know what I would have done if Marcus hadn't insisted on rescuing me." Surprisingly, he fell for it.

He smiled benignly down at her. "I will try to help you in any way I can. Follow me."

She hurried after him, hiding her smug grin behind her hand. "Hey, *this* is my room," she called when he didn't stop at her door.

He kept walking until he got to a room at the far end of the hall, turning to give her an impatient glare that made her feel about three feet tall and three years old. It was like living with Joanna all over again. "You did say you didn't have anything appropriate."

Well, she was a grown up now, and she'd prove it to him. She straightened her shoulders and marched past him, then paused as she took in the contents of the room with a silent whistle. The room was full of clothes, women's clothes at that. Why did Marcus have women's clothes? She opened her mouth to ask Allen but he distracted her by pulling out a beautiful plum-colored dress jacket and skirt. "Ooh."

"Yes." Allen handed it to her. "This should fit you." He stared at her feet and went to the wall, pressing a button. A panel slid back revealing shelves. Rows upon rows of designer pumps in various sizes stared back at her.

"Why?" she asked faintly, taking in the sight of what she hoped wasn't a sign of Marcus's heretofore-unknown predilection for wearing women's clothes. Or even something more sinister, like— Her imagination went wild at the possibilities; serial killer, pimp and stone-cold freak were at the top of the list.

"I will leave it to Mr. Bei to explain." Allen held up his hand when she began to protest. "It's his place." The firm line of his lips let her know she'd get nothing from him. He pointed to the screen at the far corner of the room. "You may change there."

Lainie dressed quickly, smoothing the skirt down over her hips before stepping into a pair of soft leather pumps the same shade as the suit. She turned this way and that to look at her reflection in the mirror stationed behind the screen. It was a perfect fit. Maybe Al had been an undertaker in a previous life.

She came out from behind the screen, twisting her hair up in the pins that he'd provided. "This fits great."

"Thank you." He paused and grudgingly continued, "You look very nice, Ms. Westerbrook."

"Thank you, Allen." She gave him her brightest smile and he gave her a small one in return. "I'll be back in a while. Shopping sucks, you know."

"Yes, I know." He sounded like he did. She wondered if he'd been the one to buy all these clothes.

Chapter Sixteen

Lainie sat in the back of the limo, alone with her thoughts. Though she'd tried to drag Mick into a conversation, she got only monosyllabic replies in return. Finally, she'd given up and allowed him to put the glass partition in place. She made him nervous, apparently. Classical music came from up front, soothing her jangled nerves on the ride into town. All too soon, they reached their destination and Mick opened her door, something she didn't think she'd ever get used to.

The store was actually an old house. The owner had renovated it just enough to turn it into a business without losing any of its original charm. Made of adobe, with the ever-present beams visible on the rooftop, the sign out front named it *The Ult*, in fancy gilt letters.

A chime rang when Mick opened the door and Lainie hesitated, knowing instantly that this wasn't her sort of place. She made good money as a freelance journalist, but not enough to shop here. She stepped inside when Mick gave her a strange look. He walked behind her, his hand pushing at the small of her back when she stopped. "Ms. Darton?" he called.

"I'll be right out!" a feminine voice called from somewhere in the back of the store. Lainie looked around while they waited.

The floors of the sumptuously decorated foyer were black and white parquet tile that gleamed brightly in the sunshine.

One wall held an original Georgia O'Keeffe if she wasn't mistaken.

Dresses lay in what at first glance looked to be a careless manner over wingback chairs. Hats were stacked on ottomans, gloves were fanned out on a coffee table, and shoes were sitting on the mantel and the hearth of the large fireplace. When Lainie looked closer, she saw that the fabric was draped artfully, and the hats were more a still-life composition of color and texture. The shoes were bright spots in the earthy room, like jewels on display. Necklaces swayed back and forth on the hooks of an antique hall tree. There were no traditional display racks, just beautiful furniture used to hold equally beautiful clothes and accessories.

A woman came out of the back and stopped short at the sight of them both. "May I help you?" Her lips firmed and her frosty tone didn't invite Lainie to stay.

"My name's Lainie and your shop was recommended to me by—"

"I am not open to the public, madam, but by appointment only." She wore her raven hair swept up in a smooth chignon. Pearls at her neck and on her earlobes softened her severe black suit only slightly.

"Ms. Darton?" Mick interceded. "This is Ms. Westerbrook. Mr. Bei should have called?" He made the statement into a question.

"Oh!" She smiled for the first time and Lainie blinked at the transformation. Her bright blue eyes sparkled with delight. "Why didn't you say so before?"

"Why does it make a difference?" Lainie wanted to know.

"Oh, you know men." She waved her hand around airily. "My husband hates for me to work, but we compromised. I only see his friends' wives and significant others."

"Pleased to meet you." Lainie's feeling of defensiveness eased. "My name is Elaine Westerbrook."

"I'm Charlotte Darton, it's very nice to meet you. Marcus spoke so highly of you on the phone."

"I'm sure he did." Lainie smothered a groan. Who was she kidding? If this was the type he consorted with, how did she hope to fit into his world? Maybe it would be better to leave after the ball. He would think she used him, but that was better than finding out just how unsuited she was to his lifestyle.

"Ms. Westerbrook." Ms. Darton was speaking.

"Please, call me Lainie."

"Fine, Lainie it is, please call me Charlotte then." The woman led her into another room, filled to the brim with ball gowns, with beads, feathers and in some cases, fur trimming.

"I don't think I should—" Lainie began, wondering at the price of all this stuff when a beautiful turquoise dress caught her eye. Strapless and gauzy, it was pretty much the most wonderful thing she'd ever seen.

Charlotte noticed the direction of her gaze and smiled. "Come, you must try it on."

Lainie followed her into one of the dressing suites. They were much larger than rooms, with a chaise lounge and two overstuffed chairs. The far corner held three antique standing mirrors angled enough for her to see herself from all sides.

She watched as Charlotte spread the dress out on the lounge and then turned. "We'll get you into it and make sure no alterations are needed."

Lainie unbuttoned her suit jacket and slid it off, hurrying over to the dress. The skirt had to go and unfortunately so did her bra. She moved to put the dress over her head and let the other woman fasten it in the back. Lainie kept her head down and wondered what Charlotte thought of the marks on her body. If she noticed it, she gave no sign of the fact.

"We'll get all the extras to go with the dress, if you want it, that is." She put her hands on Lainie's shoulders and led her to the mirrors.

Lainie took in her reflection and smiled. The bead-encrusted bodice caught the light, twinkling with every breath she took. The soft fabric, shirred to the waist, nipping in tightly before flaring out gently to the floor. Silky and light, it moved fluidly when she swayed. She felt like a fairytale princess going to the ball with her own prince.

Of course, right now, the prince was pissed off at her, but she could fix that. "Oh, yeah, I want it."

Charlotte's smile widened and she went off to find the shoes and underwear to compliment the dress. As if anyone would see her panties except Marcus, if he straightened up and flew right.

"Do you need anything else?" The other woman's voice brought her from her reverie.

"I need some other underwear and things. My house was broken into and the thieves vandalized my stuff." Lainie couldn't repress a shiver at what had been a very personal violation. If it was Caulder who ordered the break-in, she'd find out and he'd pay.

Chapter Seventeen

Marcus sat at his desk and twirled his pen over his fingers. It was an exercise in both dexterity and relaxation. Lainie's words had hurt much more than he wanted to admit. "This whole mess", she'd said. He supposed it could be thought of as such. But, he liked it this way. Messy and wild and a little off center. Her smart mouth made him laugh more than he had in a long time. Laughter had never been a part of his life, love even less.

His pack loved him and they'd die for him. His uncle—wait, grandfather—loved him, but apparently he loved Lainie more. Keeping her safe had been the other man's mission in life for fifteen years. Marcus dropped the pen and put his head on the desk. What if she left after tonight? Like Cinderella, she'd disappear and leave his broken heart behind. Better than a damn shoe, but not by much.

He closed his eyes and sighed. He was fighting the moon change on top of it all. The full moon was in a few more days. Soon it would be time to howl at the sky with his fellow wolves. Time to run free in the desert with the smell of the spicy sage filling his nostrils. He loved this time of the month; it was when all his worries slipped away. But now, it was different, because Lainie was at his home, where she would stay until he deemed it safe enough for her to leave.

Marcus sighed wearily. Being Lupin was hard; he was tired of all the bullshit that went with leading the pack. He had no children of his own, but he had to bless each union within his group. When he found his own mate, he wanted to have what they had. Could he bring children into the world, knowing they were genetic mutations that could destroy and maim? If they were like him, they could do some good in the world. Who was he kidding, what good did he do? Marcus closed his eyes wearily. He was just so lonely, and when Lainie had come back, he'd thought she was the one. Apparently, she didn't share this line of thinking. "A mess". Well, shit.

Staying in human form all the time, never losing control used up a lot of energy. He did it automatically, but still, it made him tired. Sleep pulled at him and he didn't fight it. Laying his head on his arms, he closed his eyes with the scent of her teasing his nostrils.

The scent grew stronger and he frowned but didn't open his eyes. She smelled so good, he wanted to lick her all over, nibble and suck and... Hell, he was as hard as a rock.

Someone stroked his hair, pushing the strands away from his face and he sat up, blinking at the vision sitting on his desk.

"Hi." Lainie grinned shyly.

"Hi," he grumbled, before clearing his throat. "What are you doing here?"

"I thought we'd eat a late lunch together." At her words, he glanced quickly at the clock on his desk and saw that it was almost one in the afternoon.

"I could eat." He refused to meet her eyes. She'd hurt him, but he'd be damned if he let her see that.

"I brought it with me. I hope you still like..." She paused and slid over until she was right in front of him. She planted one foot on each arm of his chair.

He glared at her. "What are you doing?"

"What does it look like?" She raised her brows and leaned forward with her elbows on her knees. The jacket gaped open slightly and showed him she wore nothing more than a bra beneath it.

He looked closer and noticed the tiny lavender-colored flowers embroidered along the top edge of some damned bits of lace surely invented to torture him. His pants no longer fit in the crotch. Unwillingly, he let his eyes fall to her legs. "I like the boots."

They were black and to the knee, making the suit look less business-like and more sexy. She let her legs fall open a little farther and he swallowed hard.

She wore a pair of panties that matched the bra, down to the flowers. He caught himself counting the flowers and bit his lip. "What are you up to?"

"Oh, just wanted to see you, is all." She reached out and grabbed his tie, pulling on it until he leaned forward between her upraised knees.

"Are you trying to seduce me, Ms. Westerbrook?"

"Is it working?" Her fingers found their way into the opening between the buttons on his shirt. She lightly scratched him with her nails.

"If I say no, what happens then?"

She jerked on his tie and pressed her mouth to his. Her tongue ran over his lips and then delved inside. She licked and sucked on his mouth. He barely suppressed a moan. "I try harder," she answered when she finally released him.

She leaned over until she was in danger of falling into his lap. Her knees were almost above her shoulders. His eyes crossed when her panties became wedged between the slick, bare lips of her pussy. “You look pretty hard right now, though, Marcus.” She grinned playfully at him.

He didn’t notice because he was pushing her skirt up to her waist. “When did this happen?” he asked, or roared rather. He slid his hand into the side of her underwear and cupped her now hairless sex.

She fell back from the force of his movements and stared up at the ceiling. His hand moved up and down her mound, caressing her bare skin.

“I did it today. You know it wasn’t that way when you left this morning!” She wiggled when he still didn’t take his hand away.

She throbbed for him to thrust his fingers inside her and make her come for him. Hell, she’d almost done that on the way up to his office just by imagining his face when he saw what she’d done.

When he still didn’t speak, she leaned up to see his face. “What is it? Don’t you like it?” She tilted her head to one side. “It’ll grow back.”

“Who—” He broke off and took a breath. “Where did you get this done?” When she didn’t answer he growled.

“At a salon, I got my hair done too.” She tossed the long glossy strands over her shoulder.

He narrowed his eyes, unable to see any change in her hair, not that he gave a damn about that right now.

“Oh, my legs too.” She wiggled them at him one at a time. “Your business associate’s wife, Charlotte, recommended it to me, in fact. The staff there is very professional.”

"Was it a man or a woman?" He punctuated his question with a soft squeeze and she tilted her hips up against his hand. "Tell me." With a slow movement she was sure was meant to torture her, he pushed his fingers just inside her. His thumb circled her clit in soft, feathery strokes designed to tease, not satisfy.

"It was a man!" She'd have confessed it was the president of the United States if he kept doing that. "I think he'd like you better, if you get my meaning."

"What?" Marcus paused and tried to figure out what she'd said, not an easy feat when his fingers were buried inside her pussy. "Oh."

"Oh?" She started to move away. "You know, I'm not your property. You haven't made me any promises, and I—" She squealed when he tore the underwear off and stuffed them into his pocket. "Marcus! Those were brand new!"

He was no longer listening to her. Instead, he cupped her with his hand, fascinated by the sight of her stretched out on the desk. "You said you brought lunch?" He spread her open, the glistening folds parted like a flower to reveal the bud of her clit.

"Yes," she whispered.

"I'm having dessert first." His mouth was on her before she could think up a reply. He lapped at her clit, spearing it repeatedly with his tongue, making her thighs tremble with each lick.

He sucked hard and she gasped, her pussy weeping, the creamy juices pooling on the desk. He'd make her want to stay; he'd keep her so damn satisfied she'd never want to leave him.

He pushed her legs farther apart until her feet fell off the chair. With her legs hanging down, the top of her mound was much more prominent. He pushed it higher and bit down softly, enjoying the shudders that racked her frame.

"Oh, yes." She sighed when his teeth moved back and forth.

He sucked on the smooth skin, enjoying the fact that this just gave him more space to work with. He lightly spanked it and she squealed coming up off the desk toward his hand.

He slid his hands under her ass and lifted her to his mouth, flipping her legs onto his shoulders. She scrabbled for purchase but he didn't give her a chance. "Open the jacket, let me see you." He whispered the command, but she sensed the thread of steel despite the softness of his voice.

Her fingers trembled when she rushed to spread the jacket open. "Take off the bra too, you're good at that, if I recall." He flicked her clit with rapid motions of his tongue when she hesitated. Her head fell back and she groaned, twisting and writhing in his hands.

She finally got her fingers to work. "Slow," he rasped, his mouth almost touching her. His gaze was boring into hers, watching her follow his commands.

She licked her lips and pushed the cups out of the way. She managed to get up on her elbows but he jerked her back down. "Marcus."

"Touch them for me." He began to lick her again. She cupped her breasts in her hands, squeezing them like he did.

He held her up with one arm wrapped around her leg, letting the other fall to the arm of the chair. It squeaked slightly when he moved. "The nipples too."

Her skin flushed pink from the combination of embarrassment and arousal. She tweaked her nipples, rolling them, pulling them hard. He rewarded her by thrusting his fingers inside her pussy. He used the same rhythm that she used to play with her breasts. His cock was about to explode but he wanted her completely at his mercy before he took her again. She writhed twice more before he stopped.

He undid his pants and turned her over, forcing her down on the desk with her legs spread wide. "Your pussy is wet, Lainie. Wet and hot and open for me. Beautiful." He pulled the jacket down over her arms, stopping at the elbows, effectively trapping them when he twisted the fabric in his hands.

Her ass was soft and round, and the skirt rucked up around it made it seem even more like forbidden fruit. He bit her hard enough to leave a mark. She said his name in a breathy whisper as he smoothed his hand over her ass then slapped it.

"What did I say about that?" she asked with a frown.

"What do you think you can do about it is the real question, darlin'." He freed himself and thrust into her. The hot, hard length of his cock filling her made her come again.

Her juices trickled out onto his belly and then down to his balls. For the rest of the day, he'd be able to smell her on him, as would any other of his Wolfkin. They would also smell him on her, which was even better.

When he didn't move, just kept rubbing her ass with his hand, she chanced a look back over her shoulder. When her eyes met his, he began thrusting inside of her and spanking her ass at the same time. The edge of the desk brushed against her clit with each movement, and her breasts swung over the cooling marble surface.

Each of the sensations combined to heighten her arousal. Stars exploded in her vision. He changed hands and started on the other cheek of her ass, the slaps a little more rough. Each one stung, but warmth was spreading to her pussy. She squeezed him tight, slowing his strokes slightly. He grunted and angled the head of his cock to hit her G-spot. Lainie bit her lip until she drew blood. He began to pull out of her; she felt it and squeezed harder to keep him inside.

"No, honey—" He bit off his words when she did it again. He roared when he came. The walls of her sex clamped around him almost painfully. A rush of heat, followed by cold chills raced up and down his spine and he spurted his seed deep inside her. He fell back into his desk chair, still embedded deep within.

At the resultant jostling, another orgasm jolted through her sex. He groaned, holding her shuddering body close. He was locked in place until nature took its course and allowed him to slide free.

"Lainie." He kissed her cheek and tasted the wetness of her tears. "I hurt you."

"No, no, you didn't, really." She sounded faint and dazed.

He grinned at her and ran his hand up and down her newly bared flesh. "I like this," he finally admitted. "Next time, I want to come with you and watch them do it though."

She shook with laughter. The sensation wasn't unpleasant at all. He twisted her so she was sideways on his lap.

She gasped when his shaft moved inside her, still hard and swollen. "I liked that, do it again." She pulled his face down to hers for a kiss.

"You're gonna be the death of me," he gritted out between clenched teeth when she had the audacity to wiggle her ass against him.

"Come on, you're still as hard as a rock. Just do that pulsing thing a few more times." Her eyes were glowing with what he thought could be love, but maybe it was just good sex.

He made his cock flex inside her and she arched her back, rocking her hips. She moaned.

"You are insatiable." He fought to catch his breath.

"You did this to me," she informed him haughtily. "I was a good girl until you corrupted me with your big old—" He smothered the rest of her sentence with his mouth.

Finally, he was able to free himself and, after righting their clothes and cleaning up, he remembered the food. "I'm starved," he announced in hurt tones, as if it were her fault.

"I said I brought food." She moved to the couch, her hips swaying provocatively. The fact that she wore nothing underneath made him hard all over again. He'd restrain himself for now, sating one hunger with another, at least temporarily.

As they ate, he watched her. She picked at the seafood pasta on her plate and nibbled on her bread. Finally, she looked up at him. "Marcus, about this morning."

"Yeah?" He paused with his fork halfway to his mouth.

"I didn't mean us, as the mess. Although, we do get a little messy, at least, I do."

"I like to clean you up." He thought it only fair to tell her this fact.

She wrinkled her nose at him. "That's not what I mean, though, I like that too." He swallowed hard at her distant expression. "No, I was talking about Caulder and my house getting torn up. I never meant us. We are... I don't know what we are yet, but I like it, the mess and all."

He wanted to believe her, and she looked sated and happy right now. But, despite his whole gender's thoughts on the matter, sex wasn't everything. Though he could hear his Y chromosome screaming in righteous indignation at this suggestion, he wanted more than that with her—he wanted everything.

"Marcus?" She tapped the back of his hand. "I asked you what time we need to leave for the ball. I want to get it over with."

“I’ll stay here and finish up. I have my tux in the closet, so, around six. I’ll come home to get you, and we’ll go together.”

She captured his hand, squeezing it. “I’m excited. I’ve never been to one of these things. I mean, I know I’m going for a different reason, but...” She looked down and blushed. “I’m really glad that I’m going with you.”

“I’m proud to escort you, ma’am.” He gave her his best cowboy drawl and grin. She laughed and they finished their meal in silence.

Chapter Eighteen

Marcus paced the foyer with his hands clasped behind his back. He paused in front of the large mirror on the hall tree and fiddled with his hair. He'd opted for one of the collarless shirts so he wouldn't have to deal with a bowtie. He hated the damned things. Instead, he was being slowly strangled by the stupid shirt buttoned up to his chin. What a damn choice.

His shirt studs were made of jet, each one gleamed in the light of the hall, matching the color of his eyes. He was going into enemy territory. He would have gone to this function whether Lainie asked him or not. He'd have gone so as not to lose face.

To not show would make him appear cowardly; he refused to back down to this asshole. How dare he hold the ball so close to Marcus's own territory? Jacob Caulder's businesses and pack were based in New Mexico, far enough away so they wouldn't overlap. And yet, here the bastard was in Tucson, almost at Marcus's backdoor, flaunting it in his face. "Son of a bitch," he seethed, his eyes turning gold with his anger.

"Marcus?" Her voice floated down from the top of the staircase.

The fire in his eyes banked only to reignite in a different place when he turned his gaze up at her. She glided down the stairs in a cloud of blue green fabric. With each step she took, she sparkled. "Lainie." He moved to the foot of the stairs. "You look beautiful."

She paused and smiled at him; his heart stopped beating then started again at a much more rapid pace. "Thank you. You're beautiful too." She shrugged her shoulders, drawing his attention to the golden smooth skin and her breasts and—

He scowled. "Elaine," he snapped, and she stiffened. "Where is the rest of the dress?"

"This is it!" She came down the stairs, the romantic mood broken.

"Are you forgetting a shawl? Did Charlotte neglect to give you the turtleneck that went with the skirt you're wearing?" Marcus put his hands on his hips and glared.

She'd stopped on the second stair so her eyes were level with his. She put her hands on her hips as well, and the fact that her breasts bounced up and almost out of the top of the dress distracted him. "I love this dress. It's the prettiest thing I've ever owned. My own prom dress wasn't this nice. I doubt my wedding gown will even begin to compete, so you'll shut up and like it!"

"Huh?" *Wait, what about a wedding?*

"Oh!" She threw up her hands and his smile widened. "My God! You're overdosing on boobs! Stop it, look at my eyes!" She stalked the rest of the way down the stairs, and he wondered if getting out of the line of breasts would help.

It didn't. "I can see your navel!" he gasped.

"You can't!" She looked down and pulled out the dress to see if maybe he was telling the truth. Marcus leaned over to see, too. There was a choking sound in the sudden silence. Lainie clasped her bodice back to her breasts.

Allen stepped from the shadows. "Mr. Bei, the car is ready." He said nothing else, but his gaze spoke volumes. Marcus's lips twitched and he grabbed her hand.

They practically ran from the house and slid into the limo so fast they almost bowled Mick over. Once the car was underway, they looked at one another and broke out into peals of laughter.

"He's like a disapproving schoolteacher," Lainie choked out when she finally subsided.

Marcus snorted and shook his head. "Well, at least we know you won't fall out of the dress."

"How's that?" she asked.

"You did the bounce test when you stumbled on the way out the door," he pointed out.

"You were dragging me. I don't think my feet touched the ground at all." Her eyes were shining and her face was flushed. She looked so beautiful that his heart ached. "Why are you staring at me like that?"

"Nothing, just looking at the belle of the ball."

She made sputtering noises and waved her hand, dismissing his comment.

But he moved to take her hand in his. "I mean it. You are the most beautiful woman in the world to me. Inside and out."

"Marcus," she whispered. "You are a dangerous man."

He jerked back in shock, wondering what she knew. "How so?"

"I could fall, easy." She squeezed his hand bringing his attention to their intertwined fingers. Hers seemed so small in comparison. He liked the contrasts between them, he was hard where she was soft.

"I'll catch you, Lainie."

"Really?"

"Always." He rubbed her knuckles and smiled when she shivered. "I love the way you respond to my touch."

"I love the way you touch me," she admitted easily. "You are so sexy, Marcus." She kissed him softly. "Handsome and kind and hmm."

He stroked the tops of her breasts. The tempting mounds of flesh trembled with each breath she took. He could smell her perfume was floral and soft but underlying all this was the sweet, musky scent of her sex, and it was torture. "'Hmm'? What's that one mean?" he teased, keeping his voice light.

All he really wanted to do was toss her down on the seat of the limo, maybe on her belly on the opposite side. He'd throw that skirt up over her head. His cock hardened when he imagined her ass in the air, her pussy spread wide for him to fuck her until she screamed. If he tried it right now, she'd have a fit about her hair and makeup, but it gave him something to look forward to on the trip back home.

"It's how you make me feel, now stop it." She moved away and straightened her dress.

Lainie kept her hand in Marcus's the whole time, drawing strength from him to calm her nerves. She had a feeling that tonight would change her in some way, forever.

As a reporter, she went with her hunches, her gut instincts, whatever you called them. More often than not, she was right. This made her good at her job, that and the determined way she went after the truth. Marcus would call it stubborn. She preferred tenacious.

Words were her weapons, after all. With them, she fought against injustice whenever she could. Sweatshops, price gouging, illegal imports, political corruption, none of them were safe from Elaine Westerbrook. She'd made sure that her name was one that struck if not fear, then at least irritation in the hearts of those who profited off the misery of others. And now, she had a personal stake in her story.

Jade Marks was missing, maybe dead by now. Lainie shook her head even as she thought it. She wasn't dead. She'd know it in her heart. She had the strangest feeling this story concerned her as well. She fought the fog that always permeated her brain when she tried to remember.

"What are you thinking about that has you scowling?" Marcus's deep voice cut into her thoughts.

"Jade. She's so smart, you know. She was going to change the world."

"Everybody wants to do that," Marcus pointed out.

"She studied anthropology. She'd laugh and say she was studying the earth's most virulent parasite but she loved people, children especially. The children took most of her money when she went off on her trips. She's been to Cambodia, Ethiopia, India, everywhere. I envied her, somewhat." Lainie shivered, instinctively seeking his warmth. "Now, I feel guilty. The first thing I thought when she called and that thing—" Her eyes fluttered when she tried to talk about it.

Marcus noticed it and knew it was her fighting against the hypnosis or whatever Joanna and David did to her.

She continued, with a dogged expression on her face. "The first thing I thought was that I was so glad that it wasn't me. I would be so scared."

"You don't have to be scared. I'll protect you." Marcus's words sounded formal, because they were. It was a vow that he intended to keep. "I—"

Mick opened the door, cutting off whatever he'd been about to say. It was probably for the best, he'd been about to make a declaration, one of possession and devotion. This wasn't the time or place. The enemy was within, and he had to be ready for anything.

He helped Lainie out of the car. The ball was being held in the city's largest hotel, to raise money for hunger in some obscure Third-World country. While his company contributed to charities, he didn't do it for the publicity like Caulder did. A stray thought occurred to him that proved Lainie's wild theory correct. Caulder used his pet cause to travel to out-of-the-way spots and check out prospective humans for his experiments. Who would miss them? Disgust washed through him at the very idea of using people. To cover it up with a false charity made it even worse.

The fountain was lit up and the water splashing soothed him, if only slightly. The hair on the back of his neck stood up, telling him that someone was watching them. He searched the facade of the building and at the topmost window, a shadow moved, confirming his suspicions.

Marcus squinted in the growing gloom then snarled as the shadow tilted his head at a familiarly arrogant angle. His father was here! That son of a bitch Caulder had the audacity to parade the deposed leader of the pack in front of the new leader. He refused to take this insult lying down—

He stopped his thoughts of vengeance and looked at Lainie. Tonight, he'd do nothing but watch her. However, he'd make sure Jacob Caulder knew of his displeasure at the soonest opportunity available.

He gave Lainie a mischievous smile and looped her arm through his. "Come on, *darlin'*." His emphasis on the endearment made her eyes sparkle. "Let's go and show these people what they're missing."

"What do you mean?" she asked when they reached the top of the stairs.

His grin got even wider. "We'll be the envy of everybody here."

"Um, why?" She frowned, still puzzled. But she was no longer as nervous and that was his aim.

"We're both here with the hottest people in the room," he whispered right before they reached the entrance. He put his hand on her lower back and left it there, showing everyone, including his father, just who she belonged to.

Chapter Nineteen

Samuel watched as his son moved through the room with Elaine on his arm as if he had every right to touch her. He gripped the banister so hard the wood creaked beneath his hands. Splinters bit into his palms, but he ignored the sting.

Instead, he stayed in the shadows. High above the ballroom, he had a vantage point so that he could watch those he wished without being seen. Marcus had seen him. Samuel knew it but he couldn't bring himself to care. The boy, the usurper, cast him out of his own kingdom, never to return. And now, he flaunted Samuel's own Breeder beneath his nose. "Damn you."

Marcus smiled down at her and she returned the gesture. The whole display was sickening, unworthy of a Bei, not to mention a Lupin. Never show affection while in public. When they got out on the dance floor his son took her into his arms. Though Samuel wanted to turn away, he found himself glued to the sight of her.

She belonged to Marcus; it was obvious in every line of her body. The way she tilted her head toward his, looked into his eyes and leaned into his touch. Samuel vowed to make Elaine his again, if only temporarily.

Samuel wasn't above forcing himself on her to get her with his child. She'd be afraid to tell Marcus who the father really was. Women hid those things, instinctively. Hadn't Diana done this as well? The bitch had lied. Those puling pups were some by-blows she had attempted to foist off on him, but he knew the truth. None of his seed could have been such abominations. He refused to believe it.

Marcus was his son. He was strong and cunning, a son to be proud of, in other circumstances, but then he'd turned on his father, hadn't he? Samuel watched for a few more minutes, his mind whirling with thoughts of revenge. He smiled down at them. "Soon, you will pay, both of you." He turned on his heel and left the balcony.

Below in the main ballroom, Lainie remained oblivious to anyone but Marcus. She moved within the circle of his arms, content to enjoy the moment for now. Soon, she'd have to go and find Mr. Caulder or one of his many subordinates and question them. But for right now, she was attempting to look like any other partygoer.

She forced herself to mingle, aware that her escort watched her closely. She danced with a few of the more influential people of Tucson. All she got for her trouble were a few indecent proposals and a grope or two. Through it all, she kept looking, hoping to find something that screamed conspiracy to her. Yeah, right, like there was going to be a big old honkin' neon sign pointing the way to her story. She sighed and looked down at her glass of punch, wishing it were something stronger.

"Aw, come on. You don't have to give up yet." Marcus pulled her into his arms as the band started to play a waltz. She let him lead, the feel of his arms around her made her breathing quicken and her heart thunder in her ears.

He must have noticed because he leered down the front of her dress. "When can we go home?" he asked with a little boy expression on his face that didn't fool her for an instant. Little boys had much different toys to play with than a grown woman. She readily admitted, at least in the privacy of her mind, that he could mold her with his hands. She cast about for an innocuous topic of conversation to distract herself from her lustful thoughts. "Marcus, you dance wonderfully."

"It's all in the hips." He winked at her.

She noticed him scanning the room and leaned closer to him. "Who are you looking for? Is there an old flame that's going to come up and scratch my eyes out?" She looked around suspiciously.

"None would dare." He laughed.

"Am I that much of a badass?" She felt smug until his next words burst her bubble.

"No, but I am." He still seemed distracted.

"Is there someone here you don't want to see? If they come up, give me a signal. I'll get the cramps or something," she told him, willing to take one for the team.

"How would they know?"

"I'd tell them, in full and vivid detail."

He threw back his head and laughed and every eye in the room turned in their direction. So much for her keeping a low profile. She glared at a few of the more interested looking women, just to make sure they knew that he was hers. Lainie stumbled as that thought struck her right between the eyes.

"Are you alright?" Marcus's embrace tightened, solicitously.

"Y-yes. I just remembered something is all." As if she'd ever been able to forget it.

"What's that?" His hand inched up her side, getting infinitesimally closer to the bottom of her breast. For one thing, he was dangerous to her equilibrium, not to mention her sanity, and for another he was an octopus.

She decided to keep that to herself. "Just a file I have to transfer when I get home. Hey, by the way, where is my backpack from the other night?"

"The one you had when you were trying to make a break for it?" He arched his brow at her.

"Um, yes."

"I think it's in your room, why?"

"Just wondering." She put her arms around his shoulders and fiddled with the hair at the nape of his neck. "Pretty man, you know, you have the longest eyelashes." She made a jealous moue with her mouth. "I think you use mascara."

"I'm all natural." He twirled her in a circle. "No artificial additives or preservatives." Marcus moved them toward one of the curtained alcoves that contained seats for the people to rest and discuss their business privately. He seated her then started to sit in the chair beside her.

A sardonic laugh halted him in mid-motion. "Now, Marcus. You know better than that. There are always additives. For people like us, especially."

Marcus snarled as Jacob Caulder stepped from the shadows with a sinister smile on his face. "Caulder, I didn't think you'd show up tonight. I wanted to applaud you on your choice of seconds."

"Small world and all that." Jacob leaned over the back of her chair.

She sat motionless, the tension in the room alerting her to the fact that everything wasn't as it should be. Her instincts screamed at her to run, but she refused to back down. His handsome exterior did nothing to hide the rotten core she could sense beneath.

Jacob's brows rose as he admired the view down the front of her dress. Marcus's teeth ground together, audible in the small, closed space.

Jacob just smirked. "Speaking of seconds, nice of you to bring a snack to the party. Did you bring enough for everybody?"

Lainie stiffened and opened her mouth to give him what for when she met Marcus's eyes. She subsided, and glared down at her hands instead. Marcus looked relaxed, bored even, but she knew he was angry.

"Ms. Westerbrook, as your date is being impolite, allow me to introduce myself." Jacob came around to the side of her chair and took her hand in his. "My name is Jacob Caulder, and I am very much at your service." He kissed her knuckles and gazed into her eyes with his own cold blue ones.

She noticed that Jacob put her between himself and Marcus and thought how telling that was. The chicken. She straightened her shoulders and blinked at him innocently. "How sweet. And here I thought I was setting myself up for an insurmountable task." She leaned forward as if to speak to him in confidence. "I know it's really a man's job, but you see, I have this need to know."

"To know what?" Jacob started to draw back; perhaps he had some inkling as to what she had in mind.

"Who do you think you're fooling?" She narrowed her eyes. "You've reached the end of your rope, Mr. Caulder. I feel it's only fair to warn you that I am onto you. I will find out what you've done with them and when I do, you will be sorry you were ever born."

"Really?" His smile was slow and sharp. "What are you going to do?"

"I'll yell it from the rooftops."

"What exactly will you yell?" He looked innocently puzzled, but Lainie didn't buy that for a second.

"You have my friend, I want her back. If I have to go through you to get her, I will. And in the meantime, I'll take your little empire apart, brick by brick."

"You have no proof behind these allegations, Ms. Westerbrook. I suggest you use your pretty little mouth to please your man and keep it shut. Otherwise I'll sue you and your paper, am I making myself quite clear?" He glared down at her.

"Yes, very. I'll get proof, and if you think I don't know about Sam, you've got another think coming. I know what he's doing. The public will know about it too, when I'm done." Venom dripped from her words.

"She's cute, Marcus. I hope she's a good fuck to make up for this tendency to run her mouth though, otherwise, I pity you." He laughed when his words hit their mark.

Marcus stood and moved to stand beside Lainie's chair. "Pity me all you want, Jacob. Just do it from the other side of the room, preferably the other side of the fucking planet."

"Be seeing you." Jacob stood to go then stopped and gave Lainie a thorough once over. "You know, she's almost worth the trouble. But, I'd suggest buying an industrial-strength gag for that smart mouth though." He laughed and shook his head, before slipping through the curtain.

She snarled and started to go after him but Marcus stopped her by standing in front of the chair and hemming her in.

"You will sit down and be still. Don't." He put up his hand when she opened her mouth to protest. "Listen to me. I won't have you chasing after that man."

"I wouldn't piss on him if his guts were on fire." Her teeth were clenched so tightly a muscle in her jaw ticked.

"Yeah, I hear you, and I do sympathize, but you can't do this in the open. Caulder is an important man, powerful, untouchable. Until you prove otherwise, he's a shining example of the perfect businessman. And David has a lot to answer for about your potty mouth."

"He's a thief and a marauder of innocents." She drew herself up in the chair.

"Marauder of what? Lainie, you sound like a damn spinster who's spent the night with a thesaurus. Calm down, keep your cool and come back to fight again. He has people in this room who will kill you without a qualm. I can protect you, but I'm not invulnerable."

"He's here." Her voice quivered for the first time.

"Who?"

She took a deep breath and let it out. "I know it's your father. I felt him looking at me earlier."

"How do you know it was him?"

"It makes me feel sick when he looks at me. It gives me the willies. I'm sorry, I know he's your father and all, but I can't stand him." She shivered and rubbed her arms.

He knelt in front of her and took her hands in his. "I know you can't. Believe me, that fact is one of your main attractions." His bitter laugh made her jerk.

"What?" She tilted her head to look into his eyes. Old pain and new resided there.

"Honey, he isn't a nice man. You know that. What do you think is going on?" he asked her for the first time.

She took a deep breath and tried to gather her thoughts. Caulder made her see red. His head on a platter was her choice off the menu. Samuel's balls would be a nice salad course. "He's experimenting on them, to make them into something different." When she said it something inside her snapped. Like a small crack in a dam that held back her thoughts, her dreams and her memories. Something was coming, she could feel it.

Marcus sat back on his haunches at her words. He kept his mouth shut waiting for her to go on.

"He's doing some sort of research. I had someone on the inside, but they turned up dead." Her eyes narrowed at the memory of the pictures from the paper's photograph files. The ones that even they didn't dare publish. Devoured, mauled, bloody and very much dead.

"Let's get the hell out of here." He stood suddenly.

"I thought you'd never ask." She sighed and took his hand.

"Don't you like the high life?" He led her as quickly as possible toward the exit.

"No, I'd rather just stay home with you, if you must know." She looked over her shoulder and gasped. Right behind them were about ten men. All were large and all looked like they meant business. But the worst of it was, in the lead was Samuel Bei. She hurried after Marcus, looking back every time she had a chance. Samuel kept moving through the crush of people, his eyes never leaving her face. The blood left her head in a rush and she fought against a wave of dizziness. He mouthed something at her and smiled. It struck dread in her heart, even as short as it was.

The word was simply, "soon".

Chapter Twenty

The ride home was silent. Lainie stared pensively out the window, thinking of what she'd learned tonight. Samuel was up to his old tricks again. Her eyes drifted shut and she sighed. Long ago, she'd thought of him as a nice man. She'd learned different soon enough.

Once, she'd hoped he would be her father-in-law. When you were a little kid, all you knew of getting married was that you and the other person were together. Marcus was the person she'd most wanted to marry. She'd been ten, but she'd known she wanted him to be with her, protect her, make her happy. As an adult, to be truthful, she still wanted those things, but she also knew that she had to bring something to the relationship besides just sex.

There was more to Marcus than met the eye. If he had a secret, which, he must, then how could she really trust him? She'd told him her own secrets, well, most of them, but what had he actually told her about himself? Why did he run around naked, and how did he do that thing with his penis? She was no virgin, but no man had ever done that before. Also, there was the way she responded to him. The more forceful and domineering he became, the more she submitted to his every whim and desire. Fear welled up, choking her with its intensity. What wouldn't she do for him? And what if he decided to take advantage of this weakness she seemed to have? Questions circled in her head until she became dizzy and sick. "Uh oh, I feel sick," she choked out.

"Mick, pull over, now!" Marcus's voice was urgent.

Mick pulled off onto the shoulder of the road and Lainie hurried out: bending at the waist, she took deep gulps of the still night air.

Marcus's soft footfalls sounded behind her. "Here, this should help." A cool wet cloth settled on the back of her neck and she sighed in relief as the nausea began to lessen. He held out a half-empty water bottle still cold from the tiny refrigerator.

Taking a cautious sip, she waited for a minute before she stood. "Sorry." She flushed with embarrassment. "I just got so upset at that ass Jacob."

"He makes me sick, too." Marcus swiped the cloth over her throat and cheeks. "You think you can get back in the car now?" At her nod, he put his arm around her waist and led her back to where Mick stood waiting.

The chauffeur looked worried. "She's fine." Marcus smiled at him. "She's been getting carsick since we were kids. It was awful."

"Shut up," Lainie grumbled. "I didn't do it that often. But you always laughed."

"Yeah, I did," Marcus admitted. "You always got carried away about it. It wasn't like it was your fault."

"I know." She shivered as a breeze slid over her skin, chilling her. "Can we go? It's dark. What if there are wild animals out here?"

"I'm not afraid," Marcus told her. "I'm the scariest thing they'll ever meet."

"Dear God." She snorted as she slid back into the car.

Marcus shoved her over and made her put her head in his lap when they got going again.

"Sir?" Mick's voice cut through the silence. "I think we're being followed."

Sure enough, lights were coming up at them at a high rate of speed. "Shit. Step on it," Marcus commanded.

Lainie tried to sit up, but he pushed her back down. "What's happening?" she began, only to be interrupted by a loud pop and the shattering of glass. Marcus slumped down on the seat, his body covering hers. "Marcus!" Warm, sticky fluid dribbled onto her cheek and she smelled the unmistakable coppery scent of blood.

"Be still, Miss Lainie." Mick's voice was no longer soft but hard and full of rage.

"He's been shot." She fought the panic that threatened and slid to the floor, keeping her body well out of range of the windows. Tearing a long strip off her skirt, she frantically searched for Marcus's wound in the dark confines of the car. Another shot rang out and glass sprayed in from the side window.

"Hold on." The car swerved to one side as Mick fought to steer.

She focused on Marcus lying so still but she couldn't see a damn thing. The car swerved more sharply, throwing her across him. Her hand skidded across his shoulder and came away sticky with blood. Marcus groaned, but she was grateful she'd found the wound. She pressed the material against his shoulder but it soaked with blood too quickly for her peace of mind so she tore off more and applied that to the wound too.

"Hold on," Mick said again. This time there was the scream of metal on metal and the car shuddered with the impact.

She looked out of the shattered window and a pair of glowing amber eyes stared right back at her. Someone in a large black SUV was trying to run them off the road.

Without a thought, she hurled the water bottle at the moving car. She was shocked when it connected with the man's forehead. She let out a triumphant whoop at the resultant *thunk* and muttered curse then took off her shoes and threw them too. One hit the doorframe and the other went through the other car's window. She hoped she put someone's eye out. Too bad she couldn't get boomerang action with those babies.

Mick howled with laughter. He hit the accelerator and the limo leapt ahead of the large SUV.

"Here they come again," she yelled.

This time they hit the limo dead-on. She clutched at Marcus when they began to slide down the steep incline. The car rolled over. It all seemed to happen in slow motion; Marcus's weight pressed her against the ceiling then the floor. Metal shrieked and glass shattered. She didn't have time to do anything but hold onto his body for dear life.

The car came to rest on its roof at the bottom of the ravine with Lainie trapped beneath Marcus's unconscious form. Her head hurt but it was a miracle she was alive at all. She tried to get out from under him, but he had her pinned.

Lainie turned her head to one side to look out the one remaining window. The moon was almost full, she thought idly, and then wondered if she had a concussion because of what else she saw.

A shadow, large and looming, and coming closer.

A growl came from the other side of the car. She froze.

Maybe she was hallucinating. Yeah, she hoped so. Or dreaming. Or—

A large furred paw stepped into her line of sight.

"Holy shit!" she hissed and increased her struggles to get out from under Marcus.

Outside of the car, clearly visible on the stark red rocks, were big furry creatures like the one in her nightmare. And, she recalled with sudden vivid clarity, like the one that took Jade. One of them was a wolf, but the rest were something in between. Werewolves had stepped out of the myths and legends to scare the hell out of her. They stood on two legs, and there was growling, lots of it. The car rocked back and forth and more of the furred feet appeared on the side closest to her and Marcus.

"Damn," a deep, gravelly voice said from above her line of sight. "The gas tank's busted."

One of the werewolves leaned down to peer at her. His large furred head filled the window.

She blinked rapidly, thinking if she did it enough, he'd disappear.

"Hi there, sweetie, I think it's time to blow this pop stand." Despite the deepness of his voice, it held a southern drawl and sounded faintly familiar.

She squeaked when a pair of black-furred hands tipped with some seriously gnarly claws reached into the window and grabbed her by the shoulders. He ignored her frantic protests, pulled her out and set her on her feet.

She stared up into his bright amber eyes and swallowed hard. Easily two feet taller than she and heavily muscled, he was one monstrous wolf dude. He snarled, showing off a set of long ivory fangs. Fangs? Shit fire and save the matches! This was worse than any horror movie she'd watched from between her fingers. He was broad and big, and if she wasn't mistaken, leering at her. Ew!

"I'll be damned." He leaned down for a closer look, then a surreptitious sniff. "It's Lainie!" This was met with a few chuckles from the other big wolf, men, er, things.

"This ain't old home week, dude. Get Marcus out before the car blows up." The big silver werewolf shoved them aside and Lainie took in the reverent way he lifted Marcus out of the wreckage. "When we find out who the fuck did this shit, they're gonna pay." Silver wolf snarled, showing some impressive fangs of his own. Nice dental plan.

"What are you?" She tried and failed to keep the quiver of fear out of her voice.

"Wolves, sweetie," the black one answered, squeezing her arm gently. "Well, right now, Wolfkin, except for the throwback over there." He indicated the lone "wolf" of the bunch. That was to say the one that looked like an actual wolf, if you discounted his size and the weirdly knowing yellow eyes that stared out of his silver-furred face.

She stood frozen with shock while they stripped Marcus out of the shirt and jacket she'd thought he'd looked so handsome in earlier. As the moon struck his bare flesh, she was horrified to see fur growing out of his smooth skin. He moaned and his mouth opened to reveal fangs growing longer before her very eyes. Marcus was one of them? A sense of betrayal made her blood boil, unfreezing her paralyzed muscles.

Mick came around the side of the car and Lainie waited for him to shoot these freaks of nature. Instead, he lowered his head in a sign of submission and whined. Low, menacing growls reverberated from deep within the silver one's chest. Somebody was in trouble, and she had a niggling suspicion that it might be her.

With that thought screaming through her head, she did what any woman with more than two brain cells to rub together would do in her situation. She rammed her elbow into fur boy's belly, lifted the hem of her tattered skirts and ran like hell. If she wasn't so scared, she might have laughed at the comment she heard from the black Wolfkin.

"Dammit all to hell. Why do they always run?"

Was he serious? She didn't stick around to find out, just poured on the speed, attempting to distance herself from the nightmare her life had just become.

Chapter Twenty-one

Someone or something howled her name in the distance. Not enough of a distance for her peace of mind, though. Damn, why did she throw her shoes away again? She pondered this as she stepped on yet another rock. One of many that were surely throwing themselves into her path on a mission from whatever gods she'd pissed off in a former life.

In the past few minutes, she'd begun to believe in reincarnation for the simple fact she knew she hadn't been bad enough to deserve this. She must have been worse than Hitler, Nero and Judas all rolled into one. Whoever it was had screwed her in this lifetime for damn sure. And she didn't even get a jar of Vaseline either!

A particularly sharp rock sliced through her heel and pain shot up her leg. She hopped around, curses punctuating every bounce. "Ow! Fuck, shit, damn!"

A rustle in the brush beside her was all the warning she had before the black-furred beast stepped out to block her path.

Lainie ran in another direction only to have another werewolf, this one gold, outflank her. She whirled in place, her breath coming in short gasps. "Son of a bitch."

"Now, sweetie, you know it's not nice for young ladies to use that sort of language." The black Wolfkin shook his long furry finger and made a *tsk* sound at her.

"Fuck you," she snarled, looking for a weapon to use against them. She wouldn't go down without a fight. They'd know she'd been there.

"Ooh, baby, can we?" Mr. Smartass of the Year put his hands on his chest and grinned.

"Shut up, Jordan," an exasperated voice said from behind her.

She screeched and whirled again, but a pair of huge arms covered in silver fur wrapped themselves around her like a vise. Her head was pressed against his chest and she could barely breathe. She froze when the name finally registered. Jordan? Jordan was Marcus's cousin. This was too much. She bit him on the chest, ignoring the mouthful of fur.

"Stop it," Silver told her.

"Let me go!" She wiggled, but he hefted her up until her feet left the ground. Fur was sticking up her nose, ick.

"We can't, Lainie." The patient tone did it.

She exploded with rage and raked her nails down his cheek, ripping into flesh with sickening ease.

He roared, holding her until she brought her knee up in a move that never failed. He may be a fucking monster but he still had balls. At least, she thought so; she hadn't really taken the time to look.

He howled and dropped her like a hot potato. Yep, balls, and they'd been flatted by the knee of steel. She landed flat on her ass in the dirt and wasted no time in scrambling to her feet, but a long arm shot out of nowhere. It didn't have fur; it was tanned, golden and heavily muscled. He grabbed her by the hair and stopped her without so much as a grunt when she fell back against him.

The big muscled freaks probably all took steroids. She was so doing an exposé on that shit when she got back to her office. "Steroids make you grow hair in strange places and bay at the moon." That would be the headline, by God.

She finally figured out that the arm belonged to a naked man, and hell's bells, he was hot! She raised one brow and gave him a long look from the neck down. If she was gonna die, she wanted to do it looking at beefcake. She struggled and finally turned her head upwards to catch a glimpse of the face of the Adonis. "Ack! Gross, you're naked!"

David's brow shot up to his hairline. "Well, no shit, Sherlock." Unfortunately, for him, this might not have been such a good time to show his natural talent for sarcasm.

She pivoted, shoving her hip against his, and flipped him over her back onto the ground. Grinning with relish at his startled whoosh of breath, she stomped on his belly using it as a springboard to run away again.

"Goddamnit." He sighed in exasperation and glared at the ring of amused faces staring back down at him. "Why the hell did I ever teach her that shit?"

The others were saved from answering by the sounds of scuffling in the bushes, then a yelp. "Ow, she fuckin' bit me!"

After some growls and curses and a lot of screaming, Jordan came back into the clearing with her squirming body slung over his shoulder. Lainie was still growling when he put her down and shoved her onto her knees.

"She bit me," he repeated, rubbing his shoulder. Suddenly, he put his hand to his furred chest. "What if she's contagious? What if I..." He paused for dramatic effect. "What if I become a—Oh, I just can't say it." His chest heaved and he shuddered. "A girl?" He ended with a whimper that did nothing to improve her opinion of males in general and these Wolfkin things in particular.

"Idiots." Lainie spat out black fur and sneered. "I hope you catch PMS you big, fat, furry freak!" She stood and kicked him in the shin, forgetting about her wounded foot until it was too late. They both howled.

"Ow. Bitch. The years ain't sweetened your disposition in the least." He pushed her back down on the ground.

"Forgive me for being a little put out when a bunch of furry men chase me after I've been in a wreck and to top the cotton, David's naked!" She made a gagging sound and shielded her eyes.

"She said you're gonna have PMS, Jordie." This came from the silver one. She had her suspicions about his identity, and that big golden one too.

"Don't call me Jordie, Benji." His snarled reply confirmed it.

Lainie shot to her feet and glared at her former pursuers. "Jordan and Ben. And who is that there?" The gold one ducked his head. "It's Stephen! The whole time you were all these things and I never knew it?"

"Yeah, well, Lainie, we, uh..." Ben rubbed the back of his neck and looked at the ground.

"We uh?" She put her hands on her hips and screeched. "You all lied to me. David!" She turned on him, glaring at a point over his shoulder. "You of all people hid this from me for over fifteen years. How could you?" Her eyes filled with tears. "And Marcus too?"

They all nodded and that was it, she lost it, not that she'd had a grip on her temper for the past five minutes or so, but before that she'd been terrified of being eaten or worse by these things. Now, she knew exactly who they were and she knew David, or she thought she did, she realized she was nominally safe. She saw red. "And you, naked ass. You're the throwback, aren't ya?"

"Yes, damn it, I'm the throwback! What are you going to do about it, Elaine?" David roared, his eyes glowing in the moonlight.

A lesser woman would have probably fainted. As it was, all the males took a step back. However, Lainie finally concluded that her whole life had been one big lie. Someone was going to pay and a strip off David's ass was just the beginning.

Her voice was flat and quiet after the echoes died down. "I'll tell you what I'm gonna do. I'll get a shotgun and fill your ass full of buckshot, that's what!" She stepped up to stand toe–to-toe—well, not that close, there were bits in the way—with him. "And for God's sake, put some clothes on, that's just so wrong on so many levels that it ain't funny."

"Young lady."

"Oh, don't young lady me, David Lyingshit. When I had those bad dreams about those—" she pointed at Ben and he flinched, "—things, you said I was just imagining it all." She punctuated each word with a poke to his chest. "You. Lied. To. Me."

"Get me some damn clothes." David's voice was soft and calm. One of the others threw him a pair of shorts. "Honey, I want you to calm down." He put the shorts on and reached out to touch her but thought better of it.

"Shut up. I hate you." She turned and wrapped her arms around her middle. "I thought you were my friend and all you wanted to do was damage control." The tears that had been threatening fell in earnest now. She picked up the hem of her ruined dress and wiped her eyes.

"Yeah." He put his hand on her shoulder and ignored her attempts to slap it away. "You know I love you." He pulled her into his arms.

She resisted at first then gave in with a watery sob.

"At first it was just to make sure you didn't remember, but then you happened." The smile was evident in his voice. "Sweet little Elaine. God, I'm so sorry, if I could change it, I would. But I did what I thought was best to give you a normal life."

"Normal how? I have bad dreams, David. Really dark and scary ones. I had some freak tear up my bed and all my underwear. That isn't normal." She sniffed back the tears. "How did you do it?"

"Do what?" His casual tone didn't fool her one bit.

"Make me not realize what you and these dickheads really were? And just what in the hell are you?"

"Hey." Jordan took offense at the dickheads comment.

David sighed, a big gusty one filled with regret. "It's a long story."

"I'll make time." The stubborn tilt of her chin made him rub his face wearily.

"Fine, but we'll do it after we get you and Marcus safely to the house." David gave her a long look. "I guess it's past time anyway. I tried to hold off as long as possible."

"Marcus!" She put her hands to her mouth. "He's been shot! What if he's dead?" She turned to head back the way she'd come.

And then he stepped into the moonlight. He was taller, broader and way more hairy. His nostrils flared and he lifted his lips in a snarl that made her tremble with the urge to fall to her knees. The others all backed away, their heads bowed before the glowing yellow gaze that landed on each one in turn. An instinctual part of her recognized that he was the leader yet another part of her rebelled at the very idea of bowing down to anyone. He'd lied to her, this whole time. He'd hidden a very important fact. He was a big, fat, lying werewolf!

"Stay away from me," she snarled and stalked away from them all.

He jerked her off her feet and held her against his hard, furry chest. "You can't leave, Lainie." His voice was different, low and deep, guttural.

She steeled herself to show no emotion, especially not fear. "Let me go."

"Never." He sounded like he meant it, too.

Marcus's arms cut off her air. She wiggled, but he ignored her, simply turning back to face the others with her hanging over his wrist like some freaky oversized charm bracelet.

David stepped forward and tipped her chin up so he could stare into her eyes. "*Okohke.*"

That one word made her whole world narrow down to a small point of light. She floated, with nothing to anchor her to reality. Then, Marcus shifted her in his arms, jostling her back to awareness.

The crack in the dam holding back her memories got another fissure. She kept still, limp in Marcus's arms. They spoke as if she wasn't there, which was fine in her book. With an effort, she kept her breathing even and slow.

"Damn it. Why did this shit have to happen?" Marcus hefted her up and put one arm beneath her knees. Her head lolled back until he placed it on his shoulder with a tenderness that made her chest ache. "What were you doing out here anyway?"

Jordan answered with his usual sarcasm. "What the fuck do you think? It's wabbit season."

"Now she knows." He sighed and sat on a nearby rock with his burden still draped over his lap. He stroked his fingers down her cheek, unaware of the cauldron bubbling inside her mind.

From deep within, things began to shine through the cracks. It was as if a wall had blocked out the memories of things she shouldn't have heard or seen. David and Joanna had done what they thought was best, but in the long run, it was all for nothing.

She took a deep breath and the fissures widened. Another breath and parts crumbled. The first thing that came through was the smells. Antiseptic, steel and wet fur. Fur? Why not, she thought with a mental shrug. Apparently, she'd been around these Wolfkin things before.

No, there was something else. Bright lights, and being restrained. She'd felt fuzzy, drugged by someone, who? Then the images slammed into her so hard she caught her breath.

Samuel Bei swept into the room and smiled benignly down at the tiny girl who lay in a dazed stupor on the table. "Elaine?" He tapped her cheek. She forced her eyes open and squinted in the glare. All she saw were blurred shapes.

"Give her the serum. I'll be back in an hour after it's finished going through her system." His voice was soft and controlled, soothing. He'd been very nice to her ever since he'd rescued her on the night of the fire. She'd been five; he'd bought her a teddy bear and some dolls. She liked him.

As he was leaving, he told the nurse, "No one is to come into this room but me, is that understood?"

"Yes, sir."

There was the rattling of metal and then a sharp sting in her arm. The woman soothed her when she cried out. "You're a lucky girl. The Lupin has chosen you for his future bride."

Her skin went hot and tingled for a few minutes. She squirmed but couldn't move. Her arms and legs were held by leather restraints. She was on a stretcher like the ones at hospitals. Was she sick?

Her eyes drifted shut again, and the next thing she recalled was a crash. She opened her eyes and screamed.

A big bear stood in the room. She made strangled noises, and her eyes rolled back in her head when he walked up to the table and sniffed her neck. He didn't hurt her though, but that may be because the people that Samuel said kept her safe came into the room and fought with him until he chased them out with a deafening roar.

She struggled to get free again; her wrists were rubbed raw by the time she gave up and started to cry. She was just too little. She didn't like being little, but Samuel said she'd be big one day. Where was he?

"Hey." A voice interrupted her fretful thoughts. "Don't cry."

She turned her head and saw *him*. She felt strange. Her ears began to ring. He didn't look much older than her. His hair was black, and his dark eyes were slightly tilted at the corners. He looked familiar, but she wasn't sure who he reminded her of. However, she instinctively trusted him not to hurt her.

An explosion boomed in another wing of the lab. She flinched and so did he. "Let's get out of here."

She tugged on the restraints and shook her head.

He grimaced before he simply tore the restraints off with astonishing ease. "My name's Marcus." That was a nice name. Another wave of something hit her right between the eyes. She felt sick at her tummy.

Then her vision cleared and she looked at him a little more closely. He wore a flannel shirt unbuttoned over a T-shirt and a pair of old faded jeans. His shoes were scuffed, and his clothes shabby, but he was the best-looking Prince Charming she could have conjured up in her childish imagination.

"I'm Lainie," she told him, and then flushed when the sheet started to slip. She made a grab for it, but his hand was there before hers, catching it. He took off his own shirt and handed it to her, helping her button it when her fingers shook too badly to do it herself.

"Lainie, we gotta get outta here. They'll be back soon." He held out his hand and she took it, and another jolt of something slid into her brain.

"Marcus," she tried out the name, rolling it around in her mouth.

"Yeah?" He lifted a brow and tugged on her hand. When she didn't comply, he simply picked her up in his arms and started out of the room. Smoke billowed down the hall making her cough. Yells and screams came from far off, followed by a loud roar that shook the very foundations.

Marcus looked around, spied a likely door and slid inside, locking it behind them. "We'll hide here for a few minutes then get out when it's clear." Here was a large bathroom with chrome stalls that shone so brightly under the lights that it made her head throb.

"I have to um, go." She shifted from one foot to another. She'd had to go for a while.

"Well, go then."

"You have to turn around. And run the water so you can't hear." She lifted her chin and glared at him.

"What?" He curled his lip in a disdainful sneer. "God, you're such a sissy."

"I'm not going unless you do." She folded her arms and waited him out.

With a gusty sigh, he twisted one of the faucets on full blast and turned his back. "Hurry up, we don't have all night."

The sound of her bare feet slapping on the tile was loud even under the cover of the water. But she finally got finished and came out.

He turned around in time to catch her washing her hands. "We don't have time for that. Come on!"

"I have to wash my hands." She gave him a disgusted look. "Boys are gross."

"A boy got you loose, didn't he?"

"I was perfectly safe until the bear showed up. What is a bear doing here anyway? Do you think it will come back and eat us?" She paused and looked at the door. It now seemed very flimsy.

"No, the bear won't eat us. I won't let him. It's going to be okay, I promise." He seemed very brave.

She smiled at him, her ire of a minute ago forgotten.

He blinked once then shook his head. "Come on." He reached out and grabbed her arm, pulling her along behind him as he opened the door and peered out into the hall.

The images from the past began to flow through her head much faster. She caught glimpses of herself and of Marcus at various ages, then David and Joanna and finally, Samuel. He had chased her through the woods in wolf form, and then sent the Wolfkin when she was a teenager. She'd gone parking with a boyfriend on an old dirt road. That night and the memory of the roars still made her cringe.

"Lainie?" Marcus's voice cut through the darkness like a beam of light.

"What?" She refused to open her eyes. She didn't want to see the man of her dreams looking like the monster in her nightmares.

"Come on, it's time to go home. There's a truck here." He shook her and she finally relented, opening her eyes to find him back in human form.

She frowned, her brow furrowed in confusion. How long had she been out and what did she miss? The rocky landscape was deserted, with the others having long since left. Only Mick remained, sitting behind the wheel of an old Ford pickup that had seen better days.

Marcus stood before her with his hand out, waiting for her to take it. Was he going to act like tonight never happened? Did he think she didn't remember?

"What happened?" She asked, deciding to give him a chance to tell her. She took his hand, but when she started to take a step her heel hit the ground and she winced.

"Your foot." Marcus immediately swept her up. She noticed he was only wearing the tuxedo pants. They weren't torn so she assumed he'd taken them off before shifting into that Wolfkin thing. "It's going to be okay. I promise." He repeated the words he'd said to her so long ago. The voice was deeper now, overlaying the youthful hero he'd once been to her. She closed her eyes and saw them superimposed onto each other, the boy and the man. But now she knew it was a lie. It was never going to be okay again.

Chapter Twenty-two

Marcus wondered what the hell to do. She might or might not remember anything about tonight's fiasco. If she didn't, then he was home free, unless he counted the guilt of keeping her in the dark. And he felt it eating at him so much that he hurt. He rode in silence, well aware that Mick kept giving him nervous glances. At this point, he would usually reassure the other man that he'd done nothing wrong and he wasn't mad at him. Nobody would be killed or at the least disemboweled tonight. Unless you counted Marcus—if Lainie did remember, she may try to kill him. What if the hypnosis didn't take this time? Marcus took his hand off her thigh and rubbed his face wearily.

"Lupin?"

"Yeah, Mick?"

"Am I in trouble?"

It took a lot for the younger man to ask him this, and he knew it. So, he reached way down inside and found that spark that made him the leader. "No." He got a sigh of relief in return that made him recall just how bad it had been under his father's rule. That Samuel was a sadistic bastard was no great secret.

Marcus wasn't, and some thought it made him weak. He didn't agree, and when needed, he got physical enough to prove his strength. Most of the pack knew he led with his head and heart, not his fists, teeth and claws. But, when push came to shove, he shoved back.

Lainie moaned, turning his attention back to her just as they made it through the gates to his home. His house was a sanctuary and he aimed to keep it that way, for both of them. He only hoped it didn't become her prison. Because if she did remember, there was no way in hell he could let her leave.

Her eyes flickered open, then shut quickly in the glare of the portico lights. He knew she was playing possum, and he let her. It allowed him to put off the inevitable confrontation he knew had to come.

Mick stopped the truck and hurried to open the door for them.

"I mean it," Marcus reassured him.

"Yes, sir, I'm sorry." Mick's head went down and he whined softly. "They were just there." He straightened. "But, sir, Ms. Westerbrook is a fighter. She'll make you a good mate."

"I think so, too." With that, Marcus turned and went inside, giving Allen a tired promise to tell him all about it in the morning. He made his way up the stairs with the limp bundle in his arms. Her breathing was slow and steady, but her heartbeat told another story altogether as it thundered rapidly in his ears. The scent of her fear almost choked him, and the minute trembling of her body made him want to howl and smash things. All of this added up to one conclusion. She knew.

His long-legged stride made short work of the distance and soon he was in their bedroom. He smiled wryly at the telling pronoun. When had it become theirs and not his? He kicked the door shut and placed her in the center of the bed where she lay perfectly still in all her tattered finery like Sleeping Beauty. "Wake up and face the music, darlin'."

For a long moment, she didn't move. He frowned and leaned over her, intending to check her pulse. Maybe she was really sick. Right as he reached out to put his fingers on her neck, her eyes flew open and she screamed.

Lainie slithered across the bed, falling off the other side with a thump. "Son of a bitch. This has got to be the worst night of my entire life."

"Elaine?" His voice sounded right above her head.

She slowly looked up to meet his worried gaze.

"Are you all right?"

"I'm fine," she grumbled, twitching her filthy, torn skirt back over her thighs. It was unfair that he could look so damn normal. And don't forget hot as hell too, the bastard.

"Can you get up, or do you need help?" He reached down as he spoke but she drew away from his touch. He looked hurt before his expression became remote and cold. "I see."

"Do you really? Well, that's nice for you, because I don't see at all!"

"What do you remember, Lainie?"

She stood, wincing when the wound on her heel reminded her of its presence. She ignored it so she could glare down at him.

He lay on his side with his head propped up on one hand, staring at her with those warm brown eyes. He scratched his bare stomach, bringing her attention to his abs, which were distracting her from her purpose.

What the hell was the matter with her? She took a deep breath, thinking it would help. It didn't, because the wild, rich scent of sand and spice filled her nostrils. His scent.

She bit back a whimper of need and shook her head to clear it. Her skin heated and her limbs grew heavy. Moisture pooled between her legs, and she clenched her thighs together to stop the tingling sensation. Her eyes went wide then narrowed when she noticed the look on his face.

His nostrils flared and his eyes were bright gold. The word that came to mind when she looked at him was feral. He smiled at her and licked his lips reminding her of the other places he'd licked just this afternoon.

She moaned then caught herself. She refused to let her body's reaction to his rule her. No matter how tempting he was, she would not succumb. "Oh, maybe, I don't know, the fact that you had fur and big pointed ears?" She put her hands on her hips, and swore she heard him snort. "Or could it have been the fangs and claws, and if you think I'm ever gonna forget I saw David naked, you've gone and lost your rabbit-assed mind!" Her voice rose and he winced.

Maybe she was overreacting. But when you found out your date was a werewolf, you should be allowed to have a hissy fit. It should be in the damn handbook. If not, she was writing it in with a large red marker the next chance she got. "I swear! All this damn time, I've been an idiot! You're a werewolf! David's one too, which I suppose explains his doggie-style attitude about life."

"Lainie, let me explain, baby." Marcus sat up and put his hands out in a placating gesture.

A mistake on his part, which she was sure he figured out pretty fast when she launched herself at him in a flurry of arms and legs and she wasn't ashamed to admit, teeth.

"Ow! What the hell?" Marcus yelped, prying her jaws apart when she latched onto his forearm. He plopped her down on his thighs hard enough to make her grunt. "Stop it. Just listen to me, please."

"No, I'm through listening. You're gonna listen to me for a change, or I'll..." She paused. What could she do? He was probably fifty times stronger and psychic to boot. A terrible thought occurred to her. "Can you read my mind?"

"Um, unfortunately, no."

"Too bad for you." She smiled and it must have been scary because he flinched.

"Have your say. Call me a monster, a beast and a son of a bitch, it's all true." He waited a beat. "But, you're one of us, too."

She opened her mouth to let him have it with both barrels when the last thing he said hit her like a ton of bricks. She was speechless and he took advantage of this very special occasion, as it didn't come around often.

He quickly explained how her memories were buried deep down in her subconscious with the help of Joanna. At the mention of Jo's name, her shoulders slumped.

She'd been betrayed by the woman she'd thought of as her mother. A web of deceit had been woven around her memories so tightly she didn't really know what was real and what wasn't, except him. He was real. Marcus was a part of her; she didn't want that to change. "I'm one of you?"

"Yeah, in a way. You and others like you were created for our kind." Marcus ran his hand through his hair, but kept his other arm around her waist.

She was very aware of the warmth of his body seeping into hers. Was that why he felt so right? Because if he wasn't even human, why did it feel like they were supposed to be together? She shifted around to get comfortable and he groaned.

"Lainie, don't do that." His eyes were heavy lidded as he stared at her mouth. Did he actually think he was gettin' some when they had so much to discuss? Of course he did, he was a man and all men were dogs— She stopped in mid-thought and clapped her hand over her mouth.

"What is it?"

"Um, nothing, carry on." She snorted. He began to explain about the genetic factors, and why. When he said the word imprint, she jerked but he kept talking, glossing over that part.

She held her hand up. "Hold it, back up. What was that about imprinting?"

"Well, you are made for a certain family. Your body chemistry is the most compatible with them. They, uh—in laymen's terms, you have a type and you stick with it." Marcus gave her a sheepish grin.

"And what type is this?" She arched her brow at him. Before he could answer, she snorted. "Don't tell me, I already know. Tall, dark and full of shit. In other words, you. I was made for you. This sucks. I want you to know that." She folded her arms and blinked back the tears.

"Lainie."

"No, it's not fair that I can't help wanting you this much." Her voice quavered. "I've felt this way for so long and I never understood why until now." With a bitter laugh, she added, "I'm your bitch, huh?"

"No, it's not like that at all."

"Whatever. Just tell me the truth. Was I or was I not made to want you?" To love you with my whole being, she added silently.

He rubbed his mouth and squeezed her waist. Dread bubbled up from deep within her belly. She froze and waited for him to say whatever it was he was trying to get out. It must be bad because his face was pale and his eyes were dark with what she would swear was pain.

When he spoke his voice was low and gravelly. "Close, but no."

"What do you mean?" But she knew, deep down, she knew.

"Leave it to you to break training, 'cause you see, you were meant for a Bei, but not me. You were meant for dear old daddy." He smiled. "You were supposed to be my stepmom. How's that for a kick in the ass?"

Silence fell as she digested this bit of disgusting news. "Samuel?" She wrinkled her nose, then chewed on her fingernails and thought back over the newly resurrected memories. "Alright, gross." She swallowed the bile that rose in her throat at the mere thought of Samuel's touch before she continued. "The night you showed up, that's what he was doing wasn't it?" When he nodded, she added, "Thank you." It was simple, but heartfelt. She couldn't imagine the life she'd have led if he and David hadn't come to her rescue.

"You're welcome. Can I say something?" He rubbed her back, soothing her despite everything.

Unconsciously she moved closer. Before long, she was snuggled in his arms, her head under his chin with her arms around his waist. "Carry on, oh divine canine." She snickered and kept moving around until he scooted back on the bed and lay down with her by his side.

He manfully ignored her little dig at his species except to inform her, "I may be a dog, but I'm top dog, darlin'." His voice was low and warm, intimate. "I knew you were there because of my dad. I'd overheard them all arguing at the pack meeting one night about the so-called Breeders and how it was unethical. Of course, my father was all for it. But some weren't. David was one of those who were opposed."

"Of course," Lainie interrupted, and they shared a look of commiseration about David. He was unique, that was for sure. She dropped her gaze, uncomfortable with the hunger she saw burning in his gaze.

"When we got you free, he said it was best you didn't remember. I didn't know about the imprinting thing then, but David did. He wanted us to be together, if nothing else, he knew I'd take care of you."

"I don't need you to take care of me." Anger rose at his tone. "I'm not a little girl that needs protection. I'm in possession of my own mind and opinions."

"Yeah, I know." He smiled at her, his eyes filled with amusement.

"Don't patronize me."

"Wouldn't dream of it."

"Kiss my ass, Marcus."

"Now that, I would dream of, baby." He gave her that disarming smile, the one that made her want to smack him then kiss him, so she hit him before giving him a quick peck on the lips that left them both unsatisfied. That was all he was getting until she had time to think on tonight's revelations.

"I want to know how long you would have let me believe the lie."

"Forever." His answer and nonchalant shrug made her grit her teeth.

"Really? Then what, you'd knock me up and use me as a broodmare?" She went white with shock. Leaning toward him, she looked over her shoulder as if someone was listening. "Marcus!" She poked him in the chest.

He just lay there, looking dazed until she pinched him. That got a rise out of him. "What? Just say your piece; I'm tired of fighting about it."

"Will I have them?" Panic rose up in her throat, making her voice squeak.

"Will you have what?" When she began to shake, he tightened his hold on her, pulling her close.

"You know that saying, 'life's a bitch then you have puppies?' Am I gonna have puppies?" If he answered, she didn't hear it. The roaring in her ears reached its peak and her lashes fluttered. The night's events finally caught up with her. She slumped down and began to cry.

With a muttered curse, he pulled her into his arms and held her, rocking back and forth. "I'll fix everything, somehow." His mouth was right by her ear, his lips caressed her neck then her jaw. "I want you just as bad you want me. It works both ways. I need you so much, I hurt."

That was nice to know. With one last sniffle, she scooted around and spooned her body into the curve of his, marveling at the fit, like always. However, she did have the presence of mind to get in the last word. "I'm having you fixed." Then she slid into darkness, leaving him to contemplate spending the rest of his life with a woman who believed in neutering her boyfriend.

Chapter Twenty-three

Lainie's head rested on his arm. Her breathing was even as she slept. Marcus wasn't so lucky. For one thing, she was soft and warm and her ass was pressed right against his cock. For another, his arm was asleep. He slowly moved it from beneath her head and she muttered incoherently before settling once more.

Though he hadn't understood her words, the tone was clear as a bell. Be still or die. But he couldn't rest, not while the moon was high and bright in the night sky. He looked at the clock and saw it was 2 a.m. Maybe a run would calm him down. Right now all he wanted to do was sink into her and fuck her until she screamed in surrender. Unfortunately, he was also angry, unsettled and confused, not a good combo for a man with more strength than was normal. He had to remember she was only human, and easily broken.

Lainie rolled onto her back and sighed. He frowned when he noticed she was still dressed in the same tattered gown from their evening out. He'd remedy that first, then go.

He turned her over on her side and stared at the back of the dress in consternation. Who in the hell put buttons on shit these days? Hello, zippers? Finally, he got frustrated and turned her on her back. It was ruined anyway, so why bother? With a big smile, he ripped the damn thing cleanly in half.

Lainie apparently didn't agree, because she sat up and screamed. It wasn't a frightened sound, more a howl of rage. "What the hell are you doin' to my dress?"

"It was ruined, sweetie. I'm getting it off so you can rest more comfortably." He was lying to her and himself, and he didn't care in the least.

She didn't buy it either. He loved her brain, but sometimes, he wished she were a little less able to figure him out. This would be one of those times. "Bullshit." She folded her arms across her chest.

"Oh, yeah." He practically drooled.

This position just pushed her breasts up a little higher. She was naked save for a pair of brief lacy undies that he wanted to remove, preferably with his teeth. She bounced off the bed and stalked toward the door to her room. Well, it was more a hobble because of the cut on her foot.

Poor baby, maybe he should offer to carry her. With that in mind, Marcus prowled behind her without making a sound. By the time he caught up with her she was at the closet door. At first, he thought she was just getting some clothes to wear but then he saw her bags and knew. She was trying to leave him.

"Elaine?" His voice deepened.

She squeaked and turned to face him while buttoning her shirt. "Go away."

"Where do you think you're going?"

"None of your business." She ignored him, which only served to piss him off further. When she attempted to go past him with her suitcase in her hand, he wrapped his fingers around her wrist. He squeezed slowly and gently until she dropped the handle from her numbed hand. "You will take yourself back into our room, get in our bed and go back to sleep." He leaned in closer and stared into her eyes. "Am I making myself perfectly clear?"

"Let me go." She shook her hand, but he held on without even caring that she'd begun to cry. "Marcus. Let me go."

"No, I can't." He wasn't talking about just tonight. Surely, she knew that.

She lifted her hand and slapped him across the face. "Take your hands off me and get the hell out of my way. I'm not staying here as your bitch, your whore or whatever capacity you think I'll fill. I won't and you can't make me." By the end of her little speech, she was yelling.

The most frightening thing of all was that he felt nothing. Not anger, not regret, not even fear that he'd hurt her. Wait, there was one thing he felt and that was possession. She was his—that was all he cared about.

"That's where you're wrong, honey."

She blinked up at him in confusion. "Wrong?"

He bent over slightly and jerked on her arm. She fell forward over his shoulder and he stood. "I can make you do whatever the hell I want." He turned on his heel and walked back to the bedroom.

She rained blows on his back and when that didn't work, she scratched him, drawing blood with her nails.

His muscles clenched automatically, but otherwise he just kept walking back to his room, kicking the door shut with his foot. He turned and locked it then walked to the bed, throwing her down. On the first bounce she was off and running toward the outer door. Marcus grinned and leapt across the full width of the bed getting there well ahead of her.

With a snarl, she turned and made for the balcony doors, intending to escape no matter the cost. At the end of his patience and endurance, he reached out and grabbed her hair, tangling his fingers in the long, wavy strands. He wound it around his wrist, effectively trapping her in place. "Sweetheart." His tone was placating in the extreme, but he pulled on her hair so that she had to stand on tiptoe to keep it from hurting. "You know better than to run. I'll just catch you and when I do, you know what happens."

"Wh—" She wet her lips. "What happens?"

"I eat you up." He picked her up again and this time when he put her on the bed, he was on top of her before she could attempt to move again.

Chapter Twenty-four

He stared into those green eyes of hers, so wide and frightened. “Now, where were we?” He ripped off the shirt she wore and threw it aside. He covered her breast with his hand and squeezed it before pinching her nipple between his fingers.

She shifted beneath him, stilling when his voice deepened. His mouth covered hers, and he pinched the peak even harder, twisting it until she whimpered. “Hmm. You taste so fucking good.” He licked her lips, sucking on the bottom one then nibbling it.

“Marcus, I— Please don’t do this to me.”

“Don’t do what?” His fingers moved away from her breast and he slid to one side. He put one thigh over hers, pinning her legs down.

When she put her hands up to push him away, he caught them easily, holding them above her head.

“This?” He ran his fingers down her belly. “Maybe, this.” His fingers crept beneath the top of her underwear, stroking the bare satiny flesh of her mound. “Ooh, forgot you did that. But so glad you did.”

He spread the folds of her sex. She cried out when he thrust two fingers inside her, hard and fast. He twisted his hand, touching her G-spot, gliding across it repeatedly. When his thumb brushed her clit, she rocked against his hand. "You're wet and slick for me, Lainie. Admit that you want me."

"You are such a shit."

"I know." He sighed, but he didn't stop. Instead, he kept it up until her body flushed pink and she clenched around his fingers when she found her release. "Beautiful."

She moaned low in her throat and fucked his hand.

He ground his palm against the top of her mound, and she shuddered.

"Mine."

"No." She tossed her head from side to side.

He tightened his hold on her wrists and leaned down to take one of her nipples in his mouth. He sucked hard, pulling as much of her breast into his mouth as possible.

Her body undulated beneath his, rolling like the ocean. She came again and her scent filled his nostrils, teasing him with the spicy musk of her arousal. He released her breast. "Mine." He added a third finger and kept fucking her.

Her thigh muscles jerked with each successive thrust. She was crying, sobbing her release with each breath. Her heart pounded in his ears and he loved every fucking minute of it. She belonged to him. "You are mine."

"No, I'm not. Let me go. Please."

He roared and reared up on his hands, releasing her. She lurched onto her belly, intending to get away from him as fast as she possibly could. He let her go for a second before grabbing her ankle and reeling her in, slowly but surely. His mouth settled in the bend of her knee and his tongue flicked out to touch the sensitive flesh. She howled and tried to jerk away, but he held her fast with his hands on her hips, then her waist, pulling her inexorably back beneath him.

Now she was trapped on her stomach, her sweet ass pressing against his abdomen.

With each shaking breath, her skin rubbed along his. "Say it," he ground out, his fingers finding her underwear and ripping them off.

"No."

"By the time I'm done, you'll be screaming it," he promised. His mouth moved to her neck, his tongue slid down the center of her spine. She trembled but otherwise didn't move. Good, maybe she'd survive tonight. He licked his way down the base of her spine, stopping to kiss two tiny dimples on each side before he nibbled on the soft globe of her left cheek.

She made a choking noise and her fingers twisted the covers.

"My delectable Lainie. So soft, so sweet. So damn hot." His throat hurt, he wanted to roar, to howl that she was his and she'd damn well stay where he put her. Deep down, he knew it wasn't in her nature to be that meek little miss, but tonight, he needed her to be. "Lainie. Please, don't fight me." His voice lost its edge, becoming more of a plea. "I don't want to hurt you." He laid his cheek against the small of her back and stroked the soft flesh of her ass. Unable to help himself, he squeezed. His fingers drifted down between her thighs and found the soft folds of her sex still wet and hot for him. Ready. She smelled ready, she felt ready. No matter what her mouth said, her body sent off signals of a different nature.

With a low groan, he moved down between her thighs, lifting her hips up slightly. He turned and slid beneath her, his mouth finding her slit. When she screamed and writhed, he just held her still. His tongue flicked the little peak, spearing it and then circling it.

"Marcus, please."

"Please what?"

"I can't, not again."

"It feels like you just did." He spread her thighs a little wider, burying his face against her.

Her body went tight as a bowstring. She arched her back, pressing her pussy against his face. He nipped her with his teeth and she screamed and came again. "Goddamnit, you're so fucking sweet. Do it again, Lainie. Come for me again." He moved his hands away from her hips and used them to spread her sex wide. He rubbed her clit with the flat of his tongue before flicking it. She drenched him with the honeyed juices of her orgasm.

"Mmm. The taste of surrender." He came up onto his knees behind her. "Up," he commanded. When she lay still, he pulled her hips until her ass was in the air and her head pillowed on her arms.

The ripping sound of his pants was loud in the room. She flinched, but he didn't even pause, just began to slide his cock into her. She squeezed him like a hot, wet fist, her muscles clenched at the invasion before stretching to accommodate him. "So tight."

"I'm not, you're just big."

"Is that a complaint?"

"Um, no. Shut up, and get on with it." The tone of her voice had him grinning. She must have sensed because she turned to glare at him over her shoulder. "Now."

"You're somethin' else, darlin'."

She scowled at him but in the next second that expression was replaced by one of wonder.

He thrust his hips forward before rotating them, slowly grinding his cock around inside her.

"Oh. My. God," she gasped out, her breaths timed with each thrust. She began to rock her pelvis against his. "Yes."

This made her angry and he knew it. That fact that she was pissed at him but still felt this way in spite of it. "Lainie." He caressed her back, his fingers pressing into her spine. She arched into his touch and groaned.

The time for talk was over; he pulled her up so that she sat in his lap, facing away from him. He cupped her breasts, squeezing the soft mounds, tweaking her hard nipples. He pressed soft kisses against the side of her neck. She put her head to one side to give him better access. He moved inside her again and she moaned.

Her hips were flush with his, her backside fitting perfectly into the fold of his body. "You're made for me," he whispered in a worshipful tone. She didn't answer. Instead she rolled her hips again, tightening on his shaft, milking him.

He spread his thighs so that hers opened, too. She slid down a little farther on his cock. Marcus put his arms around her, holding her tight as he sat back on his heels. She cried out at this new sensation, and her muscles danced around him. He thrust up slightly and she came, drenching him.

"God," he gasped out when she did it again and again. Little bursts of light flashed behind his closed lids. He stilled for a long moment, savoring the sensation of her surrounding him, clutching him. Each breath he took made him shift inside her. His heart seemed to have moved to his cock, the pulse thundering.

His balls tightened with the next thrust and he slid his fingers between her legs, determined to take her with him over the edge. Chills raced across his skin when she arched up against his hand. His cock swelled and tingles rocketed through his balls and cock as he spilled his seed straight into her womb.

He lay there buried inside her. He pressed her face down in the bed and kept her still.

She wiggled.

He grunted and his cock twitched. “Be still, Lainie.”

“I hate you.”

“I know.” He closed his eyes when she began to cry.

Chapter Twenty-five

Marcus had a pounding headache. He winced when the pounding got even louder. With a groan, he pulled away from Lainie and looked at the clock. It was six in the morning. He could go back to sleep and not get up until the next day, except the pounding wouldn't go away.

"Get out from between that girl's legs and come downstairs!" This was roared from out in the hall by none other than David, his soon-to-be-dead relative. His head wasn't pounding after all. It was that man's massive fist abusing his door.

Lainie opened her eyes and looked around. "It's all right, go back to sleep." He kissed her temple and tried to ignore her hurt expression. She was exhausted, with dark circles beneath her eyes. Her mouth was swollen from his kisses. When he stood, the covers fell away to reveal the marks he'd left on her body. The part of him that was an animal reveled in them. The human part was horrified.

He stroked his fingers down her back and winced at the sight of a particularly colorful mark on her butt. He'd bitten her, the print of his teeth was clearly outlined. "Honey, I'm sorry," he whispered.

She turned away from him so he pulled the covers up and tucked them around her. "I'll be back as soon as I find out what the hell that old man wants."

Another spate of knocking had him jerking the door open with his pants still in his hand. "What the fuck is so important that you wake me up at this time of morning?"

David snarled. "Get downstairs right now."

Marcus followed him, hopping first on one leg then the other as he put his pants on. "This shit better be good for you to wake her up."

"Like you let her sleep."

"Not your business, David."

"Yes, it is."

"No." Marcus put his hand on the other man's shoulder and stared deep into his eyes. "This time, it's not. I mean it, you can't interfere. She's mine; she stays that way no matter what."

David stared back at him for a long minute. "Fine. You hurt her, I'll kill you. There, settled. Now come on down here with me and your damned second." He stalked down the stairs and into the den.

Marcus scratched his head groggily and followed him. He yawned a good morning to Ben who sat on the couch looking as sleepy as he felt. "What are you doing here?"

"David called and said you might need me." Ben pointed at the television just as the commercial went off and the news came back on.

As Marcus watched, all thoughts of sleeping left him. Rage burned inside, bubbling up from a place so deep and well stocked that it would probably never run dry.

The morning announcer sat behind the news desk. Usually she was perky, but today she was going for solemn. He didn't really think she pulled it off. "The bodies of Mr. Bei and his live-in girlfriend, reporter Elaine Westerbrook, were found at the scene, as was his driver. They are yet to be positively identified. As they are badly burned, it may be a while before they are. The sheriff's department is puzzled as to how the accident happened." She paused and tucked a strand of bleached-blonde hair behind her ear.

"They are also unclear on how long the tycoon has been missing. They were reportedly at Caulder Incorporated's ball last night, but officials state that the bodies were also the victim of scavengers. It appears that the area's wolf population is much larger than we thought." She attempted to smile, but it didn't quite reach her eyes. "We have comments from Mr. Bei's father when we return."

The commercials were loud, not quite loud enough to cover up Marcus's howl of outrage.

It didn't help matters when the news came back on and the first thing he saw was his father's smug expression as he stood on the steps of Bei International. Oh, he attempted to look like a man grieving over his only son, but Marcus wasn't fooled in the least.

"Mr. Bei, we're sorry to hear about your loss." A reporter thrust her microphone up into his face. "Can you tell us what your plans are now? We know you retired to let your son run the company. Are you going to come back now that he's dead?"

"How very rude." Samuel purred in a dangerously low voice and pushed the microphone back. "However, in answer to your question, the answer is no. I don't think I shall. In fact, I've had an offer today to sell to a man I hold in high esteem."

There was a flurry of activity and then, "Here he is now. Say hello to the new owner of Bei International, Mr. Jacob Caulder." Flashbulbs went off as the two men shook hands.

"No!" With a scream, he picked up the large coffee table and hurled it against the wall at the other end of the living room.

"What in the hell is this shit?" Ben bellowed. "I'm the vice president of Bei International!"

"I have no idea, but I aim to find out." Marcus started for the door only to have David stop him.

"Ah, wait." He smiled that smooth smile that had spelled the doom of more than one man. "Let your father have enough rope to hang himself. I'd love to see him twist."

"He's stealing." This from Allen who stood in the doorway. "He's not on the board any longer. He doesn't even own stock. Let him keep this up at least for the next twenty-four hours."

"Mr. Bei, what are your plans?"

For a minute, Samuel stood there as if deciding. "I want time to grieve the death of my son and his sweet fiancée, Elaine. They were to be married, it's so sad."

Marcus finally noticed his father's fury. His eyes narrowed and he watched closely. Jacob looked like the cat that ate the canary.

"Do you see?" David's voice was right beside his ear.

"I see." Marcus's smile was wide and sharp. "I see two dead fuckers. But, I'll bide my time."

With a dark look on his face, he turned to go back upstairs. Maybe if he got on his knees and begged, she'd forgive him for being an ass. He doubted it, but it was worth a try. Plus, if he was on his knees anyway, he knew of a few ways to persuade her. "Where are you goin'?" David yelled.

"I'm dead, so, I'm going back to heaven. You." He looked at Ben and pointed at David. "Kill him if he puts his foot on the bottom stair. I mean it."

Marcus rehearsed what to say to get back in her good graces. Last night, she'd cried for a long time, angry that he couldn't pull out of her, angry with herself for even wanting him to touch her. She'd raged at him, calling him a monster and a beast.

The words hurt, he'd admit it, but the fact that she'd shuddered and sobbed hurt even more. He'd pretty much accepted the fact that he loved her. Not that she'd believe him even capable of such a thing. She'd say it was lust or chemistry or else hormones.

The little brat had said all that and more in the dark room as they lay there pressed together with her voice hoarse from screaming in both passion and rage. She'd clutched at his forearm, hugging him close even when she called him every name in the book. And, he'd let her. As long as she didn't leave, she could call him what she wanted. He didn't give a damn.

He flung the door wide and opened his mouth to tell her that only to close it again when the sight of the empty bed met his gaze. He listened, thinking she might be in the shower, but no sound came from inside. He went in and peered around it to be sure. Empty.

With a feeling of dread, he moved to the room he'd foolishly put her in at first. *That pink room* as she called it in that snotty tone he loved so well. The door slammed back when he kicked it, but he already knew. It was empty as well. So was the bathroom, the closet and the rest of the house when he began to bellow out orders for her to be found.

Hours later, Marcus sat on the couch, waiting. He'd become paralyzed with anger and fear the minute he figured out she'd left the grounds. Anger at her, and fear for her if she was found by anyone, including himself. Which was why he wasn't out looking for her. He needed a chance to calm down. His emotions were out of control. He wanted to shake her and turn her over his knee and to fuck her so hard she'd never forget who she belonged to, or for that matter, walk straight again.

"I think she's gone out that little side gate, Marcus." David came back in from the garden. "I'm not sure, because her trail suddenly ended." He stopped talking then shrugged. "Plus, her scent's changed."

"What do you mean changed?" Marcus snapped, at the end of his patience.

"Precisely what I said."

"Why would it do that?" Ben came in the door from looking on the southern part of the property.

"There are a few reasons." David frowned. "One of which, I'm pretty sure you know."

"No." Ben rolled his eyes. "I wouldn't ask if I did."

"I swear, they didn't teach you younger ones a damn thing." David sighed and rubbed his face. "Fine, I'll say it. I think she may be pregnant."

Marcus's breath left him in a whoosh and he sat down hard on the couch. For a long minute, he stared into space without moving. Then he shuddered and snapped out of his daze. "Pregnant?" he finally wheezed out.

"That's what I said." David put his hands on his hips and glared.

"But how?"

"You know that's usually what happens when all you do is fuck like bunny rabbits."

"I have never fucked like a bunny rabbit." Ben scowled. "I'm a wolf and that's how I do it."

"She told me she was on the pill." Marcus took a deep breath, then another in the hopes that it would make the room stop spinning. It didn't help.

"You've got super sperm, what can I say?"

He snarled at David's sarcastic reply. "It doesn't matter right now. I want my woman back and if I don't get her, somebody's goin' to die." Marcus said it as calmly as he possibly could but the howl at the end gave him away.

"We'll find her." David jerked his head toward the door. "Ben, come outside with me."

As they walked down the path to the fence, David prodded him. "What do you smell?"

"Lainie, Marcus, Mick, us. The pack, I smell the pack."

"Right." David waited for it to dawn on him.

"One of us took her." A muscle in Ben's jaw ticked. "Who would dare?"

"I can't tell because I smell all of us here. I can't differentiate between us. Which of us is missing?" David stared down the road.

"There's me and you and Marcus, Mick—" He closed his eyes. "Jordan is missing. You think he would betray Marcus?"

David leaned on the fence staring at the road. "He is Samuel's kin, not mine. I can't vouch for him other than to say he was a good kid at one time. Ben, I haven't been here for you all and I'm sorry. But you have to help me. Marcus will lose his mind if he thinks his cousin betrayed him. If it's not true, fine, but if it is, you have to decide what to do. Don't make him kill that boy."

"I won't." Ben's expression was grim. "What if we're wrong? It might not be Jordan at all. What if it's one of the others?"

David put his hand on the bars of the fence and glared at the road. "Who else could get that close to the house or for that matter to her? Who else would she trust? You and I both know how Jordan seems. He's harmless, a flirt, the joker. Well, I can attest to the fact that the joker is wild, and he can be deadly."

"David, I can't believe he'd do it. Why?"

"Like I said, he's Sam's nephew. Maybe the old man offered him something Marcus didn't."

Ben narrowed his eyes as if thinking. David knew that as Marcus's cousin, Jordan had power without the responsibility to go along with it. To someone like Ben, this would be nirvana, but he couldn't be certain this was how Jordan felt. Maybe he wanted both.

"I'll get my stuff and meet you back here in a few." He turned and started back to the house.

"Where are we going?" David moved to follow him.

"Caulder's little place in the country."

"You know where that is?" David was impressed. It was hard to see these men as anything but the boys they once were. He believed they were good men, but he couldn't stop seeing them as the children he'd taken under his wing and taught to fish and hunt.

"In Santa Fe." Ben turned and started back towards the house, his long legs eating up the distance. He'd better hurry, David had a feeling time was running out.

Chapter Twenty-six

Lainie leapt out of the bed the minute Marcus shut the door behind him. She scrambled into her room, jerked on a T-shirt, a pair of jeans, tennis shoes and scooped up her bag on her way out onto the upper deck. There were no steps leading off the balconies. However, there was a tree she was sure she could reach from the rail. She was desperate to get away from his overwhelming personality. She sank further and further beneath his power with each subsequent minute in his presence.

Marcus was taking her over. She couldn't think straight, couldn't see straight half the time. He kept her off balance, mostly on her back so that she couldn't form a complete sentence much less think on the repercussions of finding out what he and the others really were. Then there was her own identity, genetic and otherwise, that scared the shit out of her.

He refused to leave her alone. He wouldn't just allow her to run and hide. Hell, she'd probably come back within a day or two. She'd miss his smile, the way his eyes lit up when she came into the room, his hands on her skin and his mouth on her. She shook her head to clear it and concentrated on the branch just out of her reach. She took a deep breath and jumped, grabbing it on the way down.

"Ha," she grunted in triumph and shimmied down as she'd done as a child. She'd been pretty good then, it was nice to see that she hadn't lost her touch. Unfortunately, she spoke too soon, because she missed and fell the last few feet and fell to the ground, landing in the shrubs planted at the base of the tree. "Ow, shit."

She managed to get out of the bushes and scurried away from the house, only wanting to get out of his reach, at least for a little while. She'd almost made it to that little opening when a big hand landed on her shoulder. She yelped and whirled. "You scared the hell out of me!"

Lainie backed up a step and glared at the person attempting to ruin her escape. "I was just taking a walk."

"Really?" he drawled and threw a heavy arm over her shoulders. "Let me help you with your walk."

"I don't need your help." She tried to shrug his arm off, feeling uncomfortable for some reason. Why, she didn't know. Hell, she'd known him almost as long as she had Marcus. He'd been there when she was a kid, and she'd even thought he was cute at one time.

Now, though, he made her uneasy. "Take your hands off me."

"I can't do that, Lainie. I'm sorry."

"No!" She struggled when he put his arm around her waist to hold her close. He half dragged her to the opening that had just a few minutes ago beckoned her with the promise of freedom.

Now that she looked at it closer, she saw it as something else. An entrance to hell, and the devil himself waited on the other side in a big black SUV. Jacob Caulder sat in the back with a smile on his face.

“You traitorous bastard.” She squirmed in her captor’s grip, mad enough to spit.

“Yeah, I know, but a wolf’s gotta do what a wolf’s gotta do. Dog eat dog and all that.”

“Oh yeah, that’s so fucking funny. I’m laughin’ it up. Cocksucker.”

“You got a mouth on you, Lainie.” He jerked his chin toward the vehicle that waited on the road. “He’ll cure you of that soon enough.”

Lainie met Jacob’s eyes and shivered. Unfortunately for her, the asshole was probably right. She started to scream and alert the others, but he anticipated her actions and clamped his hand over her mouth. “Now, now, you can’t be doing that.” He slung her into the backseat and Jacob’s arms went around her.

“I see the reports of your demise were greatly exaggerated.” He laughed at his own joke.

“Marcus will kill you.”

“I am waiting for him to try.” Jacob’s eyes lit with amusement. “Get in, if you’re coming.” He waited until the other man did so, then slammed the door and motioned for his driver to move.

Lainie watched the house she’d thought of as her prison growing smaller when the car sped off down the road. Funny, the farther away she got, the more like a haven it seemed. They said hindsight was twenty-twenty and they were right.

Chapter Twenty-seven

Lainie kept her eyes closed, pretending to sleep. It wasn't very hard, she was exhausted from all the running around she'd done the night before. She hadn't slept much afterward either. While Marcus had been trapped inside her, she'd taken that opportunity to bitch at him. He hadn't tried to stop her, which was telling. He let her call him every name in the book, and some new ones she'd made up on the fly.

She knew *this* man wouldn't do that. He'd beat her if she opened her mouth, probably worse. Jacob and Marcus were like night and day. Oh, they had that one thing in common; she'd figured that out pretty fast. Werewolves were much more prevalent than she'd ever imagined.

Not that she had imagined it, thanks to Joanna and David. Hypnosis sucked. All the bad dreams about those things chasing her, they really happened. They'd been bubbling up into her subconscious this whole time.

Then the fascination with wolves that always left her feeling unsettled and frightened. That too was explained away. Marcus, the man she'd decided was for her back when she was ten years old, was a different story entirely. He made her feel so alive, so fulfilled, so damn satisfied that it was almost scary. Okay, it was a lot scary. He wanted her, too, and he didn't seem to mind letting her know it.

Her thoughts stuttered to a halt. He didn't hide much else either. Now that she had a little time and distance away from him, it all started to become clearer. He cared. In spite of it all, he cared for her. He was thoughtful, kind, considerate and hotter than hell on the Fourth of July. If he lost his cool and got a little bit possessive sometimes, she had her ways of dealing with that.

She snuck a glance at Jacob from beneath her lashes. Now she knew why Marcus hadn't wanted her to leave the house. This twit had been waiting for his chance to nab her.

As for the asshole who'd just handed her to him on a platter, she knew he'd get his too. Men were idiots, werewolves seemed to be even more so. However, Marcus was her idiot and she aimed to keep him.

Now if she could only get back to him. She tried to send her thoughts to him, only to get a headache for her efforts. Why couldn't they be all psychic and shit like in the movies? Vampires were psychic. She stopped on that thought.

"Er." She licked her lips and spoke for the first time since getting into the car with Jacob. "I have a question."

He turned and smiled at her and she was struck by just how handsome he was. He still scared the shit out of her, but he was nice to look at. Too bad she knew for a fact that beneath his pretty exterior beat the heart of a true monster—and she didn't mean the furry variety. "Yes, Elaine, or may I call you Lainie?"

"Whatever. Is there such a thing as vampires?" She frowned when he began to laugh, a rich sound that filled the car. "Hey!" She struggled when he reached out and pulled her beside him.

He put his arm around her shoulders. She wiggled, but he squeezed her until it hurt. Then he sniffed her neck. Gross. "No, lovely, there are no vampires." Jacob's mouth moved over her jaw. She jerked her head away and he sighed. "Why do you ask?"

"No reason." She wasn't going to tell him that vampires were always telepathic in the movies and books. "I think I'm going to be sick, tell him I ain't lying, idiot boy!" She glared at the man on the other side of her.

"She's not."

She hopped out and lost what little she'd eaten in the scrub brush on the side of the road, crouching down with her head on her knees. "I want to go home," she mumbled to herself, realizing when she said it, she meant Marcus's house. No, that wasn't quite right. Home just meant Marcus.

"Get up and come on." Jacob sounded disgusted. Good, he'd keep his filthy paws off her from now on. Ha! He did have paws. She began to giggle and couldn't stop. He finally had one of his men lift her up and put her back in the SUV. She huddled up into a ball and this time succeeded in escaping by falling into a deep sleep.

Her regular chase dream began immediately. However, she was tired of running so she turned and faced the monster this time. "I know what you are now, so just go away."

It tilted its furry head and glared at her. A long line of saliva dripped from its huge muzzle and hit the ground. Yeck! The creature's body was covered in silver fur. The requisite broad shoulders blocked out the moonlight as it loomed over her but she'd stopped feeling intimidated.

Marcus had told her she belonged to him. Well, damn him, that meant he belonged to her. Since he was the leader, this made her— Wait, she wasn't actually sure what it made her but she was going to say it was the queen bitch and act accordingly. Drawing herself up to her full height, she glared at the Wolfkin.

"Stop following me. If you were worth a shit, you'd go do one of those Lassie things like when that boy kept falling in the well."

"Lainie."

"I mean really, how many damn times can a kid fall in the well? Why in the hell didn't they call child welfare? I think that was a big old red flag for abuse." She folded her arms and scowled.

"Lainie."

"Hush, don't interrupt me while I'm bitching."

"Elaine!"

"Ack! What?" She looked up at the Wolfkin. Only, he'd changed into David, thankfully clothed, as she didn't want to be dreaming of him naked. He'd become a father figure to her long ago, and that would just be nasty.

"Where are you?" he asked. "Hurry, I can't do this for long."

"I don't know, heading toward an airstrip. I heard him talking about it. Somewhere in one of the national parks, it's where they have their lab or whatever he wants to call it." Lainie took a breath and he interrupted her.

"How are you?"

"Oh, just fuckin' peachy," she snapped, her eyes narrowed to thin slits. "How the hell do you think? I'm cooped up in a car with Jacob and—" Her eyes went wide. "I have to tell you! We have a traitor in our midst. He tricked me, I'm telling Marcus on him, too!"

"We already know about it."

"What?" She stomped her foot, angry her news had been preempted. "Well, shit. Hey! Where are you going?" David was beginning to fade.

"I can't stay long; this isn't really my strength, more Joanna's." David frowned at her. "I want you to keep quiet. Don't provoke him."

"Please don't leave me." She tried to concentrate, to make him stay, and to their surprise, he began to solidify again. "Er, did you do that?"

He shook his head. "I think you did. Look, don't let your mockin' bird mouth overload your hummin' bird ass, you hear me, Lainie? He won't put up with it like Marcus does."

"I'm not stupid."

"Sometimes, I wonder."

"Hey, asshole."

"Buh-bye." He waved, and this time, succeeded in winking out of her dreams.

"He watches too much television," she grumbled aloud. Thankfully that was all she said, because when she opened her eyes Jacob was staring at her.

"Rise and shine." He hauled her up with his hand on her arm.

She grimaced when he squeezed a little too hard but got out of the car. There was a huge plane at the end of a dirt runway. It looked safe enough, she supposed. She didn't really care for flying because it made her sick. Maybe this time she'd barf on Jacob. A girl had to have goals in life.

Chapter Twenty-eight

"Why are you sleeping?" Marcus stood over David and poked him with his foot. They were on the company jet, not an easy feat, with Marcus being dead and all. Nevertheless, Kane had managed it without a problem by the simple fact that he was the pilot.

"I'm not sleeping; I'm trying to contact Lainie." David opened one eye and glared at him. "I did, by the way. If you want me to tell you what's going on, then I suggest you stop that." He shoved his hand away.

"Don't make me hurt you, David."

"When did you stop calling me Uncle David?" The other man sat up and rubbed the back of his neck. "I have the headache from hell."

"What happened?"

"I have a weak connection to Lainie because of all the times I've had to 'fix' things. Joanna is much better at it than me, but she isn't here." He groaned and stretched his arms above his head. "The point is, they're heading for one of the national parks, located in or near Santa Fe. We're gonna make it there about the same time as they do."

"Is she—" Marcus pressed his lips together and took a deep breath to keep from howling. "Is she all right?"

"Well, let's put it like this. She's bitchy and bossy as hell, so yeah, she seems to be fine." David gave him a reluctant grin. "She's more than a match for you. In fact, she considers herself the queen bitch now. I am telling you that to warn you."

Marcus smiled and sat in one of the big leather seats scattered around the plane. "I suppose she is at that."

"The two of you together." David groaned and put his hands over his face. "What the hell was I thinking?"

"Why don't you explain that?" Marcus glared at him, which didn't do much good in most circumstances.

This time, however, David complied. "Because, I knew what your father had planned, and honestly, it sickened me. So, I made sure you knew what I was doing that night. I did a little matchmaking. I had someone on the inside of the facility."

"A woman, huh?" Ben asked with a snicker.

"Yes, as a matter of fact." David sniffed indignantly.

"Why him?" Ben pointed at Marcus.

"Hey!"

"No, I mean, why were you Prince Charming material? David was in there too, right?"

"I didn't talk to her, touch her or give her my shirt to wear. All of these things appeal to the senses, hearing, touch, smell, and that started the imprinting. She stayed around him long enough for it to stick and here we are, one big old happy freakin' family." David pushed his long black hair out of his face and sighed.

"That is just so fucked up." Marcus's lips twisted. "I don't like that part."

"Why? You were just being yourself; she picked you for that reason alone. Would you rather be calling her stepmother right now?" When Marcus began to make gagging noises, David let out a booming laugh. "I thought so. Deal with it. She's still her own person; she has her own thoughts, feelings and opinions. God does she!"

"She's mine."

"I know."

"Sir?" Kane's voice came over the speaker. "We're getting ready to land."

"All right." Marcus stood. "Let's get ready." He shrugged into an old Red Sox jacket and pulled a matching cap down low over his eyes. He completed his disguise with a pair of old jeans and scruffy sneakers. He looked like any other man until you saw his eyes. They were amber, glowing with purpose and rage.

With a sigh, he put on a pair of shades and followed David out the door. There was no use in trying to hide that man's huge ass. His presence was a distraction though, and Ben helped by being a total asshole about everything from the landing strip to the baggage service.

In the chaos, Marcus slipped out of the small airport and started walking down the long highway. By nightfall, he'd have her back in his house and in his bed, where she would stay until he decided she could get up again. Maybe in a few days. Okay, probably a month.

Chapter Twenty-nine

Lainie sat in a chair with ropes around her wrists and ankles. She'd been there long enough to be getting desperate. "Hey!" she yelled. There was no answer for a few minutes, unless she counted the chorus of howls and whimpers coming from behind a thick steel door to her right.

The dark room, lit only by a tiny window high above her, was bare, with a concrete floor, the chair she was tied to and not much else to relieve her boredom. Speaking of relief. "Hey! Someone needs to let me up! I have to go to the bathroom, damn it." The last sentence was more of a whine.

"Shut the fuck up." Jacob walked into the room and snarled at her. Literally snarled. His face was losing its humanity, becoming more and more animalistic as the day waned.

A sense of dread pooled in the pit of her belly as she realized two things at once. One, he was a psycho, and two, it was the full moon. Oh, just freakin' great, she was trapped in the room with a crazy doggie that had what amounted to super rabies, could her day get any worse?

As if in answer, the huge steel door slammed back on its hinges like it weighed nothing at all. Framed in the dim light from the warehouse proper stood Samuel Bei smiling unpleasantly.

"Hello, Elaine. So nice to see you aren't dead after all." He sauntered into the room, pausing to give Jacob a long, thoughtful once-over. "When were you going to tell me this bit of news?"

"When I thought the time was right." Jacob stood with his back to them both, looking out the window at the darkening sky.

"And when would that be, pray tell?" Samuel's mild tone didn't fool Lainie one bit. She'd heard it before, after all, at times when he was being the most sadistic to someone. Cruel and taunting without even raising his voice was his specialty.

"After you finished with the other test subjects." The other man's voice held a slight sneer. "You have a tendency to get distracted with this one involved."

Samuel's gaze drilled through her, so she dropped her eyes to the floor, tensely waiting for his next move. His fingers slid across her cheek. "Finally, you're where you belong." She jerked away from his caress, wincing when his hand tangled in her hair to hold her still.

He leaned down and met her eyes with a smile that made her blood freeze. "You'll learn your manners, and I'll enjoy teaching you very much indeed." He pressed his lips to her temple. Apparently, he read her expression well enough to realize that if he tried for her mouth, she'd bite him.

"Take your hands off me," she snarled at him, pulling futilely at the bonds that held her to the chair.

Jacob's laughter echoed off the walls. "It looks like you'll have your hands full with that one."

"More than likely." Samuel sounded amused.

"I have to go to the bathroom." Lainie put her chin up and glared at him.

"Say please."

She gritted out the word past clenched teeth. He smiled and patted her head as if she were the dog. She remained quiet while he undid her bonds, and then hurried to the door he indicated.

Lainie stood at the sink for the longest time letting the water run over her hands. Dark circles were under her eyes and she looked pale and sickly, and felt it too. She wasn't surprised. How else should she feel after being kidnapped by werewolves?

She could probably outwit Jacob because he thought with his dick first and his brain second. Unfortunately, Sam was a cold, calculating bastard who scared the shit out of her. He'd hurt her, she knew that. He'd do what he had to so she'd come to heel for him. The most terrifying thing about him was that he was always in control of his emotions, be they rage or lust.

Seeing him brought back memories involving fights between him and Marcus. When she'd first come to stay with them, right after she'd been freed from the lab, father and son had fought. Not physically, but verbally, with sharp words even more frightening for their quiet intensity.

Marcus had no such control in her presence; he'd lost it around her more times than she could count. However, that lack endeared him to her even more.

A knock interrupted her musings on the differences between father and son so she quickly turned the water off and hurried out before they decided to come in and get her.

Sam stood on the other side, waiting. "Too bad I can't trust you to behave." He made it sound like it was her fault he had to tie her back up.

She rolled her eyes, but said nothing, meekly letting him lead her to the chair. He tied her hands behind her first, making noises about the marks on her wrists. "Amateurs."

"She's been pulling on the ropes." Jacob came to gloat beside her chair. "Little Ms. Nosy."

"Piss off," she snapped, and hissed when Sam tightened the rope around her left foot. "Where is my friend Jade?"

"I'm sure she's around." Jacob shrugged his shoulders.

"She's in her cage, where she belongs." Sam gave him a look, which Lainie couldn't interpret. If she didn't know better she'd think it was censure.

"Is she? I may have to go and visit the menagerie before I go."

"If you go near her again, I'm not going to be responsible for the consequences." Sam loosened the rope slightly before moving to her other leg.

"Is she all right?" Lainie waited until the man met her eyes. "Please tell me."

"She is, now." Sam's mouth tightened and he said no more.

Tears welled in her eyes but she blinked them back, refusing to let them see her cry. She sniffed once. "Can I see her?"

"That wouldn't be wise." He moved away and walked back toward the door. "Jacob, where is our other guest?"

"Asleep. Or knocked out, whichever you prefer."

"I'll be back after I've taken some samples." Sam punched his code into the door and opened it. The cacophony of howls and whimpers halted abruptly at his rough-voiced command.

Unfortunately, this left her alone with Jacob, even worse, tied to a chair, unable to get away from his taunts and threats. "Ms. Westerbrook, ace reporter, the crusader for justice. Tell me—" he whirled and came to stand over her, "—how does it feel to know your freedom of speech, thought and even movement is at an end for the rest of your natural life?"

"Fuck you."

"Talk about an offer I can't refuse." He knelt and put his hands on her legs.

"Gah, you're lame." She twisted around but couldn't even move away from his touch.

At her words, his hands tightened on her thighs until she had to bite her cheek to keep from crying out. "Lame? I can show you lame. Your friend Jade was lame after I broke her pelvis. You wanna know how I did that?"

Her head jerked around at the mention of her friend's name. She held her breath as he continued. She tried to shut his words out. But he continued to speak, saying foul, terrible things. Surely, he lied. If he was telling the truth, Jade was dead and her whole ordeal had been for nothing.

"I hate you. I hope you burn in hell." She finally got the words out past the rage. "I will personally see to it that you roast for what you've done, you cocksucking, motherfucking son of a bitch."

A slap across her face stopped the litany of curses. Tiny lights danced in her eyes, dazing her long enough for him to grab her hair and pull her face up to his. His mouth covered hers, taking possession of it until she bit him. Blood, sweet and coppery, filled her mouth. She laughed when he finally freed himself.

He raised his hand to strike her again. She glared up at him, waiting for it. "Do it, asshole. Hit me, beat me, do whatever makes you feel like a man. You make me sick."

"Why don't you let me show you what happens to those that piss me off?" Jacob bent to untie her—her plan from the start. "Your new master may be my second, but never forget, I'm the first in this pack. Even Sam can't protect you from me."

"I don't need him to."

Jacob grabbed her arm. "You keep thinking that. Let's go and see what trouble we can stir up."

With that, he jerked her along behind him through the door. When it opened, the smell of it hit her first, making her gag. Feces, urine and God knew what other odors assailed her nostrils. One of the most prevalent was blood, which didn't bode well for her. She refused to show him her fear. Instead, she tamped it all down inside and lifted her chin. "You need to get someone in here to clean this place."

Jacob only shrugged and led her down a long, dark hallway to another thick steel door. As they passed through it to another hallway, she noticed that it was lined with cages and shadowy forms shifted behind the bars. When she peered closer to one of those nearest them, a pair of green eyes glowed from within. She gasped and drew away.

His chuckle made her hackles rise, as did his words. "Don't get too close, this isn't a petting zoo."

His fingers flew over the keypad almost too fast for her to see the numbers he'd pressed. Almost, but not quite. Lainie kept her eyes averted from his so he wouldn't see the gleam of triumph in them. He didn't know she'd seen and she refused to give away her ace in the hole.

"Sir?" A voice drew his attention from down another hall to the right.

"Yes?"

"There is something on our security monitors."

"Damn." Jacob looked at her with regret. "This way." He drew her down a second hallway much like the first, coming to a stop in front of a door with a small barred window too high for her to see inside. "Here we are. You can keep our other guest company."

"No!" She dug in her heels, but it was no use. Without much effort, he shoved her inside and slammed the door with a resounding clang. "Let me out!" she yelled, beating on the door. His footsteps faded in the distance then were blotted out by howls that grew louder before cutting off abruptly, telling her he'd shut the outer door, leaving her alone. There was no keypad on this door, not even a knob on this side.

She put her forehead on the cool metal and sighed. "Could it get any worse?"

Apparently so, if the low growl coming from behind her was any indication of how her luck was going to go. She went absolutely still and closed her eyes. "Damn." The noise just got louder, so, she squared her shoulders and turned. If she died, she'd face her killer and hope to die quickly, and as painlessly as possible.

Chapter Thirty

After a long wait in what had to be the dirtiest gas station bathroom Marcus had ever seen, Ben called and said they were on their way to pick him up. Surely all this secrecy wasn't necessary. If the situation weren't so serious, he'd think this was David's idea of a joke.

He waited in the shade of the cinderblock building and tapped his foot on the ground impatiently. Just as he thought they'd gotten lost, or more than likely stopped to get something to eat, they pulled up in a white-panel van that looked like a serial killer's wet dream.

To make matters worse, David was hanging out of the passenger window whistling. "Hey, cutie, wanna ride?" Marcus ignored him, opening the door and motioning for him to get in the back. Being leader did have some perks.

Soon they were speeding through the desert, having narrowed the location of Jacob's lair down to a small mountain range just east of Santa Fe. The land was supposed to be included in the state parks, but somehow, the other Lupin got around that, with bribes, more than likely.

Right now, Marcus couldn't care less. The information came from a local stray who hated Jacob. After he'd been assured that his name would not be mentioned, he'd given up the location. It seemed he'd left the pack after a falling out. It was surprising he still lived. Unless you counted the fact that he was an outcast. This was even worse than death to most werewolves. No social interaction with others of his kind had to be horrible.

"Are the others meeting us?" Marcus didn't get an answer, so he peered around the seat to see what they were doing. David studied a map as if it held the secrets of life and Ben played with a contraption that looked like a cross between a gun and a camera. "I asked a question."

"They'll be there," David answered without looking up.

"What are you not telling me?" Marcus glared at them both.

"Why would we keep things from you?" Ben answered the question with one of his own.

"Talk."

David sighed gustily. "Fine. It was an inside job. One of your own took her."

"Who?"

"We aren't sure." Ben still looked down at his hands.

"Yes, you are, or you'd be telling me. Who is it?"

"It's Jordan." David's voice was flat and hard. "He took her straight to him. He betrayed the pack. We'll do what we have to when we get there."

"No, you won't." Marcus's fingers gripped the dash so tightly that the leather began to dent, and then tear. "I'll personally tear him limb from limb."

"We aren't a hundred percent sure." Ben seemed to be speaking from a distance. Anger that had been simmering dangerously below the surface exploded, his vision narrowed to a small point. Then, the colors disappeared.

"Hold it together til we get there." As David spoke, control began to slip away. Marcus's animal side tugged at him. It wanted to be free to go on a rampage. He'd kill them all, Sam, Caulder and even Jordan, the man he'd thought of as a brother. The two of them had practically been littermates.

Marcus shut his eyes tightly and took deep breaths. Little by little, he pushed the rage back until he regained control of his dual nature and opened his eyes. Whatever showed in them must have been bad, because the two men in the back flinched. "When we find him, I want him." The guttural voice wasn't the same that soothed and seduced Lainie. If she could hear him now, she'd run screaming in the other direction. He wouldn't blame her in the least. She'd said he was a monster. Right now, he felt like one.

Chapter Thirty-one

Lainie couldn't see anything, but she could hear it. The noises were continuous, low and filled with menace. She slid into the corner farthest from the sound and strained her eyes to see.

A bulky shape was barely visible in the middle of the room. She squinted, but still couldn't make it out. The sound escalated before it just stopped. She took a deep breath and waited. Nothing.

It started again, and then turned into a strangled yelp. Pain, the individual was in pain. Lainie crept forward, slowly easing her way to the center of the room. She approached cautiously, unsure as to what this thing was or if it was a threat. Finally, after what felt like hours, she forced herself to speak. "Hello?"

"Lainie?" His voice was the barest whisper. Nevertheless, when she heard it, a bolt of joy made her smile despite their situation.

"Oh thank God it's you. What happened?" She put her hands out, blindly feeling her way forward. Soon, her fingers touched warm flesh. "Are you all right? Did they hurt you?"

"Not too bad. You need to get out of here."

"I'm not going anywhere without you." She ran her hands up the metal edge of whatever held him in place. She found a thick manacle on his wrist and cursed.

"Go."

"Oh, shut the hell up," she grumbled as she felt around until she reached the back where her questing fingers encountered buttons. "I wonder what happens if I push these?"

"Hey, wait!"

Too late, she depressed them one by one and the clank of the manacles releasing echoed through the room, followed by a thump and a groan.

"Oops, sorry." She ran toward the sound of cursing and groaning. In her haste she tripped. "Damn!" Luckily, she landed on something soft.

"Dear God, you broke it. I'm paralyzed and now, my fuckin' dick's broke too. Shit."

"Oh, shut up!" She dragged him across the floor, intending to hide him and come back, if only she could get out of the room.

"And you pulled my hair."

"Stop whining."

The argument would have continued indefinitely except for one thing. As she put her arms around his shoulders, the door flew off the hinges and slammed down on the floor so hard it skidded into the far wall.

Large male shapes came into the room. Lots of them. "Shit." She frantically pulled him behind one of the large metal tables. "You're heavy, lay off the freakin' tacos."

"I know you didn't say I was fat. Just be still." He succeeded in twisting around to cover her with his body, trying to protect her.

"Where is he?" The voice that bellowed through the room was so deep it rattled her fillings.

"There." Another voice, as deep but not as loud answered. The bolts that fastened the table to the floor didn't prevent the intruders from jerking it up and tossing it aside like a child's toy.

"You stupid bastard. Get away from her."

Jordan lay on top of Lainie, naked except for a pair of brief cotton shorts. Lainie squirmed and stared blindly upwards with eyes so wide and frightened it made Marcus even angrier. "I said, off!" he roared.

Ben and David flanked him. He hoped like hell that they could get Lainie out before he ripped his cousin's head off and ate it.

"What the hell?" she screamed and clutched Jordan tighter when Marcus bent down and tried to pull the other man off her.

With one hand on the man's neck, he lifted them off the floor. When he attempted to shake her off she held onto the other man like a tick, refusing to let go. Marcus pulled them close to pry her loose and she bit him. When he jerked on the leg closest to him, she squeaked and tightened her hold. He slid one hand between them.

"Get your hands off that!" Jordan slapped at him. "Perv, stop groping me and get us the fuck out of here."

"Yeah," Lainie said in a muffled voice. She had her face pressed against Jordan's chest almost as if she were hiding.

"Turn off the light," Marcus finally ground out. "Let him go, Lainie, and stand over by the door. After I'm finished killin' him, we'll leave. I wanted to stretch it out, but we just don't have the time." He turned the full force of his glare on Jordan. "How dare you put your hands on her?"

"What the hell are you talking about?" She didn't seem scared. If he didn't know better, he'd think she sounded pissed. Something wasn't right here. "Is it because he was on top of me? Don't you trust us? And besides, that is just ew."

"Hey! What do you mean ew?"

"Not helpin', Jordan."

"Oh, sorry." Jordan grinned at Marcus and it made his heart lurch in his chest. Regret replaced anger.

"Why did you do it?"

"Do what? Yeah, dude, I woke up and said, hey, what am I gonna do today? I know! I'll go get captured and let them strap me to some freaky bondage thing and stick needles in my arms. Gross." Jordan winced and tried to turn his neck.

Marcus's fingers elongated enough to reach all the way around Jordan's throat, his claws curling into both sides of his neck. "Tell me you didn't set this up, that you didn't take her from me."

Lainie finally let go of Jordan, if only to glare up at him. "I thought you knew who it was! I tried to tell David but he got all snotty about it."

"Who was it then?" Marcus let his cousin's feet touch the floor. When the other man's knees buckled, unable to support him, Marcus pulled him into a brief hug. With a whispered apology, he set him on the floor in the corner.

"Me," came a new voice from the doorway.

Marcus whirled to confront the person he'd always thought of as one of his best friends. "Stephen? But why?"

"Why?" Stephen shook his head and sighed before his face twisted in an angry snarl. "Because, I'm tired of being looked over time and again in favor of Ben, the golden boy, or even worse Jordan, the joker." His tone left no doubt as to his thoughts on the other two men.

"You would take her from me because you felt slighted?" Marcus started forward. "You could have talked to me, you stupid son of a bitch."

"The time for talk is over." Stephen smiled, and stepped to one side. Werewolves poured into the room behind him.

"Well, hell yeah, finally, a fuckin' fight!" David yelled and began to rip off his clothes.

Chapter Thirty-two

Marcus threw back his head and howled long and loud. Then he stared down at her and Jordan where they sat huddled against the wall.

"It'll be okay, I promise." He wore scuffed sneakers, a flannel shirt and jeans. Almost the exact same thing he'd had on the night he'd rescued her the first time. She hoped that was a sign of the outcome of this battle. However, her gut told her the stakes were much higher now and the odds were stacked against them.

David's form began to waver and small lights flew around him. His long black hair rippled, blown by an unseen breeze. The air around him darkened as if he were drawing all the available light into his body. Then, within the space of a heartbeat, he was no longer a man, but a huge brown grizzly.

"Oh. My. God," Lainie breathed out.

"Yeah, he thinks he's one sometimes," Jordan grumbled. "Come here. I'll try to protect you as best I can. I can't change yet. But I'm regaining some of the movement in my legs a little at a time."

"You got feeling in them?"

"No."

"Then why were you bitching about your weenie being broke if you couldn't even feel it?"

"Ow."

"What?" Lainie put her hands on his face. "Is something wrong?"

"You reminded me of it. Now it really hurts."

"Shut up, twit." David's roar drowned out the rest of their conversation and they turned back just in time to see him charging toward a large group of the other creatures.

The wolves came at him, attempting to get to Lainie and Jordan. But David knocked three of them off their feet with one swipe of his massive paws.

"His foot's as big as my head." She was astounded at this. "I thought he was a wolf."

"He is." Jordan pushed them farther into the corner, jerking her out of the way of Stephen's decapitated head. It hit the wall with a squelching sound before it slid down, leaving a bloody trail.

Lainie watched in horror as it changed to something between man and wolf. The combination was sickening. "I'm going to hurl."

"You puke on me and I'll never let you live it down," Jordan promised.

A large hand wrapped around her upper arm and hauled her to her feet. Without even looking around, she shoved the heel of her palm upwards at his face, recognizing him just as he blocked her punch. "Mick!"

"Come on, ma'am. Mr. Bei says we have to get you out of here." Mick shielded her with his body.

She peered around him to see the chaotic battle as it raged around the room. Marcus was in the thick of it too, having shifted into his larger Wolfkin form. She tensed when one of the others charged him, but he was ready. Grinning, Marcus ripped its arm off. Using the limb like a grotesque baseball bat, he slammed it into the creature's face, breaking its neck with a resounding crack.

She stood frozen to the spot, watching with fascinated horror. When Mick pulled on her hand again, she snapped her gaze back to his face. "No, we can't leave Jordan here."

Mick made a sound between a whine and a growl. "Ma'am."

"I won't leave him."

"Go, damn it." Jordan glared up at her when she turned back to look at him.

"No."

"Fine." Mick leaned down and picked the other man up, slinging him easily over one broad shoulder. He turned and reached out his other hand for her to take.

She did, but not before she pulled a metal object from its slot in the wall. At least she'd have a weapon of some kind. But it brought all new meaning to the old saying, "if you can't run with the big dogs, stay on the porch".

Chapter Thirty-three

Lainie curled her fingers in one of the belt loops on Mick's jeans as they made their way back through the dark hallways of the warehouse. In the other hand she still held the metal object she'd taken for protection.

"Hey, what's that in your hand?" Jordan turned his head to look at her from his upside-down position over Mick's shoulder.

"I don't know. It's heavy though." She swung it in an arc.

Jordan's eyes narrowed then he grinned. "Umm, I know what that is. One of Jacob's people mentioned it in front of me to scare me."

Lainie held it up and looked at it closely. It was about six inches long, made of smooth metal that widened into a circular phalange at the end before narrowing into a convenient handle. "It reminds me of those nightsticks the cops have."

Mick looked over at her at the same time that Jordan answered. "Nope, it's an anal probe."

She let it fall with a clang and gagged. "Ew. Gross."

Jordan laughed until she wiped her hand in his hair. "Hey!"

They walked in silence for a few minutes, down the hall. "This place is huge. Where are all the damn windows?"

"We're underground, Ms. Westerbrook," Mick answered, giving her a strange look.

"Well, how was I supposed to know that? They blindfolded me before we ever got here," Lainie defended her ignorance.

"I was knocked out," Jordan put in with a tone that seemed to say that he'd won this contest.

"Shush."

"You don't shush me; I'm the eldest of this group," Jordan snarled.

"Yeah, I guess that's why we gotta carry your old ass out, huh?"

"Lainie, that's a low blow. Kicking a man while he's down."

"But you aren't down, I'm carrying you," Mick pointed out.

"Hush." Jordan poked the other man in the back.

"Don't you be mean to him." Lainie smacked Jordan in the head. They'd been quiet so long, but as they hadn't met anyone, all were beginning to relax.

"If you hit me again, I'm telling Marcus to give you a whippin'."

"You will not!"

"Ah, the foibles of youth." The voice that came from the dark stopped them in their tracks.

Mick immediately backed Lainie into a corner, letting Jordan slide down to the floor with a thump. "Bet you wished you'd kept the anal probe now, huh? Wuss." Lainie ignored Jordan's muttered comment except for "accidentally" stepping on his leg hard enough to make him grunt.

Samuel stepped out of the shadows at the far corner of the room. At his side, a huge red wolf lowered its head and growled at them, showing long gleaming fangs that Lainie was quite sure could tear off her leg with one chomp.

"Damn, that's one big bitch." Jordan sounded awestruck.

"It's a girl?" Lainie whispered back, both of them peering through Mick's legs. "How can you tell?" When he didn't answer, she turned to see his leer. "Oh. Ew."

"Ew? Not even, she's fine." He peered closer. "Nice eyes too."

"Uh huh, you were looking at her eyes." They were pretty though, a bright aqua, almost turquoise, that glowed eerily in the dimness of the vast room.

"Elaine, come out of there and nobody has to get hurt." Samuel stared down at where she crouched.

Not by the hair of my chinny chin chin. She didn't say it out loud, doubting that Sam would get the reference and unwilling to give Jordan any ammo about her having chin hair. Instead, she shook her head and waited.

Mick only stood there, head lowered and shoulders hunched. A low growl emanated from deep within his chest.

Sam seemed to be surprised, if his expression was anything to go by. "You would dare? I knew you when you were a pup."

"I'm not a pup now." Mick didn't seem intimidated. Hell, he had Lainie beat. Sam's stern visage, combined with the big, scary bitch dog were enough to make her quake in her boots, if she were wearing any.

"Let me have her. They'll never have to know," Sam cajoled. The wolf at his side snarled, and stepped forward only to stop at another growl from Mick.

Her eyes met Lainie's and she let out a small yip. "Yes, that's right, girl, that's her." Sam petted the top of her head.

Jordan shuffled slightly, pulling her attention from the wolf and her master. "I'm getting the feeling back in my legs. Maybe I can shift." He began to concentrate; sweat broke out on his forehead.

"Don't strain yourself." Lainie meant it. He'd gone ashen and his mouth was tight with pain.

"Elaine!" Samuel's voice made her jerk. "Come out of there. They won't stop you. All of it will be over. I promise they won't be hurt if you do."

"Okay, just back up." She shifted to go around Mick's legs but he put his hand down to stop her.

"No."

"I'll be fine. He won't hurt me and if I do what he says, he won't hurt you two either." She smiled at Jordan. "Be sure to tell him I love him. I never got to say it." She paused and turned back. "And tell him to hurry his ass up and come get me."

Then before either man could say anything else, she slipped out of the corner and ran toward Sam. When she got within his reach, he pulled her close. "Thank you so much for your cooperation in this matter. When I regain my position as Lupin, your actions will be taken into consideration."

Dear God, she'd gone over to the Vulcan side, straight to Psycho-Spock. He possessed all of the logic and none of the morals that went with the fictional character of one of her favorite TV series. However, she didn't harbor any illusions that he'd treat her well. Oh, crap, now she was talking like him in her head.

"Come along, Elaine. You too, Jade." With that astounding revelation, he jerked her arm, pulling her along behind him.

Her mind began to work furiously. Was it possible to turn a normal human into a wolf? She looked at the canine as it walked beside her, its big tail occasionally brushing against her leg. She didn't seem ferocious now. In fact, she was almost friendly.

The trio moved toward the exit and Lainie chanced a look down into the wolf's eyes. "Hi there," she whispered and got a snarl in reply. Well, hell, so much for a touching reunion.

"Elaine, do not attempt to communicate with her in this form. She is unstable." Sam's voice held no inflection but some note alerted her to the fact that he wasn't happy about whatever had caused this.

"Why is she unstable?"

"Incidents occurred which were beyond my control. Some of which make her skittish of being in her human form." He pushed the door open to show a set of steps leading upwards.

Lainie had no clue where they were. She'd been carried in here trussed up and blindfolded, so she didn't even know how to get out. This, combined with the big bad bitch that stalked beside her, kept her from running away. Once they got outside, she hoped to get the opportunity to escape.

Samuel's hand tightened on her wrist when they came to yet another door. "Where are all the people?" she ventured. They hadn't met anyone, which was strange.

"Not many know about this place. And the ones that do are fighting with Marcus." Sam's tone changed when he said his son's name, leaving her with no doubt about how much he hated him.

"He'll win, you know. And when he does, he'll come after you." Lainie sounded calm, surprising herself. Then when she thought about it, she found she really did believe it. Marcus would win, and he would come for her, no matter what. She knew she was smiling like a loon and didn't care. "He loves me."

"He doesn't love you. He wants you. It's called chemistry." Sam scoffed at her notion of love. "I would know, as I created it."

"Bullshit." Lainie kept her goofy grin in place. "He does." The wolf sidled closer to her and she put her hand down to touch the fur on the ruff of her neck.

"Believe what you wish." Sam pulled her through the last door, out into the warm desert night before stopping to glare down at her.

"Where are we going?" She dug her toes in the dirt, hoping to slow him down. "I need shoes, unless you want to carry me."

Sam kept looking around in all directions, then, finally, almost as an afterthought, up at the full moon over their heads. "Beautiful, isn't it?" He pointed upwards. "When I began my experiments so long ago, I never knew it would make me a slave to the moon's phases. Much like women, I feel its pull too."

"Yeah, PMS sucks, huh?" Lainie edged away from him slightly. His mood was pensive, almost sad, but she wasn't going to put any bets on him staying this way.

"Hmm. Come here, Elaine." He crooked his finger at her.

She shook her head and took a step back. "Tell me why you took me away from my mother."

"Your mother?" His lips curled in a sneer. "Your mother had you at my behest and then just handed you over for a pittance."

She slowly shook her head. Joanna's memory blocks no longer worked. "You're lying, I know it. I remember the fire."

"You remember incorrectly."

Lainie began to shake. "You killed her, didn't you? You killed my mama and you took me." The wolf whined and pushed at Lainie with her shoulder, moving her away from Sam.

"Nonsense. That was an old nightmare. You've had it for a long time. I used to come and soothe you and tell you stories when you were just a little girl." He looked benign, but she wasn't fooled. Behind that civilized veneer, he was just as fierce as he professed Marcus to be. At least with Marcus, the ferocity was tempered with emotion, compassion. This man could be savage without remorse.

"Why?" She kept her voice low and soft. She was afraid, sensing the anger simmering in him. It was as if the moon drew it from deep down within.

His movements became more agitated. His features sharpened with hunger and rage. However, at her question, he snapped back, at least temporarily. "You were to be the mother of my new dynasty."

As if this idea made him happy, his eyes began to glow. "Then, Marcus came in and stole you from beneath my nose, with the help of David, of course. I should have killed that creature when I had the chance. Instead, I let my own scientific curiosity keep him alive to study."

"What about your son? Do you wish you'd killed him too?"

"I was proud of Marcus. He's strong, brave and intelligent. But, he has this streak of nobility that I have always found to be highly inconvenient." He shook his head as if sad about the fact. "I tried to weed it out, but David always seemed to be able to keep it from being eradicated no matter what."

"I see." Lainie swallowed hard.

As Sam talked of David and Marcus, he started shaking.

Desperately, she searched the area for possible hiding places besides back inside the warehouse. The moonlight illuminated the flat landscape that went on forever. Sam wanted a baby. The act that she'd have to commit with him to get it made bile rise in her throat and she shuddered. "No." Her voice was thick with suppressed terror.

"Your wishes no longer matter, Elaine."

“Did they ever?” She took a deep breath and held it for the space of a few heartbeats.

“No.” He rolled his neck back and forth as if to release tension in his muscles.

She watched him warily, waiting for his next move. Only the three of them stood out here. The battle that raged behind them could have been happening on the moon for all the disturbance it caused here. She was alone, isolated and terrified. In that one moment, she knew that she’d never submit to what he wanted. She’d rather die. She didn’t try to tell herself that she could prevent it from happening, but she could control the outcome. He’d have to kill her.

He reached out and grabbed her before she could even blink. The reflexes of these men still had the ability to surprise her. He didn’t hurt her, just pulled her to his chest. He wore a lab coat and a button-down shirt, incongruous with the savage look on his face. “I won’t hurt you, if you don’t fight.”

She bared her teeth at him. “If you think I’ll lie down and take it, you’re dead wrong. You may have made me a bitch, but I ain’t your bitch.”

His arms tightened and she had to fight to breathe. With a whispered order for her to be still, he tried to kiss her. She jerked her head away but one of his hands twisted in her hair to hold her in place.

“No.” She clamped her jaw closed, resisting him to the end.

He hissed her name again, but she closed her eyes, blocking him out. His mouth pressed against hers, and when she refused to open for him, his fingers slid around and pried her jaw open.

She kicked futilely at his shins, earning bruised toes for her efforts.

"Stop it." He looked into her eyes for a second then swooped down again. This time he succeeded in putting his mouth on hers and the first wave of nausea hit her. He literally sickened her.

Her body reacted to his nearness, violently. When she heaved, he pushed her away from him. She fell, catching herself on her palms with a wince. They stung, but otherwise she was unhurt. "I..." She took a shaky breath and let it out. The nausea subsided as if it had never existed.

"What did he do to you?" Sam crouched down and pinched her chin between his thumb and fingers. He sniffed her neck before pulling away.

"I don't know what you mean. I got sick. I couldn't help it," she babbled, terrified of the look on his face.

His eyes were hard and flat, and his stony expression didn't bode well for her immediate future. "You're useless to me now." His gaze moved up and down her form, lingering on her stomach then her breasts before pinning her with a glare. "It's of no consequence, I'll fix it."

"Fix what?" She didn't get an answer from him, but in the next second, it didn't matter because she heard the most beautiful sound in the world—Marcus's voice howling her name.

She wasted no time, just kicked out, catching Samuel in the sternum with her heel. He let out a satisfying woof as he lost both his breath and his balance.

Lainie rolled to her feet and did what was fast becoming a habit for her. She ran like hell in the other direction, hoping that this time, she'd get lucky and get away.

Unfortunately, she'd only taken about three steps when someone swept her up and threw her over their broad shoulder. "Put me down, you asshole!" She put both her fists together and slammed them into where she thought the kidneys were.

"Ms. Westerbrook, please." Without as much as breaking stride, Mick patted her leg. "We have to hurry."

"Mick?" She reared up and glared. "Where's Jordan?"

"He's in a safe place." He began to run faster, jostling Lainie around on his shoulder.

"I can run too, you know." She grunted.

"No time."

"Why?" Her answer was an explosion that rocked the very ground beneath them.

She stared in horror at the plume of fire and smoke belching from the hole that used to be the lab. "Marcus!" She kept screaming his name until it turned into a howl that rivaled any wolves'.

The repercussion from the explosion lifted Mick off his feet and threw them into the air. He wrapped his arms around her and held on, tumbling to the ground. A sharp pain followed by a cold sensation on the back of her head had her gasping. "Ms. Westerbrook?" His voice faded in and out; she swallowed thickly and tried to answer. Her tongue gained about twenty pounds and then, everything went black.

Chapter Thirty-four

Marcus ran through the corridors, looking for one particular man. When he found him, he would personally rip him to shreds. Once upon a time, he'd looked up to him, physically and otherwise, but no longer. He stopped in the dark gloom of the front of the warehouse and stared. Once upon a time, he'd called him, "Daddy".

At the sound of his voice, Samuel whirled in place. "Hello, boy." He wore that smug, patronizing look that always made Marcus want to slink back into his room and hide when he was a kid, but no more.

Marcus took in the half-healed scratches on his cheek. He could smell Lainie's scent on him. Rage took over. He didn't think, didn't speak, he just reacted. He lifted his head and roared before charging at Samuel.

Samuel feinted to the left and hit him across the neck with a blow that would have killed a human and perhaps another werewolf as well. "You're such a stupid boy." He kicked him in the ribs, lifting him off his feet. "Always playing fair. Why don't you fight me in that Wolfkin form you're so proud of, hmm?"

"I don't know, maybe I'm scared you have Wolfkin envy." Marcus righted himself and grinned. "I'd hate to make you feel inadequate." He punched Samuel with both his fists in the chest.

The force of his blows knocked Samuel off his feet and sent him skidding across the warehouse floor but he flipped back up and stood watching him, waiting. "I won't be for long."

"What does that mean?" Marcus narrowed his eyes. "You can't change into that form."

"Yet." Samuel ran at him, jumping up at the last minute to kick him in the face.

Marcus ducked, catching the blow in the side of the head.

"Idiot." Samuel slashed at his son's abdomen with his extended claws.

Marcus hissed in a breath as the pain blossomed. He stood still, waiting for the wound to heal. He couldn't help but feel smug when surprise flashed in his father's eyes at the quickness with which the cuts disappeared. "Now, Daddy..." he stalked forward, "...is that any way to treat your favorite son?"

"You aren't my son," Samuel hissed, his teeth growing into fangs. "Not anymore."

Marcus grinned at him. "That's the nicest thing you've ever said to me."

Samuel backhanded him, his claws raking a burning path across his cheek. Marcus only laughed.

"Elaine was to be mine!" Samuel charged him. At the last minute he lowered his shoulder and rammed it into Marcus's abdomen, shoving him into the wall.

Marcus's skull cracked against the hard surface, but he refused to show him how much it hurt: instead, he goaded him further. "Ain't that just too bad. I got there first, now she's mine." He brought his fists down on his father's back, relishing the sound of bones snapping.

Samuel went down on one knee, panting for breath, then lashed out, catching Marcus in the thigh with his claws.

“Where is she?” Marcus grunted, shaking it off. “What did you do to her?”

“She's around, somewhere. I'll get back to her when I'm done with you.”

“You hurt her and I'll...”

“She's mine, not yours.” For the first time, his father's control slipped. The rage boiled to the surface for him to see. “I waited and watched you court her, placate her. You catered to her every whim. She's spoiled and willful because you didn't do what you should.”

“What the hell was that?”

“Subjugation.” Samuel made his first mistake and stepped in close enough for Marcus to grab him.

“Like you did my mother?” He wrapped his fingers around Samuel's neck. “Every damn day, you made her cry. Did you know that? Did you even fucking care?”

Samuel gasped and put his hands between Marcus's forearms in an attempt to lever them apart, but Marcus had a lifetime of hatred to lend him strength. “Somehow, I doubt it.” He pressed his thumbs against Samuel's windpipe, smiling as it began to buckle under the strain. “Let's see if I can make you care, Daddy.”

“No,” his father rasped out. “I didn't care. The bitch...”

Marcus rammed Samuel's head against the wall, laughing at the hollow thud it made. He squeezed harder, and noticed that his hands began to change. “You're getting your wish, I'm shifting.”

Marcus's muscles loosened, his bones became denser, elongating in some places, and growing shorter and wider in others. His lips thinned and his muzzle grew, sprouting black fur that surrounded long ivory fangs made to rip and tear.

As his nails grew, one punctured his father's throat. Blood welled in the wound before trailing down his hand into the fur that sprouted from his formerly smooth skin. His disgust for this man was so great that he didn't even have the urge to drink it.

"So, Daddy, how do you like me now?" He tilted his head to one side, his long ears twitching back and forth. "Did you say something?" He put his hand to the side of his head. "Oh, that's right, you can't talk. Too bad. If you could, I bet you'd say how proud of me you are, how much you love me and how sorry you are for trying to kill me and take my woman."

Samuel's eyes bulged.

"Fuck you." Marcus shook him. "You hurt my mama and you hurt me. Hell, you hurt everybody you ever came in contact with."

The wound on his father's neck healed enough for him to respond. "I made you. I created..."

"Run!" David's voice came from far away, but it was getting closer and fast.

Marcus turned and watched David flash by and then shrugged. "Wonder what he's in such a hurry for?" With an almost negligent wave of his hand, he ripped Sam's throat open again.

Samuel's eyes drifted shut then widened again.

Marcus sensed someone behind him and started to turn. He got a quarter of the way around when a large furred arm shot out and grabbed him around the neck, dragging him off his prey. "Take your hands off me!" A loud blast and plume of fire drowned out his roar.

The last thing he saw was Samuel Bei slumped against the wall with blood running down his ruined throat, and that was all right by him.

Chapter Thirty-five

Marcus left the burning ruin of Jacob Caulder's lair kicking and screaming. "Take your damn hands off me, you fuckin'..." He paused and glanced around. "Oh."

"Yeah, oh." Ben shook the soot off his fur and glared. "David likes pushing buttons."

The remaining pack members poured out of the opening, coughing and sputtering.

David sniffed the air, sniffed again, then narrowed his eyes and spat out a chunk of black stuff on the ground. "Shouldn't have them if they're not supposed to be pushed. How was I to know it'd blow the place sky high?" He grinned unrepentantly.

With a grimace, Marcus stepped around it and began to look for Lainie. There was no sign of her. "Lainie!" he finally howled. He got a reply, after a fashion.

"Come and get me the hell out of here, right now! I think there's a lizard in my hair!" Jordan's panicked tones had them all hurrying toward the sound of his voice. It was a cave, half-hidden behind a huge slab of rock.

With a grin, David slipped inside the small opening.

"Hey! David, if you put that lizard down my shorts, I'll—" A high-pitched yelp cut off his words and seconds later, the huge black wolf that was Jordan's other form bounded out of the cave.

"I thought that would help you change, chicken shit." David's laughter grated on Marcus's nerves.

"I want Lainie," Marcus seethed. "Stop fuckin' around and find her."

"She's not here."

This new voice had him whirling to face its owner. A woman stood naked as the day she was born, covered with nothing more than her long red hair. She glared at him with blue-green eyes that glowed in the darkness. He was proud of the fact that he actually noticed the color of her eyes. Hell, he was in love, no doubt about it now.

"Where is she?" He kept his voice low, putting his hand back to stop the others from advancing. The fear in her eyes was apparent, the wildness she fought to keep at bay.

"Someone took her away."

"Who?"

"A short lady, with gray hair."

"Who are you?" He put his hand out to grab her but she sidled back out of his reach.

"Jade?" David broke in; Marcus spared him a glance and saw that he looked dumbfounded. "What happened to you, honey?"

At the sound of David's voice, she trembled, and in a flash, transformed into a large red wolf and ran, disappearing in the dark desert night.

"*That* was Jade?" Marcus glared at David as if it was all his fault.

His uncle seemed far away in that moment, staring after her as if he wanted to chase her down. "Yeah, but when I knew her, she couldn't change into a big red bitch."

Marcus didn't have time for another mystery right now. Only one thing was on his mind. "Who took Lainie?"

"Use your nose, it's Joanna." David put his hands on his hips and glared. "Let's go home and I'll make some calls."

"Joanna better not be doing what I think she is," Marcus warned.

"She'll do what she thinks she needs to, nothing more, and nothing less."

"Maybe it's for the best." Ben stood beside Marcus while Jordan sat at his feet and whined.

A groan from the underbrush interrupted their argument. They found Mick lying there, blinking groggily up at the sky. With another groan, he rolled to his feet, swaying slightly.

"Someone grabbed Ms. Westerbrook. I'm sorry, Lupin." He gave him an apologetic look before bowing his head.

Marcus plucked the small dart out of the side of Mick's neck and held it up in front of his face. "I think she came prepared for anything. Right, David?" But his grandfather just transformed, this time into an eagle that lost no time in flying away from the pack.

"You son of a bitch, you can't take her from me again! I won't let you!" Marcus screamed into the night. He shook his fist at the sky. The only indication that David heard him was a slight dip of his wings before he glided out of sight.

Chapter Thirty-six

Lainie slid out of her car and headed into the grocery store. She wanted something, she just wasn't sure what it was. The past three weeks had been strange. Joanna came to her house and asked her if she could stay. Of course, she'd said yes. However, the woman made her nervous because she watched her closely, as if monitoring her or something.

When she'd asked her what the problem was, Joanna's answer hadn't made sense. "I'm doing something once more, and if it doesn't work, they can all just kiss my ass."

She looked a little older, but not much. Her hair was silver and short, highlighting her dark eyes and accentuating her sharp cheekbones. She was a striking woman, but she wasn't the most comfortable of companions at times.

Lainie sighed and pushed her cart ahead of her. She'd been having strange dreams since Jo showed up too. In one, there'd been a large black wolf, in another she'd dreamed of Marcus. Though she hadn't seen him in ages, the dream had been vividly erotic and she'd woken up wet and achy. Damn, the man still had power over her after a decade.

Suddenly, it came to her what she wanted. "Ice cream, chocolate, extra dark." With a happy grin, she motored over to the frozen foods aisle and grabbed a half-gallon of Chocolate Brownie Overload. She frowned in thought. "Peanut butter."

She scurried back the way she'd just come and rounded the corner. There were a few carts down this aisle so she abandoned her own to get to the peanut butter. "Yes, come to me with your creamy goodness." Her voice went down an octave as she grabbed it off the shelf.

She whirled and started back to her cart but stopped and slowly turned when she spotted a large shape from the corner of her eye. He'd attempted to duck behind the other end of the aisle, but wasn't fast enough.

Her heart beat a rapid tattoo as she grabbed her purse and zipped around the corner. Nobody. But she didn't give up, instead, she ran to the neighboring aisle. Sure enough, there he was, tall, blond, cute and way too young to be stalking her. She lunged forward and caught his belt loop. "Hold it." He stopped, his form dwarfing hers. Damn, he was huge. However, she wasn't scared at all. In fact, the feeling inside her was more akin to joy.

His shoulders slumped and he slowly turned to face her. "Hi, Ms. Westerbrook." His face was familiar to her and he knew her name.

She hissed out a breath and went pale as the memory slammed into her. "Mick."

He quickly took her arm and started out of the store. She let him guide her to his vehicle.

"Ma'am?" He sounded worried.

She didn't answer. She was too busy remembering everything that happened. Joanna had come and picked her up. Lainie recalled the arguments, loud, long and angry. She'd thought Marcus was dead. Finally, Joanna agreed to "fix" her again. However, she said if it didn't take this time, they were on their own. David said that Marcus had gone feral. He'd spied on the pack and heard the rumors of his madness.

When she figured out Marcus was alive she'd briefly attempted to struggle against the other woman's mind control, but finally succumbed into a darkness that seemed like an old friend after all these years.

The sight of Mick brought it all tumbling back. Either she was getting better at fighting the mind control, or stubbornness was a deterrent. Either way, she wouldn't lose Marcus again.

"Lupin told me to watch you," Mick told her, snapping her out of her haze. He sat there rubbing her wrists with a worried frown on his face.

She sighed. "I can't believe I'm saying this, but take me to your leader."

Chapter Thirty-seven

Marcus sat on the rock formation that was his throne and glared. He was their leader, the king of this pack, yet they'd all come to the decision that he'd be better off without Lainie.

"Do you mean to tell me that you think you can dictate who I mate with?" He sat, stunned, after the last of the elders spoke his piece on the subject.

"Yes, Lupin. She's weak, a human, no less. And though she is providing you with an heir, we don't think it is advisable for her to be allowed into the pack." This came from Joel, one of his father's most hated enemies.

His father, who was missing and presumed dead. God, Marcus hoped he was. If nothing else good came out of all this bullshit, Samuel Bei's death would make it all worthwhile—most of it, anyway. The ache he felt on hearing Lainie remembered nothing that transpired while they were together still had the ability to rob him of his breath.

He had Joanna to thank for that. Apparently the woman felt his mate's distress from where-the-hell-ever she'd been holed up all this time. It brought her out of hiding just long enough to grab her baby chick, take her home and block her memory.

With a wry smile, Marcus pictured what would happen when Elaine found out she was pregnant. The bitchfest heard round the world was only the beginning. He had to believe that she would remember it all. If not, then he may as well just give up and die right now.

But, Mick was there, out of her sight, never far away from Lainie. Marcus wouldn't have any of his enemies stealing her away. No, he wanted that honor all for himself. Unfortunately, he may have to give up his throne to do it. Was he ready to toss all this away for the love of his life? You bet your ass. He opened his mouth to tell them where to shove the position as leader of the Arizona pack and all the headaches that went with it.

"Hey, dumbass, think about what you're doin'."

At the low-voiced order, Marcus glared over his shoulder. "What are you doing here?" he snarled at David.

The man grinned, his teeth flashing in the moonlight. "I'm just here to make sure you don't pull some stupid and immature stunt. Something I'm sure you're goin' to regret one day."

"You don't have a fuckin' clue how I feel, nor do you even care. I love her, with my heart and my soul, and you just ripped her out of my life, again. Even worse, you ripped me out of her life too." Marcus was so furious he wanted to tear his great-grandfather to shreds. "Does Lainie know she's pregnant? Did you at least tell her that?" Marcus prodded.

"Hell no." David shuddered. "You have got to be out of your mind." He gave another shudder, and then winked. "I decided to save that little honor for you." David's smile was mischievous; however, Marcus didn't have time to mull it over because all hell broke loose.

Chapter Thirty-eight

"If you don't back off, you're gonna be featured on the cover of the next NRA magazine as a rug, I'm not playing!" Her voice carried over the crowd, drawing the attention of supporters and detractors alike. "Take your filthy paws off me!"

"Ohmigod. The bitch is back." Jordan put his face in his hands and sighed.

Ben leaned forward, smiled and shook his head.

Below the raised boulder that was his throne, he could see a strange phenomenon happening. The crowd stirred uneasily. Not many would actually attack a woman who carried a baby, especially not their leader's child. All turned around to face the back, then parted in a wave, at the forefront of which was Mick.

That was one indication of the owner of the voice, and if that wasn't enough, the words only helped him to the inevitable conclusion. Elaine was here. "Back up, bitch. I bet you have ringworm. You need to see someone about that back-hair problem you have. Yeah, blow it out your ass too, sister."

When the growling started, he stood to intervene, but, before he could even take a step, David put his hand on his shoulder. "Let her deal with it."

"They're right, she's too weak. They might hurt her." His heart climbed into his throat.

"Just wait."

"I tell you what, you tear my favorite shirt, and it's on like a neck bone. Making me come all the way out here, in the dark. I swear I saw a lizard bigger than my leg back there. I think he was smoking a joint. Mick, forward, march." Her voice remained strong and angry. It didn't quaver, only got louder.

Mick stumbled, and then continued on, pushing them out of her way like a human bulldozer. However, he didn't stop the ones that came in behind her, intending to harm her.

Marcus clenched his fists, readying himself to leap into the crowd to defend her to the death if need be. Jordan stood with him, as did Ben. It warmed his heart to see the show of support from his friends.

The howls and yips grew more frenzied. The bitches would tear her apart. They were angry anyway, because he'd chosen a human, albeit a Breeder, instead of one of them. "I said back up; don't make me tell you again." She heaved a sigh. "Alright, is that how you wanna play it? Fine! Bad doggie!" A small humming zap sounded, followed by a yelp. After that, the circle around Elaine and her shield widened. "That's more like it."

Finally, she stepped around Mick and stalked up to stand in front of Marcus and the others. In her hand she held a Taser gun, which she'd put to good use. The smell of burnt hair and the wounded looks the Weres cast in his direction attested to that.

She shook her weapon at David, who had the intelligence to look scared. "Hi, honey. I'm home." She smiled, but Marcus took note of the hellfire in her eyes. She was pissed off and no amount of groveling was going to help.

"Hi yourself, baby, I've missed you." He shoved his hands in the pockets of his jeans and grinned down at her.

"You missed me, huh? I guess there was one thing that you didn't miss." Her long hair was up in a ratty ponytail and there were dark circles under her eyes, but she looked more beautiful to him right now than he remembered her being. Even with the impressive snarl.

"Um, what?"

"Let's just say, that on your last visit to the Temple of Lainie, you left a little something behind." She pointed at her belly. "When in the hell were you coming to get my pregnant ass?"

Uh oh, she knew about that too. "I—" he began but she cut him off.

"You let them take me away again." Tears glimmered in her eyes, but she didn't let them fall. "You'd think I was a mushroom as much as I've been kept in the dark and fed a steady diet of bullshit. Well, I'm not takin' it no more, you hear me?"

He couldn't help but grin. Even in the middle of a fit, in front of his whole pack at that, she made him smile. "I love you, Lainie," he whispered.

That took the wind out of her sails. She frowned for a minute then opened her mouth. He forestalled the rest of her rant by jumping down from the rocks to stand in front of her. "I didn't think you remembered me, and I was told it was best for you if it stayed that way." He stroked his fingers down her cheek.

"What a load of crap." However, she stepped into the circle of his arms easily enough. "I love you too, Scooby."

Marcus filed the insult away. She'd pay for it later, when he got her into bed. He noticed the eyes of his pack on them; some were frowning, but most seemed impressed by what she'd just done. "How'd you figure it all out?"

"I was at the grocery store. Oh shit, I forgot my ice cream!" She pouted for a second. "Anyway, I saw big boy over there, as if I could miss him." She glared at Mick, who shuffled his feet and grinned sheepishly. "And everything sort of fell into place."

Marcus looked at David, who was looking everywhere but at him. Aha, so, she'd passed the test and this was how. He breathed a sigh of relief. "You're home now, that's all that matters."

"I guess so. But if I ever have to say what I said to Mick, ever again, I'm going to skin someone," she grumbled. "Cheesy bullshit."

"What did you have to say that was so awful?" He pressed his face to her hair and inhaled deeply.

"Take me to your leader." She huffed out an exasperated sigh and cocked out her hip. "How cliché is that?"

That startled a laugh from him. His head fell back and the noise echoed around the small valley. Some of the others joined in, but a few naysayers remained.

"Bitch," one of the younger women, he thought her name was Carley, hissed. She'd had her eye on him for a while. She pushed her blonde hair out of her eyes and showed Lainie her impressive canines.

Lainie held her chin at a regal angle. "Honey, that's Queen Bitch to you and don't you ever forget it." She wiggled the stun gun meaningfully. "Unless you want another taste, you'd better back that shit up."

"She's right, back up." This came, astoundingly enough, from Charlotte. While her husband was rather high in the pack, she usually kept silent. Now, she came forward to stand beside Lainie. "If you don't, I can make you wish you had."

One by one, the females came to stand beside the Lupin's chosen mate.

"Charlotte," John growled meaningfully at her.

"Oh, be quiet. It's silly to think that we can't be civilized enough to deal with a Breeder in the pack. She makes him happy." Charlotte glared at them all in turn. "He's done so much for us; can't you do this one thing for him?"

"I can." Allen stepped up beside Lainie. She grinned and put her hand on his arm. Allen gave her a small nod before turning to glare at the assembled pack once more.

"None of you have to stay. I won't have you hunted down; I won't think less of you." Marcus's voice rang out. "I'm your Lupin, but I'm not a dictator. By that same reasoning, you won't dictate who my mate is. My head, my heart, my very soul belongs to her. If she goes, so do I." Lainie drew in her breath but he squeezed her hand, asking her to remain silent. She pinched him, but otherwise, complied.

Finally, all of the elders, including John, said a collective "aye". Cheers followed, turning into yips and howls beneath the full Arizona moon.

She turned to him and smiled. "I never got to tell you just how beautiful I think you are in all your forms."

"Thank you, Lainie." He let out a breath, unaware how much it meant to him to hear those words until she said them.

His cousin brushed past her in wolf form, his black shaggy coat identical to Marcus's own. "Hey!" She grabbed him by the scruff of the neck. "Who is this?"

"Jordan."

"Who came into the bathroom with me that first night?" Jordan, always up for a good scratch, leaned against her. She readily complied, but kept glaring at Marcus.

"Oh, that was me." He smiled back at her, ignoring his cousin's wolfish snickers.

"You're a pervert." She put one hand on her hip and tapped her foot on the ground. Jordan butted her hand to remind her of her duties. "Oh, sorry."

"Well, yeah." Marcus grinned unrepentantly.

"I guess I'll forgive you just this once, Scooby," she said, still scratching Jordan's neck. His tongue lolled out and his eyes closed in ecstasy.

"Excuse me, but that's mine." Marcus shoved him away. "I get all the good scratches; you go find your own woman."

Jordan tossed his head and stalked off to join the others in the hunt for the ever-elusive rabbit. The rest watched her from a distance, but he knew that soon they'd all clamor around her; she'd draw them into her web just as she had him.

Lainie grinned. "Honey?" Her voice was pitched low.

Marcus leaned down and kissed her, sinking into the warmth of her mouth. They stayed that way for a long time, before he raised his head. "What were you saying?"

"You're going to turn all furry in a few, right?" She looked away and bit her lip. Was she frightened of him? He knew that she wasn't of Jordan, but they'd always fought, and that probably helped ease a lot of her fear.

"Yeah." He slid his hand through his hair, and sighed. "Later on, I will."

"I guess this means that you have PMS too, huh?" She looked up at him mischievously.

"You're gonna get it." He lunged for her.

She squealed and danced backwards, sliding around David and peering from behind him. "Promises, promises."

David groaned and shook his head. "I'm going to be naked in about five minutes. That's your final warning."

"Ew." She wrinkled her nose and took off running.

Marcus ran after her, leaving the howls of his companions behind. She laughed as she turned to make sure he kept up. He let her get a little ahead, before he poured on the speed and grabbed her. He swung her up in his arms and carried her toward one of the more private areas. “Oh, look, a blanket.” He wiggled his brows at her.

“Hey, where did this come from?”

He sniffed the air right before he lay her down. “Allen.”

“I don't want Allen to know we have sex.” She tried to wiggle away but he was too fast for her.

“I think it's a little late for that.” He put his thigh over hers and pinned her down on the ground. “I'm so glad you figured it all out.”

“Yeah, I'm not happy about that test thing. Like the Emergency Braincast System. This is a test. This is only a test. If it had been an actual cock-up, I'd have never remembered a damn thing.”

“Joanna and David cooked it up. They said if you were strong enough to break the psychic bonds, you'd get here. Only then would the pack accept you. This has been the longest three weeks of my life.” He grimaced. “It's all David's fault.”

“You like blaming him, don't you? Blame him for the Taser in my purse too.”

“It is his fault, he set it all up,” Marcus insisted.

She smiled up at him. “I know, I remember the exact words he said.”

“What?” His fingers slid beneath the hem of her shirt to rest on her belly. It was barely even round, but soon, she'd be big with his child.

“‘Damn it, Joanna, don't make it too hard. I gotta see my grandbabies sometime.’” She gave a fair imitation of David's voice. "Then, I went all foggy for a few days, and woke up in my house with no memory of anything. Where's Sam?"

"He died in the explosion, or we think so." He pulled her close.

"Good." Her bloodthirsty tone made him smile.

"I thought he hurt you and I went crazy. It just got worse when I found out the truth. The pack council forced me to stay away from you. They argued that if you weren't strong enough mentally to break the bonds, then you couldn't lead the pack with me." Marcus's eyes glowed with the rage he still felt.

"I'm too stubborn to forget you. So, don't think you'll get away that easily. And you were right, you know."

"How's that?" He pulled the ponytail holder out of her hair and slid his fingers against her scalp.

She closed her eyes and purred. "You promised it would be okay, and it is. I love you."

"Damned if I don't love you too, even if you are crazy as hell." He smiled in the face of her mock glare. He could practically see the gears turning in that brain of hers.

Sure enough, she tugged gently on his hair to bring him closer. "I thought you said something about me getting it."

His hands cupped her ass, pulling her hard against him. "Oh yeah, thanks for reminding me."

She giggled seconds later when her sweats flew into the branches of the tree above their heads, soon followed by her shirt. "It is my job as ruler, to remind you of your duties."

She lay on her back in nothing but a pair of underwear he was sure she wore just to make his brain melt. He sat back on his heels to stare in appreciation before sliding them off. "What are my duties?"

"That." She sighed when he skimmed his fingers back up her legs. "And t-that," she stuttered when he spread her open and thrust his tongue inside her. "Ohmigod, that. Please."

His tongue halted her words and her breath for a long moment. His husky laugh sent her over the edge. She muffled her scream, biting the edge of the blanket.

She squirmed, but he held her. "Mine." He slid his fingers inside her, flicking her clit with his tongue before he suckled it.

She stiffened, moving her hips up against his mouth, mindlessly responding to him. He loved every damn minute of it, and drank her down greedily. He almost came when she did; the smell and taste of her made his cock so hard it hurt.

"Yeah, and that too," she said a few minutes later, after she stopped writhing beneath him. She seemed subdued as he rolled onto his back in an attempt to gain control of his reactions.

He didn't want to hurt her. The fact that she was pregnant scared the shit out of him and he told her so.

She hooted at that comment and came up on her knees. "I'm pregnant and queen of all I survey." She threw her shoulders back, drawing his attention to the lush fullness of her breasts. "You will bow down and worship me."

Were they getting bigger? He squinted and decided that, yes, they were. Maybe this pregnancy thing wouldn't be so bad. "Yes, you're my queen," he agreed, his hand snaking out to capture one full mound, stroking the distended peak.

She arched her back and smiled right before she took his cock in her hand. "Then, this shall be my scepter." She leaned down and licked him, swirling her tongue along the broad head before sucking him in her mouth.

"Hell, yes," he gasped out, tangling his fingers in her hair. She squeezed his shaft as she sucked, her teeth grazing the sensitive flesh on the underside of the flared tip. “Damn, Lainie, stop.”

She did, pulling back with an audible popping noise. Her smile widened as she threw one leg over his hips and slowly slid down onto his cock. Her pussy stretched over him, embracing him in a fist of warm silk.

He shuddered and closed his eyes at the sensation only to open them wide when she clenched her inner muscles around him. He watched the play of the moonlight on her skin as she rode him here beneath the trees. Her head fell back as she abandoned herself to him totally.

The warmth of the night was no match for her heat. Their bodies moved in perfect tandem, thrust for thrust as the pressure mounted. She had her legs clamped tightly around him, refusing to let him go. With a wicked smile on her face, she moved her hips in a slow circle, grinding against him.

That was just enough to send him over the edge. With a shout, he released his seed inside her, thrusting mindlessly until he couldn’t move anymore. His cock swelled inside her and he heard her groan, “I could get used to this.”

“You’d better, there ain’t gonna be nobody else doin’ *this*.” He lightly smacked her ass.

“Ha.”

“Ha? I’m the boss, not you. You might be the queen, but I’m the king.” He frowned.

“The big bad wolf, huh?” She snuggled closer, apparently enjoying being tangled together.

“Damn right,” he told her in the hard, mean tone he employed to intimidate everyone from shareholders to the subordinates in his pack.

For a second or two, she at least attempted to look frightened then sputtered with laughter. "Oh my, what big teeth you have." Putting her chin on her hands, she gave him a mischievous grin and used her inner muscles to squeeze his cock, hard.

He yelped, and his eyes rolled back in his head. However, he still had the presence of mind to answer, "All the better to eat you with, my dear."

By now he should have known she'd get the last word in, after all, this was Lainie, the love of his life, the center of his world. "Damn, I hope so. But I ain't coloring my hair red, so get over it."

He'd never get over it, and as long as she was here, by his side, he didn't want to get over loving Lainie.

About the Author

To learn more about Jenna Leigh please visit http://www.jennaleighzone.com. Send an email to Jenna Leigh at jennaleigh35@gmail.com or join her Yahoo! group to join in the fun with other readers as well as Jenna! http://groups.yahoo.com/group/Southern_Fried_Romance_Writers/

Loup Garou

© 2006 Mandy M. Roth

Lindsay Willows craves a simple life. One where she can make a difference without drawing too much attention to herself. As the daughter of both a vampire and a fay, the cards were already stacked against her. Finding out she's the supposed mate of a dark fay prince doesn't help matters. Especially when there are those who will stop at nothing to prevent her from mating with a prince she's never even met.

When Exavier Kedmen, the incredibly sexy front man for a world-famous band, shows up wanting her to go back to a field she left three years ago, she can't explain the strong feelings that surface for a man she barely knows.

Lindsay finds herself confronting demons from her past, coming to terms with the ones in the present and finally looking forward to a future with the man she was created for. And she discovers evil doesn't care who it hurts to obtain its goals but even the evilest of things fear something, or in the case of Exavier, someone.

Enjoy the following excerpt...

"Hey, who wouldn't want to see me gyrate on a pole?" I asked, sarcastically. "Doesn't everyone sit around waiting to see me make a fool of myself?"

Backing up fast, I slammed into something solid. A warmth laced with soothing power wrapped around me. My breath caught and for a moment, I could do little more than stare at Myra with wide eyes.

"We never have to wait long for you to make a fool of yourself." A slow smile spread over her cocoa-colored face. She winked and my brow furrowed.

Turning slowly, I found myself staring up into the blue eyes of one of the sexiest men I'd ever seen. He had to look down at me and that alone was enough to do it for me because at five-nine, I had trouble finding a man I could wear pumps with and not be taller than them. This stud was about six-five so there was no way I'd end up taller than him. His tousled black hair hung to his strong chin, putting emphasis on the tiny dimple there.

I had difficulty tearing my gaze from his thick, corded neck and found my willpower only worsened as I dropped my eyes lower, tracing his broad chest displayed nicely in a snug navy T-shirt with a faint outline of a dragon on it. The thing looked like it had been worn several hundred times but I knew it was a designer piece instantly. The inner shopper in me applauded.

"Umm, sorry." As I went to move away from him, he took hold of my arm and sent fire shooting up it. My breath hitched as my inner thighs tightened.

What?

I stared at him, confused, horny, mesmerized.

He raked his blue gaze over me slowly, heating various portions of my already aroused body. “Lindsay?”

“Do I know you?”

Please say yes. Please say yes.

“Linds?”

I drew a blank and offered up a soft smile. “Again with the ‘do I know you’ because I really don’t think I’d forget a body…err…face like yours.”

A black brow went up as a sexy grin moved over his face. I got the feeling he was hiding something. If I wasn’t so shocked and horny from his sheer presence, I’d have thought to question him more. As it stood, I was a little more concerned with begging him to have his way with me than anything else.

“I believe we have an appointment.”

It took me a minute to register what he was saying. “Oh, you must be the guy from Loup Garou. Umm…?”

Myra leaned into me and whispered, “Exavier Kedmen.” The way she said it made me think I was supposed to just know him by his name. As much as I wished that was the case, I didn’t.

My eyes lingered on his sexy lips as I nodded. He tilted my chin upwards a bit, leaving me envisioning how it would be to kiss him. The very idea of sliding my tongue over his lush lips made my heart beat faster.

“Did you catch what she said? My name is Exavier. Not Blair.”

Instantly, heat flared through my cheeks. “You heard that, huh?”

He nodded.

“Well, in my defense, I wasn’t staring at your abs when you told me your name. I was fixated on your mouth, Xavs.” The second I realized a shortened versioned of his name had popped out of my mouth, I shook my head. "Exavier, sorry."

There was something so familiar about him. I kept staring, studying him for anything that would trigger a memory. Nothing came to me.

His lush lips curved upwards. I bit back a sigh.

He smiled. "I know I'm early but I was in the neighborhood and thought I'd stop in. I brought coffee."

I perked up. "Coffee?"

Turning, he glanced towards one of the two circular tables in the lobby. A travel carrier full of large cups of what I prayed was French vanilla flavored coffee sat there. I bit my lower lip and whimpered. The man was a dream come true. Sexy and bearing caffeine.

"Lindsay?" Myra nudged me. "I think I smell vanilla."

"Vanilla?" It took all I had not to moan.

Exavier nodded.

I stared up at him and did the only thing I could think of doing to a man who brought me coffee, I threw my arms around his neck and hugged him tight. Lifting me up and off the ground, he took me by surprise. I expected him to act stunned, not to play along.

Never one to want to lose the edge, I wrapped my legs around his waist and planted a kiss on his forehead. "Trust me when I say I won't be calling you Blair any time soon."

"Lindsay Marie Willows, what are you doing?" Myra asked, an edge to her voice said she was doing her best not to laugh even though she didn't agree with my choice for displaying gratitude.

"Thanking the nice man for bringing me coffee." I wagged my brows. "You know, I was just thinking about how coffee was right up there next to sex with things I'd rather be doing."

Myra smiled. "You certainly are well on your way to fulfilling both things then, aren't you?"

I glanced back at the coffee and then down at the man who held me as if I weighed nothing. Visions of licking coffee off his smooth, tawny skin came to mind. I sighed.

Myra laughed. "Oh, sweetie, I can see it in your eyes. No. It will burn him. That would be bad. Now, get down off the nice man before he presses charges."

"Hey, I hugged him. He's the one who picked me up." I tapped his shoulder. "He's also the one who is putting me down now."

Exavier set me down but kept his hands on my hips. I did my best to appear anything but happy. I think I failed.

"Okay, where was I before he went and distracted me with his lips, dimpled chin, blue eyes, broad shoulders..."

Snorting, Myra shook her head. "Gee, anything else?"

"Yes, coffee." I gave her the evil eye. "That was just low. I think you tipped him off I'd be less than receptive about meeting with him. You told him to come bearing something I can't turn down."

"What's that? A great chin? Ask to see his obliques. I'm guessing they're as perfect as the rest of him." She winked at me and wiggled her hips in a sassy motion.

"Bite me," I said, blowing kisses at her.

Snarling, Myra made fake scratching motions at me.